rebecca brooke

Copyright © 2017 by Rebecca Brooke

Cover Design by Marisa-rose Shor of Cover Me Darling

Editing by Ryn Hughes of Delphi Rose

Proofreading by Judy's Proofreading

DEDICATION

To anyone who has ever been bullied. Just remember you are BEAUTIFUL and SPECIAL. Don't let anyone change who you are. You can be anything you want to be.

TABLE OF CONTENTS

CHAPTER ONE

Mari

"Ready?"

I glanced over at Sawyer. My stomach rolled and my heart pounded in my chest, and for a brief moment, I thought I might vomit. "Not really. I can't believe I let you talk me into this."

Voices echoed from the next room over. Forget butterflies, my stomach might as well have been a ship in the middle of an ocean during a hurricane. Sawyer, on the other hand, twirled the drumstick in his hand like this was just another night in his garage.

"You can do this. You've got an amazing voice. I wouldn't have asked if I didn't think you could do it."

I swallowed hard as the sounds grew louder. My eyes shot to the door. "It's a one-time thing, right? When Jackson gets his voice back, he'll sing again."

Sawyer rolled his eyes and draped his arm over my shoulders. At over six foot, the top of my head came right to his shoulder and that was in heels. "I swear, Mari, for someone who sings on stage three or four times a year—with your own solos I might add—you have the worst stage fright."

"This is not our college choir. You've done this before."

He turned me to face him, his gray gaze gleaming under the fluorescent lights. "So have you. It's just different music."

A hand clasped around my arm. I peeked over my shoulder to see Heath; Jackson stood to his right. Jackson was the lead singer for Jaded Ivory, but lost his voice over the weekend.

"Thank you for doing this." Jackson's voice was so soft I could barely hear him.

"He's right." Heath ran a hand through his shoulder-length black hair. "We couldn't really afford to give up this gig."

"You're welcome."

There was a slight tremor to my own voice but hopefully they hadn't noticed. They'd been trying to book this gig for months. Sawyer's friend Brandon pulled some strings and got them in. If they canceled, they would never get another shot. This was their chance to get their foot in the door; into bigger, better venues.

Sawyer chuckled. "Mari's a little nervous."

Heath glanced over at me. "Why would you be nervous?"

I shrugged, going for nonchalance. Sawyer, the bastard, saw right through it.

The moment I walked into Freshman Seminar and took the seat next to him, I started the chain of events that led me here: backstage, about to sing with his band. Both music majors, it didn't matter that I was vocal while he was instrumental. He decided that we would be friends, and that's what we became.

Sawyer found me that day. The real me. The one I'd hidden down deep to protect.

Anything he wanted, I would do.

I owed him.

Which left me standing here, at a club, about to sing for the first time with a band. I'd been to all the practices, knew the songs, but I could not shake the rolling nausea because the only other time I'd ever performed on a stage with an audience was when the lights were so bright I couldn't see the people watching me. See them judging me.

"She's nervous because she'll be able to see the audience."

I elbowed Sawyer, needing him to shut the hell up.

"Really?" Monty stepped into the room, the light bouncing off the silver ring in his bottom lip. There always seemed to be more gel in his hair for a show, the spikes looking strong enough to hold the weight of a guitar. "That's the best part. Nothing gears me up more than a cheering crowd."

The gleam in Monty's eyes brought out a little of my own excitement. The same rush I got before one of my solos.

"Sawyer, you guys ready?"

I turned and had to crane my neck to see the guy. His long blond hair was pulled into a loose ponytail at his nape, drawing my attention to the way his shoulders stretched the T-shirt across his chest. A small voice in the back of my head screamed *Oh, hell no. Are you crazy?* With a huge amount of effort, I pasted on a smile. Sawyer glanced at me and smirked.

"I think we are, Brandon."

Brandon gestured toward the stage door, if you could even call it that. A wooden door that separated the hallway with the bathrooms from the bar and dance floor didn't exactly scream professional stage. But it was what it was, and that was good enough.

Heath and Jackson followed Brandon out. My eyes darted to a darkened corner and I thought about hiding in the hallway. By the time anyone noticed it would be too late to pull out and they'd have to play on without me. They might be mad, sure, but by that time everyone in the audience would have heard how great they were and it might not matter so much.

A warm hand landed on the small of my back.

"You can do this, baby girl," Sawyer whispered in my ear.

Sucking in breath after breath, his dark eyes on mine, I nodded.

Time was up. I had to keep my promise.

I let Sawyer lead me down the hall and onto the stage in a daze, the short walk giving me one last chance to calm my racing heart. The guys took their places on stage, instruments in hand, and I gave my hands a quick shake, stepping out of the shadows but still lingering on the edge of the stage. Sawyer shook his head at me, his shaggy chestnut hair falling into his eyes.

What is that all about?

Brandon stepped on stage, taking the microphone set up at center stage. "Hello, Mosley's. Tonight we have Jaded Ivory for you, with a special vocal performance from Mari.

Fuck.

I'm going to kill him.

Sitting behind his drums, using them like a shield, Sawyer's smile was so bright it reflected the lights on the stage. With trembling hands, I made my way to center stage to deafening cheers. Butterflies assaulted my stomach. There were people everywhere, screaming and jumping as I took my place on stage. Heat burned my face, but I forced a smile and prayed, not for the first time, that I didn't forget the words.

The beat of the drum started, followed closely by the guitar, keyboard, and bass, leaving me no choice but to join in.

Sweat beaded along my brow as I sang the opening song, my sounding more confident than I expected. Then another. And another. With each song, I felt my confidence growing, the tension in my muscles draining. The cheers of the crowd weren't a bad ego boost, either. By the time we'd played our set, my cheeks ached from smiling so much, but my heart was full, every nerve ending in my body was alive, and I was panting as if I'd run a marathon.

We took our bows before exiting the stage. The second I stepped into the hall, many warm, strong arms engulfed me.

"Fucking amazing."

"Why haven't you sung with us before?"

"Told you so."

"Holy hell, that rocked."

They all spoke at once, making it hard to distinguish between them. Then again, I didn't need to hear Sawyer to know his comment was the "Told you so." If he had his way, I'd never hear the end of it. He'd never let me live down being nervous before we went on. The chant of the audience seemed to get louder with each passing second.

"Umm . . . guys?"

We all turned to look at Brandon. With his brow pulled down but a huge smile on his face, he threw a thumb over his shoulder. "They're screaming for an encore out there."

Monty froze. "An encore?"

The question in his voice surprised me, as did the giddy way the rest of the guys slapped each other on the back and traded high fives.

"Don't encores happen all the time?" At least every concert I'd been to had one.

"Maybe if you're Mumford and Sons, but not usually for small bands like us, playing in a bar." Sawyer wrapped an arm around my head and pulled me down, rubbing his knuckles over my head. I squealed and pulled back, my hands pawing at my hair, which was sticking out at all angles.

"Listen." Brandon stepped to the door and cracked it.

"Mari! Mari! Mari!"

My whole body turned to ice. The guys stared at me, mouths agape.

"They . . . umm . . . They can't—" My eyes darted around the room. I took rapid steps backward, my heart thundering in my chest, the adrenaline rush of before leaking from me, draining my newfound confidence as quickly as water from a bathtub.

Sawyer eyed me warily. "Mari?" He reached his hands out to take my shaking ones in his arms, the strong muscles of his biceps holding me tight. "You need to breathe."

"I've . . . I've never . . ."

I shook my head, the words dying on my tongue. My face buried into his chest. There had been praise for my performances before, but most had been a calm, reserved round of applause. Chanting was something else entirely.

Sawyer's hands wrapped around my biceps and he held me at arm's length and bent down enough to catch my gaze. He flicked his head to the side, moving his hair back from his face. The gesture was so familiar, so comforting, it settled me enough to listen. "We need to go back out there. And you need to sing your heart out." His voice dropped low. "I need you to pull it together, Keys."

That nickname.

The one I'd gotten from Sawyer the first time he heard me play the piano. I owed it to him to go back out there. This was an important night for them.

I forced my shoulders to relax and although the stiff set of my back remained, a whisper in the back of my mind told me that this wouldn't be the last time I stepped on stage with Jaded Ivory.

Holding my head high, I nodded at Sawyer. Stepping out of his grasp, I rolled my shoulders back and walked around him to the stage door. With a quick glance over my shoulder, I gave him a wink and stepped out onto the stage, the roar from the crowd making me wince. I walked back to center stage, knowing the rest of the band wouldn't be far behind. As the crowd whistled and whooped, their voices combining into one loud chant, I decided to play it up. I took the microphone in hand and smiled.

"Hello, Mosley's. Thanks for having me back."

ϒϒϒ

A light rapping on the door startled me out of the memory.

"Keys, open this door."

I rolled my eyes. As the only girl in Jaded Ivory, most of the time I changed in the bathroom. I didn't get much privacy, but what little I could find I grabbed with both hands. This place was big enough to have a separate room just for me. It couldn't have been any larger than a broom closet, but it smelled a lot better than some of my previous "changing rooms."

For the last year or so we'd played venue after venue, each one bigger than the last. Each night, our audience grew. Over time, my nerves settled. Getting on the stage, hearing the audience call my name, got easier each time. Somehow, we'd become popular enough for a small record label to seek us out. Just the thought of a contract made butterflies take off in my stomach. The guy from the label contacted Sawyer last week about upcoming gigs. We'd gotten confirmation yesterday he'd be here tonight.

When I opened the door, Sawyer had his hand raised ready to knock again. A smile played at the corner of his lips as his gaze raked down my body.

"Sexy." He stepped around me into the room, the ever-present drumsticks sticking out of his back pocket. He wandered around the room looking everywhere but at me. I watched him for a moment, leaning back against the doorjamb. When he didn't take a seat or turn to face me, I snapped my fingers.

"What's with the pacing? If you've got something to say, say it."

With a flinch, he stopped moving and leaned on the small table pushed up against the wall. He pulled one of the sticks from his pocket and twirled it through his fingers. I didn't think he was even conscious of the fact he was doing it.

"Well?"

He moved his eyes from the floor to mine. "I wanted to make sure you're ready for tonight."

"Why wouldn't I be? It's not like it's the first time I've been on stage with you guys." What was supposed to be a one-time thing had turned into something permanent after that first night.

"Yeah, but remember"—he pointed the stick in my direction—"I know you better than anyone. And when it comes to putting yourself out there, you tend to panic."

I shrugged, doing my best not to think about his words or I might just do exactly as he said and start to panic. "And?"

One of his brows rose. "And? Singing for a small label isn't a big deal?"

I ran a hand through my short blond locks. "It is, but I'm trying not to think about it that way. It's just a regular show."

He smirked. "That working for you?"

I sighed and turned to face him. "No. It made me think of the first time I sang with you guys."

He laughed. "Have to say, I never thought we'd end up here."

"So much has changed in the last year." I traced a finger over the birds tattooed on my left shoulder, each one representing a moment when I'd pushed myself to be more than I thought I could. After tonight, I'd add another to the collection.

His eyes moved to my hand on my shoulder. "Yeah, it has. I'm glad you took the journey with me."

The sincerity and love that radiated from him brought me forward and into his arms. He banded them tightly around me, pressing a soft kiss to the top of my head. "You can do this. They're going to love you."

"Us," I corrected. "They are going to love *us*."

His chest rumbled beneath my ear. "You're right, they're going to love *us*." Another moment of silence passed, then Sawyer spoke again. "This could be huge. Life changing."

"I'm ready for whatever awaits us on the other side of that stage."

He tipped my chin up with his finger. "You are so much stronger than you give yourself credit for."

His image blurred before me. "I'm trying."

Swiping at my cheek with his thumb, he brushed away a tear that escaped. "Five minutes. We'll be waiting for you."

"I'll be there."

I turned to look at the small mirror I'd set up on the table and marveled at the woman who stared back at me. She was completely unlike the girl who'd left home at eighteen. The short, messy bob couldn't have been more of a contrast to the long straight locks she'd arrived with four years ago. No longer were her eyes sunken. Gone were the dark circles under them, the only black near them being the dark rim of eyeliner that accentuated the shape of her eyes. My eyes ran over the tattoos; the piercing through her brow. If I hadn't been that girl, I'd never believe it was the same person.

After years of lectures from Sawyer and our friends, I finally loved the woman I saw in the mirror and I wouldn't let anyone make me believe any different. The time had come to throw it all on the line.

Rolling my shoulders, I stepped out of the room and saw the guys waiting for me at the end of the hall. As was our own little ritual, they each pulled me in for a tight hug, then left to take their place on stage. Nothing had changed since that first night. They still made me wait to be introduced before taking the stage.

The owner of the place stood in front of the microphone. "Tonight, we have a special guest for you: Jaded Ivory."

I stepped out on stage and the chanting began. "Mari. Mari. Mari."

After a few seconds, I took the microphone in one hand and raised the other.

"Fuck yeah, Island Lounge. You guys are awesome. Just for that welcome, we're gonna have some fun tonight, right?"

Cheers filled the room.

Sawyer tapped us in. The time had come for me to do what I did best.

A lot had changed since that first night.

CHAPTER TWO

COLE

"You cannot sit in this apartment all night." Ryan kicked my legs which were resting comfortably on the coffee table.

I cracked one eye. "Fuck that. I'm exhausted."

He crossed his arms over his chest. "Whatever. It's Friday. It's the only Friday you don't have a game until the end of November."

"It's my first Friday night off since July."

"Which is exactly why you are going to get your ass off the couch and hang out." Asshole kicked my foot again, knocking it from the table and narrowly missed knocking over my water. I swung at him, my balled fist colliding with the couch cushions when he moved.

"Stop fucking kicking me."

"Not until you get off the couch and into the shower."

I groaned and he picked up a cushion and tossed it at me. Luckily I caught it. "I'm gonna get up off this couch, but it'll be to beat your ass."

Ryan dropped down next to me, leaning back, his arms resting along the top. "Dude, as your friend, I can't let you hide from the world anymore. You've already spent the last five months hanging out with teenagers every night. I need to save you from yourself."

The set of his mouth told me he wasn't going to let it go until I agreed. And he had a point.

Ever since the high school football season started, most of my time had been spent coaching the team or at work. As the offensive coach for the team, working in the school was a way to keep my eyes on the players during class. It wasn't exactly the life I'd expected as a starry-eyed eighteen-year-old, when football had been my everything.

It still was.

My rock.

My plan.

Everyone said I could get to the NFL: coaches, reporters, teammates. How could they be wrong? Fifty-year-old records went down in flames with me on the field. Maybe it was ego, but I knew I was the one other teams watched footage of, trying to find ways to beat me.

I'd thought I was invincible.

My stomach clenched thinking about the hit that ruined everything. My brain told me the pain wasn't real, but I could still feel the snap of the bone; hear it late at night when I couldn't sleep and my mind kept replaying everything, over and over.

After the surgery, things changed. My teammates came to see me, pity etched in each of their faces because despite what they might have said out loud, they knew the reality of my injury. No team would take a risk on someone with a metal plate and screws in his leg.

It wouldn't be worth the money.

There were days I'd think back and wonder how different my life would have been. If that kid who thought he was the king of school could have ever imagined this reality. I dropped my head, squeezing my eyes shut, pinching the bridge of my nose until it was just this side of painful. So many things I wished I'd done differently. The regret was like a physical weight on my shoulders.

I needed to get out of the apartment.

Sitting there alone would only make the dull, heavy feeling in my chest worse.

"Okay."

I put my foot on the floor, wincing with the moment. Two years later and there was still a twinge of pain whenever my leg sat in the same position for too long. I'd given up trying to fix it. It was just part of life now. I might be twenty-four but some days my leg made me feel like I was seventy.

Ryan sat up and spun to face me. "You'll go?"

"Fuck it. I could use a night out."

"Good. What kind of best friend would I be if I didn't help you get laid every once in a while?"

I lifted my head and glanced over at him. "Are you telling me you're worried about my poor, lonely dick?"

He watched as I let one of my brows lift and promptly burst out laughing. "Only when it makes you sangry?"

"Sangry? What the hell is that?"

"Sex-deprived angry."

It was like listening to my students sometimes. "You're a lunatic."

Ryan linked his hands behind his head. "Life would be boring without me. Now get in the shower. I'm fucking starving."

He propped his feet on the table, making himself comfortable in the exact same position I'd been in only a few minutes ago.

Dickhead.

"Leave in twenty?"

"I'm dragging you outta here in ten," he called after me.

I shook my head. There was the very real possibility that he'd do exactly that. I stripped my shirt off on the way down the hall, tossing it into my room as I made my way to the shower.

"Nine minutes and thirty seconds."

Thirty minutes later we were on our way to a bar. Apparently, he wanted to see whatever band was playing that night.

"Why do you have such a hard-on for this particular band?" I fumbled with the radio station. Ryan's taste in music was only tolerable for so long.

He shot me a look. "Besides the music being good, the lead singer is smokin'."

"You better not be dragging me to some country western line dancing bullshit."

He laughed. "Dude, I know better than that. You'd kick my ass for that shit. Trust me, it'll be totally worth it."

I crossed my arms over my chest and relaxed back in the seat. "I'll take your word for it."

We pulled up in front of a pretty large building. It looked more like a club than the hole-in-the-wall bar I was expecting.

The *Island Lounge.*

"A club?"

He shut off the engine and opened the door. "No. There's a huge bar in the center, but there's a stage in the back for the band."

We climbed from the car and I let the cool fall night fill my lungs. Practices for the season started in July and since school began, there hadn't been many nights where I'd gotten home before eight. Not too late for a week night, except when I was also getting up at six in the morning to teach for the day.

I would never give him the satisfaction by admitting it out loud, but Ryan was right—I needed a night out. Something to keep me from watching tape or Googling ways to fix my leg without the steel plate. Some days it was easier to forget, others not so much.

Ryan pulled open the heavy wooden doors. He hadn't been kidding when he said there was a huge bar in the center of the room. The damn thing almost ran from wall to wall on the sides. If it hadn't been for the tables lining each side, it might have. The stage ran the entire length of the back wall, with enough space in front for the crowd to get up close and personal with the band.

At the end of the bar, closest to the stage, sat Trevor and Mike.

Trevor made a show of slamming his beer down and slapping his chest. "Holy shit, Ryan. Did you actually get Cole to leave the apartment?"

I flipped him the bird and pulled out a barstool. "Funny. For that smart-ass remark, you're buying me a beer."

He laughed. "Fine, but you're buying the next round."

"Aren't you the one with the high-paying job."

"Yes to the job. No to the high-paying."

Ryan and I took our seats. From here we could see the stage but still hear each other without having to yell. Mike ordered a round of beers and over the course of the next hour the crowd grew to the point where you couldn't move without bumping into someone. It seemed a bit excessive for this early on a Friday night.

Screaming started all around us, as people shoved each other to get to the stage. I glanced up and noticed the band members taking the stage. I turned my attention to Mike.

"No way the Panthers are making the Super Bowl this year. Even with their picks in the draft, they still need to strengthen their offensive line," he called, having to raise his voice to be heard over the din of the crowd. I opened my mouth to respond when the piercing sound of microphone feedback interrupted.

"Tonight, we have a special guest for you: Jaded Ivory," someone from the stage called out into the crowd, who started chanting what sounded like "mar ree."

I leaned forward and looked at Mike. "If Newton plays anything like he—"

A sultry voice drew my attention to the stage. *Fuck me.*

The beer in my hand almost slipped to the floor. The chick standing on stage, microphone clutched between her hands, had to be one of the sexiest women I'd even seen. In a tight blue tank top which accentuated the curve of her breasts and legs that went on forever in skinny black jeans, she was a walking wet dream. Blood no longer ran through my brain, all of it traveling south. Adjusting myself, I grabbed my beer off the bar again and drained it, hoping to cool my suddenly heated body. All the

23

reasons Ryan wanted to come here stood before my eyes.

"Holy shit."

Ryan followed the direction of my gaze. A smirk lifted the corner of his lips. "Now you get it."

I dropped my empty bottle onto the bar, my eyes glued to the stage.

"Trust me, I get it."

Damn, I wanted a chance with her. Hopefully she'd stick around for a drink, then I could charm her into my bed.

Throughout the show, I couldn't keep my eyes off her short blond hair, barely brushing her shoulders and the tattoos that covered them. My dick surged to life in my jeans thinking of the ways I could explore each and every inch of her ivory skin, my tongue sweeping my bottom lip when the lights glinted off the small barbell in her brow. After each song, the crowd lost it. The catcalls, the cheers—all of it directed toward the singer. Every time they chanted her name—which Ryan told me was Mari—a slight blush stained her cheeks, the color accentuating her high cheekbones.

The final song ended and I reluctantly turned my attention back to my friends. Ryan's eyes were on me, like he'd been watching me the whole time.

"You gonna see how far you can get?" The laughter in his voice was unmistakable, even as he took a sip of his beer. Having gone the whole set without a beer, I gestured to the bartender for a fresh one.

"Let me guess, you've tried?"

He outright laughed this time, along with Mike and Trevor. "There isn't a guy who hasn't. She always turns them down." He gestured toward the stage with his chin. A tall guy stood near the front, about to take the steps down into the bar. "She usually sticks pretty close to the drummer there. We figure she's dating him; although, he's never threatened one of us for chatting her up."

I watched as the drummer made his way toward the bar. He was only maybe an inch or so taller than me. Maybe the guys were right and she was with him. It was hard to imagine a woman who looked like that being single.

I ceased to think at all when I saw her emerge from the back, no longer in the blue tank, but a tight white V-neck, her nipples poking out through the fabric. She stopped next to the drummer. He whispered something in her ear that made her laugh and punch him playfully on the shoulder.

The gesture one of friends not lovers. Not that I knew anything about love. The only love I'd ever had was for football. Mari stepped around the guy and took a seat at the bar. Not a second passed before a drink was handed over to her. If the drummer wasn't her boyfriend, I'd have to take my chance before another guy got to her first. I glanced over a Ryan.

"I'm gonna buy her a drink." I nodded toward the blond-haired beauty.

He raised his bottle. "Like I said—sangry."

"Dick."

I grabbed my beer and walked over to take the seat next to her. She barely glanced at me out of the corner of her eye and brought the glass to her lips. As aloof as she was playing it, I was positive I saw a slight smirk at the corner of her mouth before she took a sip.

"You made tonight worth coming out for. Can I buy you another drink?"

She lifted her almost full glass and gave it a shake, all without looking at me.

Okay, that had been a dumb question.

"Fair enough. You can't blame me for missing your full glass. I'd much rather look at you." She continued to face forward but I wasn't done yet. There was no way I was striking out with the guys watching me. I noticed the birds tattooed along her shoulder.

"Your artist does excellent work. I've been looking for a good place since I moved here. What's their name? I'd loved to check them out."

That caught her attention. A smile curved her lips and she turned slowly, eyes sparking.

Finally.

Her sapphire eyes moved to mine and she froze. Time seemed to stop as I got caught in her gaze; at least, until the liquid from her drink snapped me back to reality as it hit me in the face.

I sputtered, wiping a hand down my face to clear my eyes. By the time I managed to focus on anything, the only thing visible was her back as she left through the door by the stage.

Grabbing a napkin from the bar, I stood up and wiped the rest of the liquor from my face. When I opened my eyes again, the drummer stood in front of me, arms crossed over his chest. He shoved my shoulder, pushing my back against the bar. "What the fuck did you say to her?"

Not exactly how I expected things to go when I hit on a girl. I held my hands up, wanting to avoid a fight. "I only asked about where she got her tattoos done so I could check the place out and add to my own." I lifted the sleeve of my shirt to show the design that wrapped around my bicep.

His brows drew down, confusion clear on his face. I kept my palms up, not wanting to antagonize the guy as I braced, waiting for his reaction. Any kind of physical altercation would cost me my job.

Great, I was going to get into a fight the first time I went out in ages, and lose the one job I liked almost as much as playing football.

But the guy said nothing. He turned on his heel and took the same path Mari had taken earlier. I turned to look back at the guys. Ryan shrugged his shoulders. Trevor was on his feet, his eyes on where the drummer had exited, stage left.

Everybody in the place was fucking crazy.

CHAPTER THREE

Mari

It couldn't be. There was no way in hell the Cosmos could be so cruel as to let me have the performance of my life, only to be faced with one of the people I hoped to never see again.

But there was no denying it.

Cole Wallace was here.

The room that only hours ago seemed small now seemed minuscule, like the walls were closing in on me.

Five years.

Five years I'd spent trying to push every memory of him out of my head. To reinvent myself. To become a woman I was proud of. And the night that everything could change—the night things could finally go my way—Cole had to step into the same bar.

Mariloon.

Mariloon.

A light knock rapped against the door. I pulled my legs tighter against me, pushing myself closer to the wall, hoping whoever it was would go away. The knock grew louder, until the person was pounding on the door. Each thud sent a tremor through my body.

"Mari, open the goddamn door. I know you're in there."

I buried my face in the protective embrace of my arms, ignoring Sawyer, memories of the worst years of my life assaulting my brain even as I tried to keep them at bay.

I glanced at my phone. Shit, I was going to be late to class if I didn't hurry. Turning down a side hallway, I picked up my pace. It was the long way around, but it meant I didn't have to take the main hallway, past where the cheerleaders and football players hung out between classes.

The bell rang.

"Damn it."

"Aww, late for class?"

The hairs on the back of my neck rose. These hallways were normally empty.

My stomach dropped, but I ignored the voice and moved even faster. A hand wrapped around my arm, pulling me to a stop.

"You're already late. Stay. Have some fun."

With a shove, I was pushed up against the lockers behind me. My heart raced in my chest. I tried to control the shaking of my hands as I lifted my eyes to see which one of the jocks had decided to torture me today.

Sam Horton.

He lifted a hand to brush the hair from my face. I flinched at the contact.

"Look at that, Cole, she doesn't look happy to see us."

Over Sam's shoulder, I could see Cole leaning against the lockers on the other side of the hallway.

Sam leaned in and I pressed my cheek to the locker, the metal cool against my heated skin. I closed my eyes, afraid he was going to try and kiss me. There was a long pause before he laughed, cruelly.

"Did you actually think I would kiss you?" He sneered. "Why in the hell would I let these lips touch a freak like you? No guy in this school wants to put any part of their body near you, Mariloon."

Cole burst out laughing. Sam stepped back, tilting his head down the hall. "Let's go. I don't need a detention."

They started to move away and I felt my shoulders sag. They weren't out of earshot, though. Still close enough for me to hear Cole say, "Just tell them Mariloon tried to kiss you and you had to stop her before you could get to class."

My knees buckled and I slid down the lockers to the floor, tears racing down my cheeks. The sound of footsteps forced me to my feet and into the nearest bathroom. I raced inside the stall, slamming the lock across and sitting on the seat, my head in my hands, sobs racking my whole body. How could I go to class now? There was no doubt everyone would know what happened by now, and exactly like Cole said, it would be all my fault. They probably told everyone that I came on to Sam, hoping to sleep my way to the popular group. It was just the same as always.

The door slammed into the wall, the handle leaving a crack in the drywall, and Sawyer stalked into the room. His eyes widened and he dropped to kneel in front of me.

"What the fuck happened, Mari?"

I shook my head, unable to force the words past the lump in my throat. He pressed a finger under my chin, lifting my face.

"Did that asshole say something? Am I going back out there to kick the shit out of him?"

"No, don't do that. He didn't say anything. I just needed a minute," I choked out.

His eyes bored into me. "You are a terrible liar. Fess up right now. What the hell happened?"

I sucked in breath after breath. Sawyer knew that my high school experience wasn't the greatest. I told him about being bullied, but I never told him how bad it had gotten. He'd likely assumed it was the typical jocks vs. geeks kind of bullying. He didn't know half of the things I'd spent the last six years trying to purge from my memory. Honestly, I wasn't sure I was ready to tell anyone about some of the most humiliating moments of my life.

Sawyer took a seat next to me against the wall and lifted me into his lap. "Tell me, Keys. I can't help fix if I don't know what's broke."

I wrapped my arms around his neck, needing his strength to deal with the demons in my head. "The man who hit on me tonight is Cole Wallace, one of the assholes who enjoyed making my life a living hell."

I felt every muscle under my hands lock tight and I held firm.

"Let go, Mari. I'll be right back. I'm gonna beat the ever-loving fuck out of him."

That wasn't what I wanted at all. "It's not worth it. You attacking him only makes us like him."

"No, it makes me feel better."

I cupped his cheeks in my hands, forcing him to keep eye contact. "Maybe, but then he wins. I've spent the last few years trying to get away from that; to find the strong person inside me and to love her. I'm finally there, thanks to you. I need to show him that everything they said and did had no impact on me."

He clenched his teeth so hard, I was surprised he didn't crack one. "You know I really fucking hate that line of thinking."

I smiled at him. It was weak, yes, but it was a smile. "I know you do. But when you calm down, you'll see I'm right. I haven't seen him since graduation and it threw me. I needed a moment to freak out. Now I can face it head-on."

"Let me up, Mari." One of my brows rose. "I'm not going to do anything, I just need to move around and burn off this energy."

I backed up off his lap. Apparently, he had a lot of energy because he not only pulled out his drumsticks, twirling them in his hand, but he also paced back and forth in the room. How he managed to do both and not drop them or fall over was amazing. I stood against the wall watching him.

"Why the fuck would he come here and hit on you after all that?"

I shrugged. "I don't think he recognized me. Besides, you know as well as I do, I don't look anything like I did when we first met."

Different was an understatement. Gone were the long hair and bangs. Gone was the girl who hid in bathrooms, crying. Determined not to let that girl to the surface, I stood and walked over to the small mirror, wiping away the mascara smeared under my eyes and reaching for my makeup bag to hide the pale tone to my cheeks.

"What are you doing?"

I glanced up from reapplying my eyeliner. Sawyer was standing in the middle of the room, staring at me in the mirror.

"Fixing my makeup so I can go get a drink."

He crossed his arms over his chest. "You're actually going back out there? You know he didn't leave, right?"

I shrugged, trying to show that I didn't care. It was a façade because, really, I cared more than I wanted to admit. This was the real test.

Could I walk out there and pretend like his presence meant nothing to me?

"Let's just pack up and go. The agent already left for the night, we're not gonna play again."

I ran the tube of red over my lips, then pressed them together for an even coat. I placed the cap on the tube and sucked in a deep, steadying breath, looking at Sawyer's reflection.

"I need to go out there. I have to prove I've put all that shit behind me."

Sawyer walked over and his fingers bit into the skin of my shoulders. "You don't need to prove anything to anyone."

I held his gaze in the mirror. "I know I don't need to prove anything to you. This is something I have to prove to myself. To know that I'm the strong woman I believe I am."

He stood there silently for a moment, then bent his head and pressed a kiss to my cheek. "You're the strongest person I know. We'll go back out there—together. If it's too much, you give me the sign and we'll bail and grab food and drinks somewhere else. Deal?"

I reached up and covered his hand with mine. "Deal."

"I'll wait for you in the hall. Take as much time as you need."

When Sawyer reached the door, I called out to him. "Thank you for always having my back."

He smiled. "I wouldn't have it any other way."

The door clicked closed behind him. I reached up to wrap my fingers around the gold chain that had hung around my neck since sophomore year of high school. With everything I'd dealt with during those four years, it was a reminder of my grandmother—the one person, besides my parents, who'd believed in me. She believed in the person I would become even when I wondered if I would ever amount to anything. The jade flower wrapped in silver gave me strength when I had none of my own.

I closed my eyes and tried to relax.

I can do this.

Squaring my shoulders, I opened the door and went to face my nightmare head-on. Sawyer, true to his word, was waiting for me in the hall and walked next to me all the way to the bar, not close enough that he seemed overbearing but close enough that I knew he was there to support me.

As soon as I approached the bar, a drink was set in front of me. We'd played the Island Lounge enough that the bartenders knew what our drinks of choice were, and it was rare that we had to actually ask for what we wanted.

I lifted the glass to my lips, using it as a cover to scan the bar for Cole. I had no intention of giving him the impression I was looking for him, or, even worse, that I actually wanted him to hit on me again. The most I hoped to accomplish was for him to get the impression I thought I was too good for him. If I came off as a bitch, so be it. That didn't stop the butterflies from assaulting my stomach as my eyes scanned the room. It wasn't until I reached the end of the bar that I saw him.

The same as in high school, he stood with a bunch of roided-out meatheads. Three of the guys were laughing. A quick scan of Cole's face and I knew they weren't laughing with him. Most likely it was my drink in his face that had them in fits of laughter. A small part of me thought it was karmic retribution rearing its ugly head.

Someone took the seat next to me. I glanced over to see the dragon tattoo that wrapped around Sawyer's bicep. He'd gotten it the same time I started the set of birds on my shoulder.

The seat on the other side of me was taken by Heath. He tipped his head toward where Cole and his friends stood. "What did he do?"

"Nothing." *That I'm going to dwell on*, I added silently.

An annoyed grunt came from Sawyer. I knew he was still pissed, but I also knew he wouldn't do anything unless I wanted him to.

"Should we drag the asshole outside?"

I laughed. "No, but thank you for the offer."

Heath smiled and took the beer the bartender offered him. "I think we have a really good chance of getting this deal." He brought the beer to his lips, taking a long sip.

"I think you're right. The rep seemed more than happy when he left. Hopefully that means he's trying to sell us to the label tonight." There was slight edge to Sawyer's voice.

The guys knew exactly how to distract me. But now that they'd reminded me about the fact that we'd been watched tonight, the jitters I'd felt earlier over the rep wanting to hear us came back in full force. My face was warm and I knew it had nothing to do with the alcohol. The guy from LiteStar Records contacted us a few weeks ago about coming to one of our performances. Someone from his office had seen one of our gigs and convinced him he needed to hear us for himself. The label was small, but it was a place we could work our way up from, or stay if we were happy there.

I didn't actually meet him until after the show, but he'd been easy enough to pick out in the crowd. Wearing a pair of khakis and a polo, he didn't exactly dress like our normal fan base. After the obligatory encore, he'd come up to the stage and introduced himself as Tom Dunn of LiteStar. The admiration for our work came through loud and clear based on the excitement in his voice. Tom gave us his card and promised to be in touch at some point during the following week.

It was time to play the waiting game. Much easier said than done.

"After his reaction, I don't doubt it. He loved every song we played." I finished the rest of my glass and signaled the bartender to get me another one.

My focus had been on the two men sitting beside me, but I could feel the eyes on my back. His eyes. I knew he was watching me. For what, I hadn't a clue. There was no doubt in my mind he hadn't figured out who I was yet and hopefully he never did. The last thing I needed was for him to come to every show trying to torture me all over again. I kept my gaze on Heath and Sawyer. Every once in a while, I'd glance up to where Monty and Jack were playing a game of pool. I didn't care what I was looking at, as long as it was *never* him.

By the end of the night I was so drunk that Sawyer had to drive me home and practically carry me through the house and into my room.

"Oh, Keys, look at you." He placed me on the bed and pulled the covers up over me, which was nice of him because, with the way the room was spinning, I wasn't sure I'd be able to remember how. "You're going to regret this in the morning."

"Maybe." I tried to wink, but ended up blinking instead.

He placed a finger over my lips. "Get some sleep. You need it. I'll see you in the morning."

Sawyer backed out of the room, shutting the door silently. I heard the door to his room shut directly across the hall and sighed. It *was* more than likely I'd regret my actions in the morning. The one thing I didn't regret was making it through the night with no additional battle scars.

After all, I'd faced Cole and walked away unscathed.

And I classed that one as a win.

CHAPTER FOUR

COLE

The sound in the bar should have been deafening. With the crowd still keyed up after the show, it was odd for such silence to fill a room. All eyes on me.

"Everything all right?"

I glanced over my shoulder and saw Ryan standing right behind me, a wad of napkins in his hand. He pressed them against my chest and I took them, attempting to dry off my shirt. "Yeah, everything's fine."

"What the fuck was that all about?" His eyes were focused on the door backstage.

"Hell if I know." I noticed the other members of the band staring at me, but none of them moved from their spot. "I need a drink, and beer isn't going to cut it."

Ryan turned. "Come on. I'll buy you one."

After a few rounds of tequila shots, the guys had a good laugh at my expense. I played along, but the scene kept playing through my head because although I'd struck out once or twice over the years, I'd never had a woman throw her drink in my face. No way was I giving up. Maybe it was ego or the dry spell, who knew, but I was determined to try again.

About a half an hour later, Mari and the drummer walked back into the bar. She took a seat at the corner farthest from us, and the bartender wasted no time putting another drink in front of her. She lifted the drink up to her lips, her rigid movements belying the look of indifference on her face. Every once in a while, she'd grip the charm that hung off her necklace and look to the sky. It was a bit unnerving to be so focused on a woman I'd only met once—who'd intentionally thrown her drink in my face—but that didn't stop me. I was drawn to her in a way I couldn't explain. Even more bizarre was that her looks were only part of the draw. I couldn't put my finger on the rest.

She avoided looking in my direction for most of the night, which didn't give me much of a chance to try and win her over. I caught her glance over a few times when she thought she could cover it by taking a sip of her drink, but other than that, she kept her eyes focused on the drummer or the pool tables.

The more I thought about it, there was something about the way Mari had looked at me . . .

I just couldn't put my finger on what.

The more I drank, the more the nagging feeling that I was missing a giant red flag went away. By the end of the night, I'd had more than enough to drink. Ryan wrapped an arm around my shoulder. "Let's get you home."

"Yeah."

Even that came out slurred.

Ryan walked alongside me to the car— probably to see whether I'd make it without falling flat on my face. At some point during the night, he'd switched to water. A good thing because there was no way I was getting myself home. The inside was silent as he pulled from the lot. My eyes felt heavy. All I wanted was my pillow and some sleep.

"All right, what gives? I've seen you drink this much exactly one time before, when I dragged you out last spring break. You normally have one, *maybe* two beers. Wanna explain why you strike out with one girl and you end up shitfaced?"

"Never exactly been turned down that spectacularly."

"So, drinking enough for three people is a way to boost your ego?"

"No," I mumbled. "It's a way to forget tonight, then I can try again next time."

He snorted. "Oh, you may forget the conversation, but there is no way you're forgetting tonight. My guess is you'll be remembering it on repeat . . . throughout the night . . . on the bathroom floor."

I was too tired to argue. My eyes became heavier, the desire to sleep growing stronger with each mile we drove.

The scent of coconut overwhelmed my senses. She was like a breath of fresh air. Comfortable in her own skin. Tattoos ran over both shoulders.

"Where did you get your tattoos done? I've been looking for a good shop in the area to finish mine."

Gorgeous blue eyes turned toward me. Something about those eyes. She smirked and took another sip of her drink. Determined to taste her lips, I took the glass from her hand, setting it down on the bar.

My stomach lurched. "Oh shit."

40

Ryan pulled the car to the side of the road without question. I shoved the door open, just in time for the contents of my stomach to make an appearance on the ground next to the car.

"Jesus Christ, Cole. You couldn't keep it down until we got home?"

I coughed and wiped the back of my hand across my mouth. When I was sure there couldn't be anything left, I pulled the door shut and leaned against the back of the seat.

Ryan watched me for a minute. "Are you done? There will be no puking in my car."

I nodded, afraid to speak. There was no need for a repeat. Ryan was going to give me shit for weeks about this.

He scoffed. "We tried to warn you. No one has had any luck with her."

Ryan pulled into the lot. My stomach rolled again and I got out of the car, stumbling up and into our apartment, dropping to my knees in front of the toilet. There couldn't have been much left to throw up. That didn't stop me from puking twice and dry heaving for another ten minutes or more. It seemed as if hours had passed when I eventually managed to sit up and lean against the wall.

Ryan rolled his eyes and tossed me a clean hand towel. "Get yourself cleaned up and go to bed. I'll see you in the morning."

I heard his bedroom door close, the noise making my head throb. I sat there, my head resting against the wall, breathing in through my nose and out through my mouth. Each deep breath settled me a little more until I knew I wouldn't get sick again if I stood. Forcing myself from the floor, I splashed some cold water on my face and rinsed out my mouth. When I looked into the mirror, the pale pallor of my skin combined with the red lines running all along my eyes painted a picture something closer to a horror movie than a night out with friends.

I made my way down the hall to my room, leaning against the wall for support. Not wanting to risk any more sudden movements, I took a seat on the bed before removing my shoes and pants. My shirt was a bit more of a struggle. Eventually freeing myself from its hold, I dropped into bed. The room spun and thoughts of Mari swirled through my head.

Fuck. What had I been thinking?

ᘏ ᘏ ᘏ

The sensation of my heartbeat pounding inside my skull yanked me from sleep. With an effort, I cracked one eye and shut it immediately. Blinding light shone throughout the room. Apparently, in my inebriated state the night before, I forgot to close the shades. The room, with its white walls reflecting the light of the morning sun, only served to torment me for my lack of judgment at the bar. I pulled the sheets higher. Hopefully, the muted light beneath would give me a chance to get my bearings.

Slowly, I cracked one eye open. Then the other. The room was still bright, but it didn't make my stomach threaten to purge itself again. I'd lost my goddamn mind last night. Getting sloppy-ass drunk wasn't on my list of things to do. What the hell would possess me to do that to myself?

Mari.

Her name rang in my head louder than the jackhammer. She'd thrown her drink at me. What had I done? The same annoyance that had eaten away at me, making me drink more than my share, came back with a vengeance. Not many girls ignored me when I tried to talk to them. When it did happen, most of the time they were already in a relationship. Maybe I'd been wrong about her dating the drummer, but her freak-out still didn't make sense. Why not just say she was taken? Why throw her drink?

Clanging in the kitchen drew my thoughts back to the present. Ryan was up to something. With my luck, he'd probably broken my coffee maker. Heaving I sigh, I squinted, bracing myself for the light when I took the covers off my head. It had been a while since I'd drank enough for a hangover of this size.

Eventually my eyes adjusted enough for me to chance moving and I tossed the covers off and sat up on the side of the bed.

Nope. My stomach wasn't done with me yet.
I swallowed and sat as still as possible.
Water.
Advil.
Grease.
Everything I needed, and in that order.

By the time I'd reached the kitchen, whatever Ryan had tossed into the pan had burnt to a point it was no longer recognizable as food. It looked more like a hockey puck for an NHL team.

"What the hell is that?" I dropped into a seat at the table, deciding it was no longer a good idea to be wandering around. The smell permeated my senses, making me dry heave.

"Don't you dare puke. You got yourself into this mess and I refuse to clean up after you." He set a glass of water and a white bottle down in front of me.

So much for him not wanting to clean up the mess. I popped the top off the bottle and dropped

43

two of the tablets into my mouth, chasing them with half a glass of water. Once I knew it wouldn't come back up, I finished the glass. I hadn't realized how thirsty I was until I took the first sip. "Thanks."

Ryan nodded, his eyes narrowing on the thing in the pan. Thankfully he dumped it into the trash, grabbed a mug off the counter and joined me at the table. "Now that you're coherent, want to tell me what got into you last night?"

I shrugged. It hurt. "Maybe she *is* dating the drummer."

He shook his head. "I doubt that. She would've just told you to back off."

I scrubbed a hand over my face. "Yeah, that's what I was thinking. Can't figure out why, though."

"I've had it happen once." He leaned back in his seat. "Had nothing to do with who she was dating and everything to do with my *assholish behavior and inappropriate comments*." He made air quotes around the last part.

"I only asked about where she got her tats done. Doesn't make any sense."

He took a drink of the coffee. "Don't worry about it. There's plenty of pussy around."

"Maybe." But like any other guy, I wanted what I couldn't have.

He narrowed his eyes at me. "What are you thinking?"

I ignored him and went back to my room to grab my phone, feeling his eyes track me when I came back into the room.

"What was the name of the band?"

"Why?"

"Just tell me." I opened the web browser.

He sighed. "Jaded Ivory. You're not going to do something stupid, are you?"

I typed in their name, hoping like hell they had a website or Facebook page where I could find their schedule.

Jaded Ivory ~ Fan Page.

Bingo.

The second link led me exactly where I needed. The calendar said they had a show tonight, about an hour away.

I glanced up at Ryan. "What are you doing tonight?"

He quirked a brow at me. "Why?"

I twisted my phone around for him to see the site I was on. "Didn't know if you wanted to grab a drink?"

"You think that's a good idea?" He leaned back in his chair, crossing his arms over his chest.

"Probably not. But apparently I'm full of bad ideas."

He stared at me, waiting to see if I'd say anything else. When I didn't he dropped his head to his hands. "Fine." I smiled but it was short-lived, my mouth turning down when he lifted his head and pointed a finger at me. "But if the drummer tries to kick your ass, you're on your own."

I shrugged, knowing he didn't mean a word of it. "Get a shower. You can't cook and I don't feel like it. We'll go grab burgers."

"You're paying. It's my charge for putting up with your crazy tonight."

Ryan got up and left the kitchen to get changed. We shared one bathroom so I sat back and waited my turn, thankful when the pain relievers took effect. My skull no longer throbbing, I swiped my finger across the phone, choosing the "Meet the Band" section of the page. Each member had their own profile, complete with pictures. Mari's still didn't have any information to help me dig deeper.

"You can't hide from me," I said to her picture on my phone. "I'll find a way to convince you I'm a nice guy."

Mari

Three weeks.
Nine shows.
And no escaping Cole.

It didn't matter where we played, he showed up. I'd kept it together, afraid of what the record label would say. Tom had contacted Sawyer the day after he saw us perform, sharing that he'd convinced his bosses that we were good enough for a contract. He'd asked Sawyer for demos, which we already had ready, and passed them on to the head of LiteStar. The final contract was coming. We were just waiting to put pen to the paper.

But the excitement I felt with this development was slightly diminished by seeing Cole every time we played.

It didn't matter whether I told him to fuck off or ignored him for the night. He was like a dog chasing after a bone. He still had no idea who I was, and I certainly hadn't told him. I didn't want to tell him anything about me. All he saw was a woman who wouldn't give him the time of day. He didn't remember the high school me.

I did.

Each night he tried to talk to me. Some nights he bought me a drink, others he did his best to draw me into conversation even with Sawyer scowling at him. Every time I kept my cool and my drink in its glass.

Somehow, I had to get him to give up. The tenacious bastard didn't seem ready to quit. I'd even gone as far as to hook up with another guy, hoping he'd get the hint.

Nope. All I got was Sawyer pissed at me.

He wouldn't have cared if I'd done it for me. The fact that it was for the sole purpose of getting rid of Cole, he did not like.

I needed to find another way. The deal was everything. I'd worked entirely too hard and for too long to let one guy ruin everything.

"Mari?"

I blinked rapidly to clear my vision. Monty stood in front of me, his dark hair spiked in a million directions.

"What's up?"

His brows drew together. "You feeling all right tonight?"

"Yeah. Just thinking about when they'll send the contract over." I pushed off the wall, hoping my excuse was enough.

Sawyer had cornered me when I was too hungover not to tell him everything that had happened with Cole. Apparently, the little information I'd given him in my dressing room hadn't been enough. It took another three hours to calm Sawyer down enough that I could get him to promise not to hunt Cole down. It was a long time ago. Not that I could have seen myself forgiving him, but I also really wasn't interested in the rest of the band knowing. Some secrets were best kept locked deep down inside.

He clasped his hands together. "I know what you mean. I'd always hoped we would get our break, but honestly I wasn't sure it would ever happen."

I covered his hands with my own and leaned up to press a kiss on his cheek. "We definitely deserve it. Now let's go out there and show the crowd what we can do."

A smile pulled at the corners of his lips. "You bet your ass we will."

With a nod he stepped back, then turned and walked to the stage door. I glanced up and noticed Sawyer leaning against the doorframe, watching me. I stopped and looked in the mirror on the wall. Nothing seemed out of place. Pushing down my old insecurities, I went to the door but when I tried to step through, Sawyer lay a hand on my arm.

"Want to tell me why it took Monty a few minutes to get your attention when he was standing right in front of you? Or why you've checked your hair and makeup at least five times since you came out here."

I couldn't look at him, I knew he'd see right through the lie about to slip past my lips. He'd already seen enough to know something was wrong. "I'm fine."

Out of the corner of my eye, I saw him shake his head before letting go of my arm and walking through the door before me. My chest constricted. Sawyer never walked away from me. He pushed and pushed until I opened up.

Damn Cole.

I had to find a way to prove to myself that nothing Cole and his friends had done would keep me down. And if I wanted to remove the wedge that was driving space between me and my bandmates, I had to do that fast.

"Mari. Mari. Mari."

Now wasn't the time to dwell on ridding myself of Cole. Heaving a sigh, I climbed the stairs to the stage. I plastered a smile on my face and stepped into the light. Of course, the first face my eyes landed on was Cole's.

So much for pushing him out of my head.

It was the same every time I sang. Was my subconscious trying to torture me? There had to be a reason why he was the first person I seemed to find.

The backbeat came out louder than normal, and I didn't have to turn my head to know Sawyer was pissed. Well, so was I.

At myself.

I did the best I could to push all thoughts of high school trauma and annoyed best friends from my head and to put on the best show possible, letting all my insecurities and fear bleed out into the music.

By the time we finished one set and an encore, I was physically and emotionally drained. If I wanted, I knew I could convince Sawyer to take me home. But what would I do there? Sit in the silence and think about all the memories that wanted to take me under? To wonder why I couldn't push Cole out of my head?

No. It was time to take matters into my own hands and approach the problem in a whole new way. Tonight would be different.

"Still avoiding me?"

I glanced over to see a quirked brow over the green eyes I'd remembered so well through the years. Drink number three sat half empty in front of me. Tingles in my fingers and toes indicated a wonderful buzz, something that made the prospect of facing Cole easier. I had to admit, seeing him was getting a little more painless. The need to brace for a rebuff or nasty comment no longer washed over me—the first sign I'd had all night that I was stronger than I'd been giving myself credit for. I wondered whether his reaction would be the same if he knew I was Mariella. Maybe. Maybe not. Mari, on the other hand, seemed to be free and clear of Cole's retorts.

"What makes you think I'm avoiding you?" It was hard not to register the way the button-down shirt accentuated the muscles of his biceps. The way the fabric stretched across his clearly defined chest.

What in the hell am I thinking? Am I really checking out Cole Wallace?

"Maybe you're not. My name's Cole." His voice was low and raspy.

My head snapped up. Something warred in his eyes.

Lust?

Amusement?

Whatever it was, he'd caught me staring at him. Much to my dismay, I felt the heat rush to my face and turned away. The glass in front of me suddenly became the most interesting thing in the room.

Or I was going to pretend it was.

A warm hand settled over mine. Heat raced through me. I narrowed my eyes at the tan fingers, such a stark contrast to the alabaster of my skin.

"I've come to every show you had for the last three weeks just to see you." He gave my hand a light squeeze. "You're absolutely gorgeous. Can't you give me a chance? I'm a nice guy."

The breath caught in my chest.

Second period. The worst point of the day. Every single person in the class made it their mission to make my life a living hell. Normally, I'd find a reason to leave class, whether to the nurse's office or the bathroom. It didn't matter where I went, as long as I wasn't in the room most of the time. The teacher wasn't letting anyone leave the room so I did my best to focus on writing the notes from the board.

Of course, Cole sat directly in my line of sight.

When the phone rang, I wrapped my fingers around my necklace and said a quick little prayer that whoever was on the other end of the line would be looking for me and I could get out of there. Mr. Long stepped out into the hall to finish his conversation and my hands started to shake. Maybe if I was quiet, no one would pay attention to me. I kept copying the board, doing my best to ignore the conversations that had sprung up around the room.

"I'm not going." Jackie, one of the nastiest people in the room, shook her head at Cole.

If she didn't deserve Cole, I might have felt bad for her.

Focus on your notes.

Cole reached out and touched her arm. "Come on, Jackie. At least let me pick you up after the game? I'm a nice guy."

I caught myself before the snort slipped out. "Nice guy" was exactly the opposite description of what I'd use for Cole. I looked up to see the next line when my eyes locked with emerald green eyes. For a split second, I lost my mind and didn't look away.

"OMG, Mariloon. Are you trying to flirt?" Cole smirked.

That snapped me to attention. Jackie's brown gaze was cold and I knew hers weren't the only set of eyes on me. "No guy in this world would bother trying to get his dick in that dry virgin pussy."

Laughter filled the room.

I had to get out of here.

I wasn't that girl anymore. The past shouldn't stop me from having fun. The last few years had been good to Cole. He'd always been muscular, but the definition of his arms and chest far exceeded my teenage memory. His green eyes were molten as he watched me, waiting for my reaction.

I tipped back the rest of my drink, the alcohol burning away any protest my conscience might have had. It was time I proved they couldn't hurt me anymore; that I came out stronger and could face any one of them now.

And what better way to do that than to go home with Cole?

Each time I saw him my defenses crumbled a bit more. Not the emotional ones. I wasn't sure I could ever forgive him. This was all physical. My body craved the man next to me. One night wouldn't hurt anyone. One night to give into my fantasies.

"What kind of chance do you want?" My voice was husky to my own ears.

The pads of his fingers lightly caressed up my arm, across my shoulder, and down the side of my jaw, sending goose bumps racing over my skin. He bent his head low, teasing the shell of my ear with his tongue. "To be alone with you."

I glanced around the room, more than happy to see Sawyer preoccupied with Heath at a pool table. I didn't need his input. He'd tell me this was the dumbest fucking idea I'd ever had. That I was only thinking about it because I was drunk.

"Any suggestions where we might find some place to be alone?"

His eyes widened for a brief second, only to turn heavy-lidded. "I think we could find somewhere."

It couldn't be my place. Sawyer would be home later and if he found Cole in my bed I had no doubt he'd break his promise and give me away. Plus, I wanted the chance to make a quick getaway without him knowing where I lived.

Cole gestured his head toward the other side of the bar.

"My roommate is here, too, but by the way he's talking to that redhead, I don't think he's heading home any time soon."

I didn't give myself a chance to think. "Lead the way."

His hand slipped down to take mine and he linked ours fingers on the bar, in full view of anyone and everyone. On shaking legs, I let him lead me out to the parking lot and to his car. Sawyer had driven us to the bar that night. He'd been doing that a lot the last two weeks, knowing that I was likely to end up sloppy drunk by the end of the night. Coping mechanism my ass. All I got was a brain-pounding hangover and Cole still on my mind when I woke up.

He led me to a black SUV, the lights in the lot were too dim to tell what kind of car it was, and as we climbed in and Cole started the car, I reached up and fussed with my hair.

Instead of pulling the car out of the lot, he turned to me and without warning, brought his mouth down on mine. It took me a moment to process what was happening. The taste of the beer lingered on his lips. When my brain finally registered that not only was Cole kissing me, but that I loved the feel of his lips, I lost it and joined in, parting my lips, slipping my tongue into his mouth, taking my first and only true taste of Cole Wallace.

He tightened his grip on me, holding the connection of our lips until he abruptly broke it. My heart sank, then I saw him reach down and adjust himself in his jeans.

"Fuck, Mari. If I keep kissing you, I'm gonna blow right here in the car."

"Then take us back to your house."

He watched me for a second before throwing the car in reverse, the squealing tires throwing stones and dust up into the air as he hauled ass out of the lot.

Cole pulled up in front of a small single-story house. It wasn't huge. Again, not what I expected. The Cole I'd known had been ostentatious. When I thought of it, even his car didn't scream anything to me.

Interesting.

He made it around to my side of the car, throwing the door open to let me out. Never in my life had I expected Cole Wallace to open a door for me. The second my feet touched the ground, I was backed up against the car, his lips stealing my breath, the scenery around me spinning like a carousel. Closing my eyes, I wrapped my arms around his neck and let myself simply . . . *feel*.

In for a penny, in for a pound.

CHAPTER SIX

Mari

Desire.

The need to touch him.

These sensations and these alone overrode every other sense I had. His hips pressed against me, letting me feel how much he wanted me. My core heated, hardening my nipples until the scrape of fabric across them sent tingles of desire along every nerve ending. At the first swipe of his tongue I let him in, teasing his mouth with my own.

He moved his lips from mine, tracing them across my jaw and down my neck. A shiver ran through me when his tongue reached the lobe of my ear and paused.

"What are you waiting for?" I whispered.

He drew back, his eyes locked on mine. The connection lasted longer than I expected and for one moment I thought he might have recognized me.

When he stepped back and held out a hand to me, I took it, only a slight tremor to my fingers.

He led me into the house, down a dark hall into a room. I didn't take in much of my surroundings. The only thing I noticed was the way his jeans stretched across his muscular ass.

There was a click and a light came on, and for the first time since I was a teenager, I saw Cole in more than the muted light of the bar. Whether or not I wanted to admit it, Cole had grown even more gorgeous in the last six years.

He turned to me, eyes alight, and tugged his shirt over his head. A tattoo ran across his bicep, but what really caught my attention was the deep V that led below the waistband of his low-slung jeans. The fire in his eyes blazed brighter with each step he took toward me. Shutting my brain off and letting my body make the decisions, I met him halfway.

Our lips reconnected; the same as before, yet different. This time there was a promise.

A promise of more.

My thighs clenched at the sensual way his tongue swept against mine.

"You are abso-fucking-lutely gorgeous."

Cole's hand dipped below the hem of my shirt, pushing up until his thumb caressed beneath the curve of my breast. His calloused fingers were warm, teasing my already sensitized nipples.

My fingers flexed against his arms. "More."

One corner of his mouth lifted in what I could only describe as the most seductive smile I'd ever seen. My shirt and bra hit the floor in rapid succession. Instinct called to me to cover myself, but with an effort, I forced the notion down and let him look. He lowered me to the bed, his heavy-lidded gaze taking all of me in.

The moment he crawled on top of me, I sank my hands into his hair and took matters into my own hands. "Too slow," I said, right before I yanked his mouth down to mine.

Things went from heated to blazing in seconds. Even through his jeans, I could feel his erection pressing into me, and every time my tongue touched his he thrust his hips forward. He moved his head down to lavish my breast, sparks of pleasure shooting straight to my core. By the time he moved to pay the same attention to my other breast, my whole body was squirming beneath him.

He seemed content to torture me but after the last few weeks, I needed an end. I wanted pleasure to pour through my body until I couldn't move. I needed confirmation that I'd done the right thing—taken the right chance.

With small little nips, his mouth traveled lower down my body until he reached the button of my jeans. He popped the button and slid them down my legs and onto the floor, taking my panties with them. Cole stood and shed the rest of his clothing, his eyes on me the whole time. He was solid muscles from his head to his toes.

He returned to the bed, kissing a path up my leg until his tongue reached my core.

"Fuck me," I said, grabbing his hair and pulling him up to me.

Although more than happy to sleep with Cole, *that* seemed too intimate a gesture. "I would argue, but damn I like the sound of that."

He slid on a condom and crawled between my legs until I was consumed by the sensation of the warm heat of him pressing inside me.

I lost all ability to think about what I was doing.

The fire that had begun building earlier had morphed into a raging inferno, my body burning hotter with every thrust.

"Oh, fuck. Harder." My head moved fitfully on the pillows and I bucked my hips to meet every stroke. My muscles clenched, the pleasure I'd been looking for within my grasp. Just a bit more and I would crash over the edge.

Cole must have felt my body's reaction because he slid a hand down between us and pinched my clit. Stars danced before my eyes as every muscle in my body tensed. "God, yes," I screamed, clamping my mouth shut when his name was about to roll off my tongue.

His strokes became rapid and uneven as a groan tore from his lips and he pressed into me one last time. He clenched his eyes shut, his head thrown back over his shoulders. My chest heaved. Cole's breathing was just as heavy when he dropped down onto the bed. The scent of sweat and ocean surrounded me as the sound of our ragged breaths filled the air.

Cole pulled me tight to him, his front to my back. The kisses started at the nape of my neck and trailed up to my ear.

"You're absolutely amazing. I would love to see you again." His warm breath ghosted over my skin.

My body tensed, but I quickly forced myself to relax. So much for getting him to leave me alone. I pretended to be asleep, hoping I could sneak out once Cole fell asleep. If he was asking to see me again, I knew he wouldn't ask me to leave. I'd have to do that myself.

Eventually Cole's breathing evened out. Praying he wasn't a light sleeper, I carefully moved from his embrace and reached for my jeans. I buttoned them, then grabbed my shirt and bra, remembering with a sinking stomach that my car was back at my place and there was no way I was calling Sawyer to come get me. Picking up my phone, I hit the app for Uber and almost cheered with relief when I saw there was a car two minutes away. With only about an hour until sunrise, I scheduled the pickup, pulled on my shoes and tiptoed into the living room.

The rest of the house was still dark. I assumed the roommate still wasn't home. Lucky for me. I never was good at making small talk.

Cars lights flashed across the walls. I pushed my phone in my pocket and went out to the car. With the alcohol no longer stealing my brain power and good sense, I tried to figure out what would have possessed me to come here.

Had I really proven anything to myself? Yeah, I slept with Cole, but in the end what was it going to get me? It hadn't made me feel any more confident. How could it when he had no idea who I really was? Only one lesson was learned tonight: none of my prior sexual experiences came even halfway close to what happened in that room.

The ride to my place was quick and quiet. Thankfully, the driver didn't attempt to chat me up like so many others had in the past. My head was a mess. It had been since Cole showed up at the bar and tonight had only made it worse. I'd thought I had everything figured out.

Apparently, not so much.

With a gentle hand, I unlocked the door as quietly as possible. The last thing I needed was twenty questions. I'd be more prepared to deal with Sawyer after sleep.

The door snapped into place with almost no noise and I tiptoed my way across the living room.

I'd almost reached the hall when the light flipped on. Shock made me whirl around. Sawyer sat on the couch, still in the same clothes from the night before. A vein pulsed in the side of his neck.

"What the fuck, Mari?"

I shrugged, hoping to play it off. Nothing good could come of this conversation. "What? I went out after the show."

"Bullshit." He stood, bracing his feet apart, his eyes narrowed on me. "You went home with him."

"With who?"

"Goddamn it! Stop with the games." Anger flowed off him in waves, and if it had been a physical entity, it would have knocked me clean off my feet.

I mimicked him, crossing my arms and narrowing my eyes. "What do you want me to say?"

He raked a hand through his hair. "Be real."

"Real?" I scoffed. "You already know the answer to your question or you wouldn't be sitting here in the dark waiting for me to get home."

He glared at me. "I'm not the one sneaking out of a club with a guy who made my life miserable."

My mouth dropped. "No, you don't get to do that. This was *my* choice. You run away from your problems."

He flinched, but that momentary lapse didn't stop the venom that left his lips. "That was entirely different. And you're going to stand there and tell me that you didn't run the moment you could? I call bullshit. You forget, Mariella, that I already know your story."

He never called me Mariella, and knowing my story gave him enough ammunition, if he really wanted to hurt me. But I also knew his. Blood roared through my ears. "You're right. I ran until I learned that I didn't want to run anymore. Can you say the same thing?" He opened his mouth to speak but I kept talking. I wasn't going to give him a chance. "I wanted to prove I could do it."

He threw his hands up in the air. "I'm sure you proved that all right." The sarcasm rolled off his tongue like a coiled whip, each flick doing just enough damage. "It takes fucking a guy to prove you're better than him. Sleeping with someone to prove a point. Sounds more like you're making yourself the town whore."

I recoiled. "Fuck you."

Not understanding why he was acting that way and unwilling to let him get the best of me, I whirled around in the direction of the hall. My throat burned. Usually around Sawyer I didn't hold back my emotions. His was the shoulder I cried on. He was my safe place. My person.

Not this time.

A hand clamped around my arm, pulling me to a stop. I tried to yank my arm free but his grip was too strong. "Get off me." I enunciated each word, proud that my voice came out as strong as it did.

"No. I'm—"

"I said, get off." My voice cracked.

It was enough to give me away. The next thing I knew, he'd turned me around and brought me tight against his chest. "I'm sorry, Keys. I didn't mean it."

Unable to hold on anymore, I let go. Sobs made my whole body shake and I barely felt Sawyer's arm slip behind my legs and lift me from the floor. He sat down on the couch, cradling me in his lap. The position was comforting, yet made me feel vulnerable at the same time. I tried to stand but he held me closer. "Please, stay. I'm sorry."

62

I buried my face in his neck and let the tears fall. Sawyer ran his hand up and down my back in comforting circles. "Please don't cry."

The familiar scent of his cologne settled me. My breathing hitched and I tried to get myself under control. When I was sure there were no more tears I sat back, wanting to look him in the eye. He didn't let go, but he did loosen his grip.

"Mari, I—"

I held my hand up. What I needed to say wouldn't be easy and I had to get it out before I buried it with all the other memories.

"You're right, what I did tonight was monumentally stupid. Part of me hoped that one night would get him to leave me alone, and with that I'd be able to prove to myself that what they'd done to me hadn't broken me."

He kept his eyes locked on mine. "And how'd that work out for you?"

The light caress from his fingers gave me the strength to continue. "It didn't. But you already figured that out. It wasn't what I expected." My voice grew quiet with the realization I ignored in the car.

"What was unexpected?"

I dropped my gaze to his shirt. "I expected to feel triumphant. To feel like I won something. That I came out on top."

He pulled me back down to his chest. Needing the feel of his arms around me, I went, wrapping my arms around his waist. "Nothing about revenge of any kind is ever going to make you feel like you won," he whispered in my ear.

"I know . . ." I trailed off, trying not to think about the other things my brain had wanted me to recognize about Cole.

I snuggled into his warm embrace, taking comfort in knowing that Sawyer would always be there for me. The more my body relaxed, the heavier my lids grew. I wasn't sure how long it was before I felt Sawyer stand with me still in his arms. He carried me back to my bedroom and slowly lowered me onto the bed.

"Sawyer."

"Shhh." He bent down and pressed a kiss to my forehead. "Get some sleep. We'll talk more in the morning."

I kept my eyes closed, but in the silence of the bedroom it was hard not to focus on the physical chemistry I'd felt with Cole. The way he made me feel in his arms. With Sawyer, I was safe; protected.

Cole was different. It was like an inferno was racing through me, burning nerve endings along the way. I felt sexy and desirable.

It was only afterward the boulder had settled in the pit of my stomach. The sexual high had morphed into regret, and I was all too aware that my actions had been no better than those of the people who'd spent their lives making mine a living hell.

Not to mention, now that I'd had Cole once, I knew it wouldn't be enough.

Somehow, I'd have to find the willpower.

Somehow.

CHAPTER SEVEN

COLE

The weight of the morning hung over me like a woolen blanket. I'd gone to sleep with Mari's warm body wrapped in my arms, only to wake up in the morning to cold sheets and an empty bed.

I'd finally gotten her to do more than give me the brush off; although, something had seemed off from the moment she started flirting with me. I'd gone from being completely ignored to her trying to pick me up. Red flags went up everywhere, but with the woman of my recent desires finally giving me the time of day, I pushed them away. This was what I wanted.

And she hadn't disappointed.

Mari was something else. One taste would never be enough. I'd planned to tell her that when we woke up and I could linger over her. Never did I imagine she'd be gone when I opened my eyes. I wanted to take her on an actual date. Not some hookup in a club after her show.

I scrubbed a hand down my face and glanced at the clock. About thirty minutes until the students showed up for their next class and I still hadn't eaten anything. The cafeteria wasn't far from my office next to the gym. Better to eat now than wait until I got home long after the football game was over.

After my shitty morning, I wanted to tug the tie loose and open a beer. There were still another two hours of school left, not to mention the three-hour game tonight. With as much thought as I'd given it, I still had no idea what to do about Mari. Should I go track her down after their show? See if she'd even talk to me.

The white paint of the halls blended together while my thoughts were tied up in Mari. It wasn't until I reached the library doors that I realized I'd passed the cafeteria. Frustrated that I was letting a one-night stand mess with my head, I sighed and turned back, now having even less time.

The problem was that I didn't want Mari to be a one-night stand, which sounded really fucking ridiculous since I knew absolutely nothing about her. She'd made sure of that. And yet, there was still something about her that drew me in.

Voices down the hall caught my attention. All the kids should be in class. I made the quick right to check it out. Being proactive earned me points with the administration and sometimes with the students. Not usually, though.

The voices grew louder, one incredibly familiar. I came around the corner and stopped. Jarrod, one of the players, was leaning against the wall while Chris, another player, stood across the hall, his back to the lockers. I took a step forward and noticed a girl trapped in front of Jarrod, fenced in by his arms. Tears stained her cheeks and her eyes were squeezed shut.

I glanced down at my phone. "Shit. You made us late, dickhead."

Sam rolled his eyes. "We have Homecoming this weekend. Coach'll get us out of detention. It might cost us a few laps but whatever."

We turned down the main hall. Sam elbowed me in the ribs. "Ow, what the fuck?"

He nodded his head toward the blonde in front of us. "We're not the only ones."

"Aww. Late for class."

Sam walked up, wrapping a hand around her arm. I leaned against the lockers to wait for him to get it out of his system. We needed to get to class and I wasn't in the mood for bullshit today.

"You're already late. Stay and have some fun."

Sam moved her back against the lockers on the other side of the hall. He lifted a hand to brush the hair from her face. She flinched.

"Look at that, Cole, she doesn't look happy to see us."

I crossed my arms over my chest. Sam leaned in. She twisted her face to the side. Sam pulled his head back. What did she think he was going to do?

"Did you actually think I would kiss you?" He sneered. "Why in the hell would I let these lips touch a freak like you? No guy in this school wants to put any part of their body near you, Mariloon."

I couldn't stop the laughter that burst out. That name got me every time. A gem from freshman year. Sam stepped back, gesturing with a tilt of his head down the hall. "Let's go. I don't need a detention."

We started down the hall and I turned to Sam. "Just tell them Mariloon tried to kiss you and you had to stop her before you could get to class."

It was one way to get out of detention.

God, I'd been such an asshole.

"Jarrod! Chris! What are you doing?" I moved the rest of the way down the hall. Both guys froze for a second, before turning in slow motion.

The poor girl, whose name I didn't know, sucked in a breath, her wide eyes darting between the guys and then dropped to the floor. She bent down, snatching the books off the floor, her hands shaking.

"Coach Wallace. What's up?" Jarrod offered me a cool smile, one that didn't even begin to mask the mischievous light in his eyes.

I stopped dead in my tracks. Did they think I was going to fall for that bullshit? "Not sure. Wanna tell me?"

"We were just chatting with Kristen about going to the game tonight." He glanced over at Kristen, who immediately flinched and pushed herself closer to the lockers.

You want to keep your job. You want to keep your job.

I chanted the words over and over again in my head. A few deep breaths and I was calm enough to address the situation.

"Jarrod and Chris, go wait for me in my office." Jarrod smirked at Kristen on his way past. Chris rolled his eyes, looking bored. "And don't even think about skipping out or being benched for tonight's game will be the least of your worries."

Both their eyes widened. Jarrod opened his mouth but I held up a hand. "Save it. Now go."

They grumbled on their way down the hall, Chris throwing a well-aimed punch to Jarrod's arm. "Thanks a lot, asshole. My parents are gonna fucking kill me."

"Stop talking and move!" I yelled. I turned to face Kristen, who still stood in the hall, eyes darting around, looking everywhere but at me.

"Kristen, right?"

"Yeah." She tucked a piece of hair behind her ear. "It's fine. They were just joking around."

She didn't seem to be able to hold her hands still, playing with the papers sticking out of the top of her binder or fidgeting with the strap of the bag on her shoulder.

"No, it's not okay. Those guys have no right to treat you that way."

Her eyes snapped up. "B-but . . . You're one of the coaches."

"And?"

She shrugged and looked away. "They usually don't get in trouble. Some of the teachers ignore what they do because they're on the team."

As much as it sucked, I knew what she meant. Hell, half of the things I'd done in school were swept under the rug because of who I was. Didn't make it right. But I also knew Coach Harrison didn't put up with that bullshit and when he found out, heads were going to roll.

"Have you ever talked to Mr. Harrison about what those two were doing?"

She shook her head.

"He doesn't think that they should get special treatment. They have to earn their place on the field by more than just their ability to play."

"I guess." The slump of her shoulders told me she'd heard me but didn't believe it was true. *Damn, how long had she dealt with those two shitheads?*

"How about this? I'll talk to Mr. Harrison and deal with Jarrod and Chris. I'll write you a pass to class for ten minutes from now, so you can have a few minutes to collect yourself, unless you want to go see someone else? The only thing you have to do is promise to let me know if something like that happens again. Deal?"

She watched me for a moment, most likely afraid to trust me—to trust the former jock. Eventually, she nodded. "I'll take the pass."

After I wrote her pass and sent her on her way, I went to deal with Dipshit and Dumbass, who had wisely taken my advice and were standing outside the door when I arrived back to my office.

So much for eating.

I unlocked the door and flung it open, gesturing for them to step inside. The moment it closed behind me, they started.

"Coach, you can't bench us. We need to win tonight to get to the championships."

"We were just joking with her."

"We won't do it again."

I held up my hand and the room fell into silence.

"You're right, you won't do it again." I let my gaze fall on one, then the other. "But you won't be on that field tonight, either, whether we win or not." Jarrod opened his mouth to speak again. "Don't," I snapped. "You're not going to change my mind and once Coach Harrison finds out, you'll be lucky if this is the only game you miss. You know he doesn't put up with that shit. What the hell were you thinking?"

They exchanged a look and I shook my head.

"You know what, I don't wanna know, because the why really doesn't matter. Just because you play on the team, doesn't give you the right to treat your classmates that way. Keep it up and not only will you be *off* the team, but she'll have the right to press charges. Are you really gonna ruin your life over something stupid like that?"

Chris shook his head, his skin taking on a grayish hue. At least one of them got it. Jarrod, however, stood stock still, defiant as ever. "Jarrod, get to class. And I better not hear or see any more of that crap."

He curled his lip at me, glancing at his friend before swinging the door open and letting it slam closed behind him. I looked at Chris. "I'm gonna give you some advice, and this comes from personal experience. Jarrod isn't willing to get it together, hang out with someone else. I had a friend in high school who was a lot like Jarrod. I thought it was no big deal when he harassed anyone he didn't consider popular. He was wrong, and I was wrong to stand by and let it happen. I look back and wish I'd stood up to him sooner. Don't make my mistakes."

He nodded. "Sorry, Coach."

"Go to class. I'm going to talk to Harrison now."

Chris left silently and I slumped into the chair behind the desk. I should have known when I got out of bed that this day was going to hell in a hand basket. I grabbed my phone off the desk and sent a text to Harrison.

Me: Problem with Parker and Wilkes. Caught them bullying one of the girls in the hall.

Losing those two for the game was going to be a bitch. Two lines hit. Plays would have to be rewritten. My phone buzzed with one text after another.

Harrison: Fuck, we could have used them tonight.
Harrison: You told them they were benched, right?

71

Harrison: If not, I'm hunting them down before the end of the day.

Me: Yeah, we could have, yes I did, and no need, already had a long chat.

Harrison: Good. Can you handle reworking offensive line?

Me: I'll get it done before practice.

Harrison: Let me find Davis to deal with the defense.

I dropped the phone on the desk and got some paper to rewrite the plays as students began filing in for health class. By the end of the period, I'd figured out a way for the offense to survive a game without Chris. Hopefully it would be the last time I needed to do that.

ᘐᘐᘐ

The lights of the stadium were still on when I left the locker room. Most likely the grounds crew cleaning up after the game.

And what a game it was.

Nights like this reminded me of the excitement, of why I'd started to play. The team rallied to make up for Jarrod and Chris's absence on the field. It wasn't easy—especially when the rival team took an early lead. The guys had to fight to score that final touchdown.

With only five seconds remained on the clock and three points down, there was enough time for one last play. Jones, the team's quarterback, under pressure from the other team's defense, threw a high pass, the kind Chris usually excelled at catching. But with his ass on the bench it was up to his backup, Keith Young. I must have bitten off every nail

72

watching the ball come down, right into Keith's hands. The team surged from the bench. One more win and they'd make the playoffs.

For the first time since that afternoon, I'd taken an easy breath. Even waking up without Mari couldn't get me down.

Traffic was light when I pulled out of the lot. The frustration I'd seen on Chris and Jarrod's faces made me hopeful that they wouldn't pull that shit again. I'd made a lot of mistakes in school, but I was lucky because some of the shit I did could have ruined any chance I had before I even made it out of high school. The fear and embarrassment were written all over Kristen's face. Could they not see it?

Then again, for the longest time I hadn't seen it. I'd never paid enough attention. How many times had Sam and I done something like that?

Poor Mariella. The number of times we'd tormented her were too many to count. The look in her eyes. The fear. The same wide-eyed stare as Kristen as she braced for whatever horror might come next.

There were so many similarities. Just thinking about that poor girl's shaking hands, the way she fidgeted with her bag, with her folder. I thought about the way Mariella would hold tight to the pendant around her neck.

The pendant.

As my foot surged forward, my head almost slammed into the steering wheel. Horns blared around me. A quick glance in the rearview mirror showed headlights swerving around me. I sucked in a deep breath and with shaking hands turned the wheel until I was safely parked on the side of the road. Sweat beaded on my forehead.

A smirk rose at the corner of her mouth. She turned slowly, the lights above glinting off the

*barbell in her eyebrow, her fingers toying with her
necklace. She froze, the pendant slipping from her
fingers. A six-petal flower in silver and jade.*

So familiar . . .

It couldn't have been *her*. My luck couldn't
be that bad.

But deep down, I knew it was. If I'd looked a
little closer earlier, maybe I would have seen it.
Everything made sense now.

Mariella Cosmann was the lead singer of
Jaded Ivory.

My lungs seized in my chest, getting breath
almost impossible. I couldn't catch my breath.
Somehow, I forced myself to calm down and after
sucking in large gulps for a few moments, I sat up,
resting my head against the back of my seat. It felt as
if a five-ton elephant was sitting on my chest.

Her eyes after she threw the drink in my face
should have told me everything I needed to know.
Had I paid more attention to her that night instead
of focusing on my wet shirt and ego, maybe I would
have seen it.

I was still an asshole.

Each night I'd hit on her like she was some
kind of prize to be won. A conquest. A challenge I
needed to win. There I was preaching to the guys
today about treating people with respect, yet once
again I'd done nothing but disrespect Mariella. I'd
told them they had to take responsibility for their
actions and deal with the consequences. Now it was
time for me to man up and do that.

I grabbed my phone off the seat to see where
Jaded Ivory was playing tonight. I'd looked it up
before on my quest to get Mari, but there were too
many thoughts running through my head to
remember.

I really wanted to punch myself.

74

The venue was about forty minutes away. I glanced at the time. Nine thirty. The band would probably already be on stage, which would give me enough time to get there before the show was over. Originally, I'd planned on going home to change then going out to see Mari, but now I didn't give two shits that I was in my school polo. I needed to make all of it right. Or at the very least, try.

Why the hell did she come home with me? She'd obviously recognized me the moment she laid eyes on me that first night. Why else would she have thrown her drink on me? Each and every night I'd tried to talk to her, she'd known who I was. I hadn't had the same luxury.

As I walked into the cafeteria, Mariella stood a couple of feet in front of me. Her long blond hair hanging midway down her back. Sam and a couple of the other guys already sat at our table. Sam nodded toward Mariella's group. Taking the hint, I hip-checked her, hard enough to send her careening into her friend, their books flying every which way.

"Shouldn't block the door, Mariloon."

Half of the cafeteria burst into laughter. Mariella's pale skin brightened as the red hue rushed up her cheeks. She glanced up at me, her eyes partially covered by her bangs. I ignored her, stepping over her stuff to get to my table.

I punched the side of my fist against the wheel. The tires spun, catching, and lurching forward when they finally found purchase on the road. Lights passed by me in a blur. Red, white, yellow, green—it didn't matter. My only goal was to get to Mari.

The parking lot was full when I arrived. Not surprising, considering Jaded Ivory's popularity.

The pavement vibrated with the beat of the drums. They were still on stage.

With purpose, I walked toward the front door of the place and stopped, my hand frozen on the handle.

What would I say to her? What could I possibly say to make up for all the wrong I'd done over the years? I thought about her smile, her laugh. The way she'd felt in my arms. There was so much to Mari I'd never known.

All I could do was try. She deserved that much, even if she told me to fuck off. I yanked open the door.

It was time to man up and accept responsibility for my mistakes.

"Thank you, Brevet Lounge. You've been great tonight."

Her soft voice sent a tingle down my spine. I caught a quick glimpse of her as she bowed and waved at the audience, the short, curly hair such a contrast to the young, naive girl who'd hidden behind bangs. Not to mention the tattoos on both arms and shoulders, plus the brow piercing. Never in my wildest imagination would I have dreamed Mariella being so bold or confident. It wasn't like I'd done anything to help her come out of her shell. I was one of the people who probably pushed her into it.

As I watched her, the differences were astounding. No wonder I hadn't put it together sooner. The only two clues I'd had were the pendant and her eyes. How had I not noticed her eyes before? They were a unique combination of green and blue, almost teal in color. No doubt they'd always been beautiful, but I'd been too lost in being a popular dick to notice.

The band left the stage and maybe it was childish, but I stepped up to the bar and ordered a shot of tequila and a beer. A little liquid courage never hurt anyone. The bartender set that and a beer in front of me. I downed the shot, letting the alcohol burn a path down my throat. The familiar tingle along my nerves settled me; at least, until I saw Mari step out from the back and head toward the bar, flanked by two of the band members.

For a moment, I closed my eyes and tried to steady my racing heart. With measured steps, I walked over to where she'd stopped to talk to a fan.

"Mari?"

Her shoulders stiffened. For one moment, I had the irrational desire to pull her into my arms and hold her until I could make up for everything I'd done.

She said good-bye to the woman she'd been speaking to and slowly turned to face me. "Cole? I . . . I didn't know you were here tonight."

"Can we talk?"

Her eyes darted left to right and my stomach took a nosedive.

"Look, there's not really much to say. Sorry for sneaking out like I did. Last night was great, but we both knew it was a one-time thing." She continued to ramble on, her words blending together when I saw something flash in her eyes. Hurt maybe? Disappointment? I didn't know her well enough to tell what she was feeling. I forced myself to concentrate on her words. "So, I'll see you around."

She stepped around me to make her way to the bar. I could leave and never worry about seeing her again, but I wouldn't let myself be the kind of man who took the easy way out. So I turned and did the one thing I knew would get her attention.

ROCK ME

"Mariella."

CHAPTER EIGHT

Mari

"Mariella."

My lungs seized. I couldn't move, couldn't breathe. All I could do was stand there and hope this was a nightmare; the kind where you are naked in front of a room full of people. Shit, that dream would be easier to deal with.

The people around me were silent. Sawyer and Heath hadn't moved a muscle. Heath didn't know the story, but the tension in the air was thick enough you could choke on it so it was clear *something* was going on. Sawyer glanced over my shoulder and I knew Cole was still standing there.

How had he figured it out? Had someone told him? Sawyer would never . . .

The drum of my heart pounded in my ears. It was so loud, I was surprised no one else could hear it. Deep down, I knew Cole wouldn't leave until I faced him so I sucked in a gulp of air, tried to muster as much courage as I could, and slowly turned.

Cole took a step forward and I forced myself to hold my ground. "Mariella, I'm—"

I held up a hand. "It's Mari and don't worry about it. You don't have to say anything."

"But—"

"No buts. It's fine. We're good. I'm gonna get a drink with Sawyer."

I glanced over at Sawyer, hoping he would swoop in and save me again and, thankfully, he nodded his head toward the bar.

Cole wrung his hands together, not a sight I was used to seeing. "Please. Talk to me, Mari. Just a few minutes."

Out of the corner of my eye, I saw Sawyer and Heath take their seats, leaving one in the middle. Heath shot me the briefest of looks but then nodded once and turned. Whatever Sawyer had told him, I owed them both. "Not right now."

I turned back toward the bar and took the seat between the guys. The bartender seemed to appear out of nowhere, but I was grateful as hell for his presence.

"Can I get a shot of Jamison?"

Sawyer took one look at me, rolled his eyes and said to the bartender, "Make it a double." I glanced at him and he added, "I'm driving."

The bartender went to get my drink. I noticed Heath watching me. When I followed the path of his gaze and saw my hands shaking uncontrollably, I tucked them under my legs. There was no way I'd let anyone, especially Cole, know how fucked up my head was at the mere mention of my full name. If I had to sit there all night with a fake smile plastered to my face, that's exactly what I was going to do.

Up until the moment that name left his lips, whenever I'd seen Cole, I could be Mari, lead singer of Jaded Ivory. It made it easier to see him. I could be someone else. Exactly like I'd been last night, before I let him take me home. I didn't have to worry about seeing pity or disgust in his eyes.

Another documentary. It had to be the third or fourth this week. Most of the students went to the bathroom during class, to wander the halls and get a break from it all.

Not me. The classroom was a safer place to be. With the teacher in the room, the jocks kept their comments to a minimum. Not that the teachers did much to the athletes when they treated others like shit, but they knew there was a line they couldn't cross with an adult around. And they stayed only just behind it.

Jennifer, the one friend I had, sat a few desks over. It looked like she'd already given up on the video, when I noticed her head down on the desk. For some reason, people paid less attention to her. She was better at hiding in the shadows and going unnoticed by the rest of our classmates. I wasn't so lucky. The last thing I needed was to give them more ammunition. A picture of me sleeping in class blasted all over social media would most certainly fit that bill.

I propped my head up with my hand and turned the lined paper on my desk into sheet music. I spent the class writing music, ignoring the muted laughter coming from behind me. God only knew what they were doing. Whatever it was, the less I paid attention the better.

With a few minutes left of the period, the movie ended and the lights came on. The guys at the back of the class were still laughing, with a few snickers thrown in here and there. I looked over at

Jennifer. She'd woken up and was staring at something behind me, her eyes wide.

"Your hair," she mouthed, pointing at the back of her head.

A lead weight settled in the pit of my stomach. With trembling fingers, I reached up and lightly ran my hand down my hair. About only an inch from the top my hand ran into something sticky. Gum. But it didn't stop at one piece. As I ran my hand down my hair, I found more and more sticky lumps. The laughter behind me came in great gusty shouts.

I ran from the room, ignoring Jennifer's calls. I ran into the bathroom, which was thankfully empty because it meant no one heard the high-pitched cry that left my mouth when I saw my reflection. Small pieces of gum covered most of my head, the bright pink a stark contrast to the blonde.

I tried pulling a piece out, which only yanked on my hair, taking some of it out by the root. The tears dripped down my face, no longer from embarrassment but from the pain in my scalp. Knowing I couldn't leave the bathroom until it was all out, I locked myself in one of the stalls, biting the inside of my cheek to keep from yelling as I removed each piece of gum, creating a pile of matted, discarded hair on the floor in front of my feet. By the time I was done, my scalp throbbed and I knew without looking in the mirror that my eyes would be red and puffy. When I opened the stall door, the image I saw reflected back at me brought tears to my eyes all over again.

Jennifer walked in, my bag in her hand. She wrapped her arms around me, holding me tight. "I'm so sorry, Mariella."

"It's not your fault." My chest hitched as I sucked in a ragged breath.

She held up her bag. "Let's see what we can do about your hair and makeup."

Jennifer did the best she could with what little she had to work with. It wasn't perfect, but it was much better than walking out of the bathroom a disheveled mess. When she was satisfied, she looped her arm through mine. "Good thing we have lunch next. Let's go."

I nodded and followed her out the door. What I hadn't expected was to walk right into Cole.

"Look where you're going." He shoved my shoulder and turned his nose up at me, eyes glaring.

"Sorry," I mumbled and started to walk away.

"Maybe you should learn to keep the gum in your mouth and out of your hair." The same laughter from earlier spread through the hallway.

I dropped my head and pushed past Cole and the rest of his crew.

With that one word, he'd spoiled everything. Now I was back to being Mariella, the girl who'd been bullied. The girl to be pitied. It wasn't what I expected from him, but it was there all the same. It was clear in his eyes and the way his mouth had turned down at the corners. I didn't want to be that girl anymore.

There I sat, my head swimming with things I didn't want to remember. The room blurred before me.

I would not let them break me.

I would not let them see me cry.

Heath wrapped an arm around my shoulders and leaned over to whisper in my ear. "He's still sitting at the end of the bar watching you. Want me to have one of the bouncers boot his ass out?" The shot landed in front of me and before I answered, I grabbed the glass knocking back the contents in one swallow. The searing fire of the liquor was a welcome relief from the emotions waging war for control of my body.

"No. He's fine. He didn't realize that we weren't interested in the same things."

"Okay," he said. "If you change your mind, tell me."

I ordered another drink. Sawyer stayed silent. Heath leaned back and watched me. "How did I not know your name is Mariella?"

Time in the room seemed to freeze. Not exactly a question I wanted to answer, but I couldn't leave him hanging. He'd already offered to throw Cole out for me.

"It's my name," I said to the empty glass in front of me, "but no one's called me that since high school."

There was a tangible pause before Heath caught on. "New start?"

"You could say that."

He gestured to where Cole sat. "That mean you know him from high school?"

"Yeah," I mumbled. "Can we talk about something else?"

He contemplated that for a moment. "Yeah, but no more hiding. I didn't know your real name and we're about to sign a record deal together. What else don't I know about you?"

The bartender returned, placing the drink in front of me. I waited a moment, not wanting to share but not wanting to lie, either. "You know me. There's not a whole lot more to tell."

He played with the label on his beer bottle, his eyes focused on the task. "I don't think that's true." He looked up, catching me in his perceptive gaze. "Besides Sawyer, you keep the rest of us at arm's length. We know the surface Mari—the one you show us. But there's more to you than that. And I think that's partly our own fault."

That brought my head around. "Why would you think it was your fault?"

"It's not like we've ever asked. You hang back, let the rest of us make all the decisions. I've never questioned it because you seem happy to be there. Seemed happy."

As much as it hurt to think, Heath was right. We'd known each other for years, but I'd kept a lot to myself. Tomorrow we would meet with the agent from LiteStar records and sign a contract that would tie us together for the next five years. The least I could do would be to open up about more than just what I liked to do on a Saturday night when we weren't playing.

Heath wasn't trying to pry into stories I didn't want to share, he only wanted to know more about me. It wasn't like I was the first person to be bullied in high school and I sure as hell wouldn't be the last. Shit, Sawyer had only just scratched the surface of those stories. Then again, most people left the bullies back in high school. They didn't have to deal with their bully face to face, hundreds of miles from home, after finally pulling themselves out of the gutter.

"I'm just not good at letting people in." It was my turn to focus on my drink, swirling the liquid around in the glass.

Sawyer leaned over and whispered in my ear. "Maybe, it's 'bout time you did." The man was still saving me from myself.

"Look, Mari." Heath turned in his seat so his knees were bumping mine. "I feel bad that we haven't paid more attention, asked more questions. It's time we did. You're part of our family. You don't have to be afraid to open up to us. We want to be there for you."

My chest ached with the thought I'd pushed them away, especially with my parents and siblings on the other side of the country. It was time to build those kinds of relationships with the other guys in the band. Sawyer had already proven he wouldn't hurt me. Surely I could trust the other guys to do the same?

I sat up straighter and faced him with a smile. "Well, you know my name is Mariella, but I haven't gone by that in five years, thanks to Sawyer here." I nodded my head in his direction.

"Ah, so Sawyer is the creator of Mari." Heath laughed.

"You can say that again." Sawyer chuckled and I shot him a grateful smile. Heath had no idea how true his statement was.

I was already feeling cautiously optimistic. "How about this? You guys come over Monday after we sign the contract and I'll cook."

"You cook?" He raised his brows.

"Hell yeah, she does," Sawyer chimed in, taking a sip of his beer and elbowing me in the side.

Heath reached around me and punched him in the arm. The bottle jostled away from his mouth, beer going everywhere.

"Damn it." Sawyer grabbed napkins from the bar to clean up the mess.

"You're supposed to share this kinda shit. Why the fuck are we always ordering out?"

Sawyer wiped the beer from his jeans. "'Cause Mari isn't your maid."

Heath winced. "Sorry, Mari."

I giggled. "Don't worry about it. I know that's not what you meant."

Sawyer grumbled under his breath. "That's it, defend the guy."

"Shut up. You're just cranky 'cause you're wearing beer." I rolled my eyes, then bit my bottom lip to keep myself from laughing at his expression.

"See?" Heath taunted.

The banter settled me. It was like another night in our basement, working on music. "Hey, at least Monday night you won't have to order."

Despite the looming record deal, money wasn't exactly falling from trees; then again, it wasn't tight, either. We made enough from our appearances and website to not have to work outside the band, but we were all very aware of the fickle nature of our industry. Just because we were hot property today didn't mean that we'd still be popular next week.

"Won't have to what?" Monty walked up behind us. Apparently, they were done playing pool.

"Won't have to order dinner or eat Jackson's cooking on Monday." Heath and Monty both wrinkled their noses at the thought. "Mari's gonna cook dinner."

"Hey, I'm not a terrible cook," Jackson protested.

"Yeah, you are," Monty, Heath, and Sawyer said at the same time.

"You can cook?" Monty asked.

Heath threw his hands up in the air. "That's what I said." He sent a mock glare at Sawyer. "And apparently, he knew."

"Dude, what the hell?" Monty hit Sawyer in the shoulder. At least this time he wasn't holding his beer.

"Ow." Sawyer grabbed his shoulder. "What the hell, you assholes? Stop hitting me."

Jackson laughed and took my hand, kissing it. "I knew there was a reason I loved you. Marry me."

I rolled my eyes at Jackson's joke proposal as our group erupted into laughter.

Out of the corner of my eye, I noticed Cole sitting at the end of the bar, no drink or food in front of him, his eyes trained on me. I didn't even want to imagine what he had to say to me. Nothing would make a difference. Sawyer was right—it had been a colossal mistake to sleep with him. It accomplished nothing. I had to live with that choice, but for the night I was done letting Cole impact my life.

I brought my attention back to the guys surrounding me. The guys who were my family. The ones who would be there for me no matter what.

ᕙᕙᕙ

I couldn't sit still, no matter how many times Sawyer tried to convince me to relax. I was up before the sun. Sleep wouldn't come. I'd tossed and turned until I decided there was no way I could get back to sleep. Instead, I got up and made coffee and breakfast. Four cups later and nerves weren't the only thing making my hands shake.

"Would you sit down. You're making *me* nervous." Sawyer glanced up at me from whatever TV show he'd settled on.

I stopped mid-step, plunking my hands on my hips. "You can't tell me you're not freaking out?"

"Nah. I'm excited." He tossed the remote to the side. I looked down at his knee, bouncing a mile a minute, then back up at him. He sighed. "Fine. I'm nervous. I can't believe things I've only dreamed about are coming true."

88

I dropped on the couch next to him, feeling the weight of his arm settle of my shoulders. "I know. Not that any of this was ever a dot on the radar of my life."

I leaned back against Sawyer's muscular chest and he dropped his chin to my head. "You do know a lot of this has to do with you, right?"

Heat raced up my chest to my cheeks. Thankfully, he couldn't see it. "You guys would have made it without me."

His finger slipped under my chin, tilting my face up to his. "Not likely. Remember, we were calling in favors for gigs until you sang with us the first time."

I shrugged. "I guess I can take a little of the credit."

He chuckled. "Always the humble one."

After that, he was silent for a few minutes. The kind of silence that told me he had something else on his mind. Sawyer had a habit of thinking things through, choosing his words carefully when he wasn't sure if he was saying the right thing. Even when I wanted to scream at him to spit out whatever was on his mind, I knew I had to wait for him to be ready. A few minutes later, he spoke up.

"The other night made me wonder something."

I ran through everything about the other night, not sure what he could mean. Hopefully, it wasn't something to do with Cole. "About what?"

"Heath's right, we never really asked your opinion on all of this. We asked you to keep singing with us, but never if you wanted the deal as much as we did. I guess I wanna know if this is what you really want, or if you're just going along with it because we want it."

My head snapped up so fast, I smacked into his chin. "Ow." I grabbed the top of my head at the same time Sawyer rubbed his jaw.

"Nice, Mari."

"Sorry. You caught me off guard." I moved to my knees, cupping his face between my hands. "Listen to me carefully. None of you have ever made me do anything I didn't want to. Sure, the first time I sang with Jaded Ivory was for you. It was the only way I knew how to repay you for everything you'd done for me." His eyes narrowed. "You taught me to love the girl I see in the mirror."

He shook his head. "But, that's no reason—"

I held his face tight, forcing him to keep his focus on me. "I'm not done. Every show, every song after that, I did because I wanted to. When I left for college, singing in a band was never on my list of things I could do. It took me time, but I know now that I can do it, I've never wanted anything more in my life."

He lifted a brow, the corners of his mouth lifting. "Nothing?"

Laughing, I smacked him in the chest.

The smile on his face fell once again. "Are you okay after what happened with Cole? You've been ducking me every time I've tried to ask you about it."

Not exactly what I wanted to talk about. I'd thought if I avoided the topic all weekend, he'd let it drop and I'd escape this conversation. I should have known better.

"Honestly, I'm not sure. After all this time, I never expected him to figure out who I was."

"Neither did I. Not until I heard him call you Mariella."

I shivered at the thought. Only two people still called me Mariella, and they were my parents.

Even my sister and brother had switched to calling me Mari.

"I didn't know what to do. It's not like there's much he could say to make up for four years of torture."

"Can't blame you for that."

"Hopefully, since we haven't seen him all weekend he's decided to leave it alone." I turned, sitting back down next to Sawyer.

"I'm not sure." Even without seeing his face, I could see the question in his voice. "He was pretty persistent last time. What's there to change his mind this time. If he wants to talk to you, I'm pretty sure he's going to keep trying."

I sighed. "I can hope he stays away, but you're probably right. If he comes around again, I'll figure out a way to avoid him. It might mean leaving after shows instead of hanging out, but I won't let Cole ruin anything else for me."

"That's my girl." The smile returned to Sawyer's face.

"Now that we've taken care of your worries and we have another hour before we need to leave for the meeting, I'm going to call my mom. I haven't talked to her since before Cole appeared." I wasn't sure what to tell her about that. Mom and Dad paid for me to go to school on the East Coast specifically so I could get away from people like Cole. How he managed to end up in the same town as me instead of playing professional football somewhere was beyond me.

"You haven't told her about the contract?"

"Not yet. I haven't called her because I didn't want to have to tell her about Cole."

"So don't. Doesn't mean you can't tell her that you're about to sign a record deal as the face of Jaded Ivory."

There was a flutter in my chest. "I fucking love the sound of that."

"Good." He gave me a light shove. "Now go tell her before we need to leave."

Smiling today was easier than it had been over the last month. I stuck my tongue out at him and ran to my room to grab my phone. She picked up on the second ring.

My mom was an accountant at her own firm. If she wasn't with a client, she always answered, even during the work day. That was especially true for me. She knew once I started playing with the band that we'd be busy at night.

"Mariella, sweetheart, what have you been up to? I haven't talked to you lately, is everything okay?"

I dropped down onto the bed, lying back. This was going to be a long conversation, might as well get comfortable. "I'm fine. Things are just crazy here. Sorry I haven't gotten the chance to call you back."

She was just learning how to text, which gave me a free pass on text messages. I must have been quiet too long. "Well, are you going to tell me what you've been busy with?"

I could hear the shuffle of papers on her desk. "We got a record deal."

The line went silent. It didn't even sound like Mom was breathing on the other end. I glanced down at my phone to make sure it hadn't dropped the call.

"Mom? Are you there?"

"Really?" she breathed.

I smiled. "Yeah, really. We sign the papers today."

The silence stretched for a second or two before the screaming started. A door banged open, most likely her secretary checking on my mom's freak-out.

"I'm fine," she said to someone on the other end. "Well, more than fine. Mariella got a record deal with her band!"

The sound changed and I knew she'd put me on speakerphone. "Congratulations, Mari. That's fantastic news. I'm so proud of you." Barbara had been Mom's secretary for as long as I could remember. She was like a second mom to the twins and me.

"Thanks, Barbara."

"I think your mom has finally calmed down enough to speak. I'm gonna go assure the rest of the office that no one is causing her bodily harm." She laughed. "Good luck."

"Thanks, Barbara. I'll call later with all the details."

"You'd better."

The click of her heels grew fainter as she walked from the room.

"Have you told Dad or Luke and Cassie?"

"Not yet. I called you first."

"They're going to be so excited for you."

There was a pretty large age gap between my siblings and me. The twins had seven years on me, and were well into their own lives by the time I reached high school, thankfully missing all the humiliating moments burned into my brain.

"I promise I'll call them later. We had a little time before we had to leave so I called you." My leg started bouncing up and down on the floor.

"You're nervous."

Of course she knew. The freaking mom whisperer. The woman could read us even when we weren't in the same room as her. "How'd you know?"

"It's all in your voice. Plus, I know you. You always question yourself when you shouldn't. You have a beautiful voice and deserve everything it brings you."

My chest felt a bit lighter with that. She might always know what we're thinking and feeling, but she also knew what to say to make us feel better. "I love you, Mom."

"I love you, too, sweetheart. Now tell me how all of this happened. The last time we talked about it, you guys didn't want to submit demos to labels."

I told her about the guy from LiteStar; how he'd heard one of our songs and come to one of our live shows. An hour seemed to pass in minutes. In the blink of an eye, Sawyer was knocking on my door to leave.

"Bye, sweetheart. Good luck today. Call me later and tell me how everything goes."

"I will. Love you."

After we hung up, I went to the bathroom to check my hair and makeup. When I was sure everything was where I wanted it, I met Sawyer in the living room.

"Ready?" He dangled the keys in the air.

"As I'll ever be."

I smiled and followed Sawyer out the door on another adventure. After this, I'd need another bird tattoo.

CHAPTER NINE

COLE

I rolled over a little after three in the morning. No matter what I tried, sleep wouldn't come. Every time I closed my eyes, Mari was there. The way she looked now, with a smile on her face as she performed for a horde of screaming fans, and then the way she used to look, shy and scared. But what I really couldn't push from my mind was the way she looked tonight.

Scared.

Ready to hear something shitty from me, when all I'd wanted to do was apologize the best I could.

I sat at the bar for hours, waiting to see if there'd be a chance to talk to her. I needed her to see that I wasn't the same guy; that words couldn't express how sorry I was for the hell I put her through. No matter who she was or what had happened in the past, I was still the guy who'd taken her home and who wanted to meet up for drinks again. The guy who really wanted to get to know the girl behind the microphone.

I didn't want any of that to come off as insincere. This wasn't about redemption. I wanted to get to know her, and it had nothing to do with the fact she was Mariella Cosmann. She was just a girl I met in a bar. Not that she'd see it like that.

Memory after memory assaulted me. The thought that I'd actually treated someone that way made my stomach roll. It was like a lead weight sitting on my chest, cutting off my circulation. How had I let myself be that person for so long? Thank god that one day changed the way I saw things. Too little, too late.

I couldn't blame her for not wanting to talk to me. The way she'd frozen when I called her by her full name had sent a chill through the room, making me think she hadn't expected me to figure it all out.

By four thirty, I gave up on sleep. Throwing the covers off, I climbed from the bed and as much as I wanted to drown in a bottle of tequila, I knew liquor wasn't the right answer so I pulled on a pair of gym shorts, sweatshirt, and my sneakers. Running myself into exhaustion didn't sound like a terrible idea. The team didn't have practice until Monday. Coach Harrison was happy enough with the way they'd played last night to give them the day off.

At least, that's what he told the kids.

What he really wanted was to watch tape of the possible teams we'd be facing in the playoffs without interruption, which meant I still had to go in for a few hours. At least he didn't expect us in until ten. A few miles might be enough to get me a couple of hours of sleep.

A few miles turned into seven, but it did the trick. My eyelids heavy, I barely made it to my bedroom. Without bothering to shower and change, I dropped into bed, my shoes still on my feet.

Thanks to my ill-timed run, I was almost late getting to the school. The entire time we watched the different teams, my head was a million miles away. Dismissing the other coaches, Coach Harrison called me into his office.

"What's on your mind, Cole?" He took the seat behind his desk and gestured to the ones in front.

With a sigh, I dropped into one of the two chairs there. "Just a lot on my mind."

He nodded like he understood where I was coming from. Coach Harrison had gotten me the job teaching Phys. Ed. after he found out I'd moved here to finish my degree. Once my shot at the NFL was over, I couldn't make myself stay there. The school, the campus all filled with memories that would make me dwell on the *what ifs*, instead of the *what nows*. He told me to finish my degree and he'd take care of the rest. After I'd gotten my bachelor's degree, he set me up in a program where I'd teach for a year and become certified that way, all of it designed to get me into the offensive coaching position sooner.

He leaned back in his chair, eyes trained on me. "I figured. I've never seen you so distracted. Usually you analyze every move the defense makes. Something happened this weekend?"

I ran a hand through my hair. I hadn't planned on talking about this with anyone, but if coach was offering me the opportunity to get a few things off my chest, I might as well take it. Everything else I'd tried hadn't worked. "You could say that. I ran into someone I went to high school with."

"Ahh, never easy. Especially when you wind up far from where you thought you'd be."

My heart stuttered in my chest. This was so much more than dealing with someone who expected me to be playing professional football. Would Mari have even known that? Then again, besides not playing the game I love, I was much happier with the man I was now over the one she'd known.

"Yeah, I just need to find a way to talk to her." I rested my elbows on my knees, dropping my gaze down to the floor. There had to be a way to get her to listen to me. Apologizing to her wasn't about making myself feel better, either. I needed her to know that she hadn't deserved any of what my so-called friends and I put her through in high school. I didn't know if any of what we did had had an impact, but even if it hadn't, that shit still hadn't been right.

"The whole picture is coming together. She expected you to be a big, fancy football player." I looked up to find him rolling his eyes, the corner of his mouth lifted in a smirk. "And you don't know how to tell her you're doing more for the sport of football now than you could have done as a player."

My head snapped up.

He laughed. "Not what you expected me to say, huh?"

He couldn't have been further from the truth, but what he said had me confused, nonetheless. "There have got to be millions of high school teams in the country, how am I making that much of a difference?"

He crossed his arms over his chest, leaning them on the desk. "You don't see it because you've always been so wrapped up in playing." He pointed at me. "You're a natural, Coach. It comes easy to you. You know when to push, and when to let the players make decisions for themselves. Your plays are unique and well planned. Look at yesterday. In less than an hour, you reworked the entire front line and still pulled off a win, even missing your starting wide receiver."

"I . . . I . . . Thank you."

Even with the nightmare I'd walked into last night, Coach's words lifted some of the weight off my chest. His words told me I wasn't that guy anymore. The one who took pleasure in making other people's lives miserable.

"Don't thank me. It was always there, I'm just the guy who recognized it before you did." He gestured around his office. "This is only a starting place for you. Colleges have been taking an interest—watching you. Someday you'll be coaching a Division I school, and no one will be worried about the kid who missed his chance for the NFL. They'll talk about Cole Wallace as one of the greatest coaches in collegiate history."

College? Being watched? None of it made sense. I was just a high school coach. "I've only been coaching for two seasons. How would they—"

"They've seen it in the plays you call. In two seasons, you've completely redesigned the offensive line. Don't get me wrong, everyone in football knows your name. After you got hurt, everyone was curious to see what you'd do. You picked coaching and every college out there shit themselves waiting to see what you could do. It's not for everyone. But you? You're a natural with unlimited potential." He watched me for a minute, letting me absorb his words.

For a brief moment, all my worries about Mari were pushed to the side. "I guess I never imagined anything like that."

"Don't get me wrong, you're a great teacher. The kids in your classes love you, but you're going to do so much more with your career." He stood and came around to sit on the front of his desk. "So face your past. Deal with it and move on. This is just a stop along the way for you."

What happened to my career became pretty insignificant in light of all the mistakes I'd made, but I couldn't make Coach Harrison understand without rehashing everything that had happened, and I had no plans to do that. And yet, even without knowing the extent of my problem, he seemed to know exactly what to say to give me the boost I needed. Like most teenagers, I'd made mistakes. I just honestly never thought I'd get the chance to make up for them.

"Thanks, Coach. Today . . . that was what I needed to hear." I stood from my chair. "I'll see you Monday."

He nodded, turning to open his playbook. "Enjoy the rest of your weekend."

"You, too, Coach."

I left the school, a mixture of emotions warring within me. On one hand, an excitement I hadn't felt since I signed my acceptance letter to college with a full ride scholarship filled my chest, reinforcing the career choice I'd made when I could no longer play.

On the other, a lead weight sat in my stomach. It was weird feeling so light and so heavy at the same time. Coach mentioned being embarrassed about not playing professionally when, actually, the only thing I was embarrassed about was my behavior off the field.

The entire drive home I was too distracted to notice anything around me. A parade could have marched right in front of my car and I would have missed it. When I walked into the house, Ryan was lying on the couch, watching TV. He looked up at me, tossing the remote onto the coffee table.

"Where have you been?"

I raised a brow. What was he talking about? I was at the school every Saturday morning for practice. This wasn't something new. "How hungover are you?"

"Better than when I woke up, but that doesn't answer my question."

I dropped my keys into the bowl by the door. "At the school to watch tape. Where else would I be?"

He sat up, dropping his feet to the floor in front of the couch. "That explains this morning. What about last night? You were supposed to meet us at the bar. Don't tell me you got a second night with Mari."

I'd totally forgotten about meeting them. "No, I didn't get a second night with Mari."

He flopped back onto the couch, like the weight of the world was too heavy for him. "I still can't believe you, you bastard. After all the times the rest of us tried and you're the one to get her in your bed. I bet you saw her last night."

"I did, but not for the reason you think I did." I dropped down into the recliner.

"Why the hell else would you go see her, if not for round two?"

"I know her."

He smirked. "I'd say you know her in the biblical sense."

My chest felt tight with the admission. "No, I mean I *know* her as in I knew her before she was Mari of Jaded Ivory."

Ryan sat up in a flash, grabbing his head, most likely to stop it from spinning. He dropped his hands and glared at me. "You fucker. You pretended not to know her just so you could fuck her first. That was low, you bastard."

"I wish that were the case." I scrubbed a hand down my face, my stomach in knots. "When I knew her she went by Mariella, and she looked nothing like she does now. I had no idea who she was until last night."

He narrowed his eyes at me. "How long ago are we talking? Did she recognize you?"

"High school." I winced. "And I'm pretty sure she did."

"Why wouldn't she say anything to you?" He sat forward, eyes on the TV but not taking any of it on. He sat in silence for a moment before turning to me. "Ex-girlfriend?"

I shook my head. "Not even close."

"Okay then, what? You're way too bugged out for this to be some chick in your graduating class."

My throat tightened and I swallowed to clear it. "Let's just say my *friends,* and I use that term loosely now, used to make Mari's life a living hell."

I didn't need to explain. Ryan would know exactly what I was talking about. High schools were the same everywhere. Popular kids teased the geeks and nerds, the hierarchy stayed intact, blah, blah, blah. Didn't make it right, though.

"Shit. What kind of stuff are we talking about? It can't have been that bad."

For the millionth time since yesterday I asked myself how I could have done any of it. Not just to Mari, but anyone I went to school with. Acid burned in my stomach.

"Let's see, there was the time we smashed her guitar . . ."

Ryan's eyes bulged. "Are you telling me you were a big enough asshole to pick up her guitar and smash it on the floor?"

"Yes, and not exactly."

"What do you mean, not exactly?" Ryan crossed his arms over his chest and lifted his chin.

"I'm sorry. I've known you for years and can't imagine you doing anything like that."

I rested my arms on my legs and looked anywhere but at him. "I made a lot of mistakes when I was younger. I thought I was invincible—that I could do whatever I wanted. So yes, I was a complete asshole. But I didn't pick the guitar up and smash it."

"Then how the hell did her guitar get smashed?"

"My high school wasn't huge, but each group had their own table in the cafeteria. Or at least I thought they did." I looked up at Ryan. "Hell, the only thing I really paid attention to was where we sat and the girls we'd hook up with were."

"Okay. Most high schools are like that. Shit, I'm sure the cafeteria at your school is the same way. I know mine is."

"It is. But that day when we walked in, the table where the girls normally sat was filled with the band geeks."

One brow arched over his eye. "You're seriously gonna go with that term?"

I lifted my hands. "Jesus, I know, but it's part of the story, all right?" He waved his hand for me to continue. "Anyway, before we could take one foot in the room, Sam had the idea to screw with them for sitting next to us. We had no idea at the time they were on a field trip. Another guy, named Brian, decided to help him. We had a big game that weekend and couldn't afford for either one of them to be benched if we were going to make the playoffs, so we fanned out to keep the teachers in the room distracted."

Ryan ran a hand through his hair. "For fuck's sake. This story keeps getting worse and worse."

"We haven't even gotten to the worst part."

"Are you telling me you actually helped those two pricks screw with people?"

"Hell no. While the rest of the guys fanned out through the room, I went over to rein those two assholes in." I sighed. "By the time I reached the table, Sam and Brian were already leaning over, trying to talk to two of the girls. Brian had, of course, picked Mariella—everyone's favorite target."

"She's hot as fuck, why would you guys get off on tormenting her?"

I laughed humorlessly. "Trust me when I tell you the Mari you know and the one I went to high school with are two different people. And as big of a dick as it made me, my only focus was on football and reaching the NFL. I didn't really pay much attention to anyone who couldn't help with that goal."

"You're right, that does make you a dick."

"Trust me, I know. I've learned a lot over the years."

"What does any of this have to do with the guitar?"

Self-loathing burned through me like acid. "Sam had the one girl eating out of his hand. It didn't take long before he got bored and ended up making her cry, but Mariella wasn't falling for Brian's shit. He kept trying to get her to talk to him, but she knew better and told him to get lost."

"Let me guess, he's a big enough asshole to not take too kindly to that and broke the guitar as payback."

"No. I told you, I broke the guitar. When I saw Brian was about to lose it on her, I grabbed his arm and tried to drag him away from the table." I thought about what I said to get him away from her.

"Come on, Bri. Mariloon's not gonna talk to you. She learned her lesson last week with Sam."

Rebecca Brooke

My throat burned remembering the way she flinched away from my words. "He yanked his arm out of my grasp and wrapped it around Mariella. Out of the corner of my eye, I saw Sam moving away from the table. I was relieved I only had one of them left to deal with. I saw the girl crying, but turned my attention back to Brian who looked up at me and told me to back off. I saw his hand come up to shove me back and I braced for it. My foot caught on something, taking me down to the floor.

"Shit. The guitar."

"Yeah, my ass landed right on top of it. I was about the same size then, so you can imagine what happened to the guitar. The crunch echoed throughout the room. Those assholes were laughing their heads off as I picked myself up off the floor."

"Holy hell."

"When I looked down and saw the guitar case, it wasn't the right shape and somewhat flattened." I swallowed hard. "I still remember the sound of her scream as it filled the room, the tears streaming down her face. She grabbed the case and ran. It was later that I found out that Sam had moved the case behind me so that Brian could push me down onto it."

By the time I'd finished reliving the whole clusterfuck of a day, my coffee had soured in my stomach and Ryan's eyes were practically bulging out of his skull. "Holy fuck. Your high school friends are a bunch of assholes."

I laughed, but it was humorless. "Tell me something I don't know. Why do you think I stopped being friends with them?"

"Shit, man."

I closed my eyes trying to shut out the world. Silence filled the room, heavy enough to be a physical presence but there wasn't much more to say. I'd just revealed how much of a dick I'd used to be, and the only glimmer of potential redemption was that I'd recognized that fact.

Ryan groaned. "You're killing me. What happened when you went to see her?"

I tried to suck in a deep breath, but the weight only grew heavier with each admission. "At first, she tried to pretend it was a one-night stand . . . until I called out her full name."

"Then?"

I sighed, my head dropping back to the couch, my eyes falling shut. "Then she walked away. And I can't blame her. When I think of all the times I'd been a part of making her life hell, I want to puke."

I opened my eyes to see Ryan rubbing the bridge of his nose with his thumb and forefinger. "What are you going to do now?"

I shrugged because for as much thought as I'd given it, I was yet to come up with a plan. "Not sure. I know I owe her a million apologies that won't even come close to making up for what I did."

"You gonna keep going to her shows?"

"I don't know any other way to find her."

"You'll figure it out. Since I've known you, you've always been able to find a way to dig yourself out of some of the biggest shit piles. You'll make this right."

"I hope so."

Ryan stood, his face turning a slight shade of green in the process. "Fuck, probably shouldn't have gotten up. Need greasy food. Pizza?"

"Sure," I said absently, my thoughts still on Mariella. Ryan was right. I'd crawled out of deep holes before. No reason I couldn't do the same thing this time.

The rest of the weekend passed in a blur. Ryan tried a number of times to get me to go out, his pledges of never drinking again quickly forgotten, but I just wasn't in the mood. I didn't even bother trying to figure out where Jaded Ivory was playing. What was the point? Until I could get her to listen to me, the conversation would only end up the same way.

By the time I finished work and practice on Monday I was exhausted, every muscle protesting under the weight of the stress.

Frustrated, I found myself standing in the middle of the grocery store with no idea what to buy. It was definitely one of those days where being an adult sucked. Life was much easier when I'd been able to come home from practice and dinner was waiting on the table. Growing up, my parents had fully supported my dream of playing in the NFL; taking me to practices, night games in the cold, even dinners wrapped in foil, waiting in the oven for me to get home.

After the last week, I could have used one of my mom's home-cooked meals. Deciding on something easy for dinner, I turned down the aisle to the left. The second I turned the corner I ran right into someone, knocking both of our groceries to the floor.

"Shit, I'm so sorry."

Cringing, I dropped down to start picking things up, noticing the girl I'd knocked into crouching down to do the same. I grabbed another one of the boxes that had fallen to the floor and my hand touched hers. I looked up, startled by the jolt that ran up my arm at the contact.

Those teal eyes would give her away anywhere. She snatched her hand back. My mouth went as dry as Death Valley. This was my chance. I needed to get my shit together and start talking. She threw things back into her basket, doing everything she could to avoid eye contact.

When she reached out to take the box in my hand I let her have it, then covered her fingers with mine. She flinched, her back going straight as an arrow.

"Why didn't you tell me?"

She tried to pull away but I held tight. It might not have been the right move, but I didn't know what else to do to get her to stay and listen.

"What was there to tell?" Her voice soft, dejected. I didn't like how it made me feel. Not one bit.

"You could have told me who you were. That we knew each other."

Her head snapped up. Fire blazed in her eyes. This time when she pulled her hand away, I let her go. Rage I could understand because I knew it was something I deserved.

"Told you who I was? For what?" Although the store was fairly quiet, I didn't miss the heads of the few other people in our aisle turn in our direction. "So I could see the look of disgust in your eyes when you realized it was Mariella Cosmann in your bed?"

I flinched, taking a step back as if she'd slapped me. "That's not what I would have done."

She dropped her basket, stalking forward. By now people were coming from other aisles to watch the show. "Oh really? Are you telling me that everything I remember is wrong?" Mari shoved my shoulder, making me stumble over my own two feet. I hadn't even tried to stand my ground. She could do whatever she wanted to me as long as it made her feel better.

I held my hands up. "I meant now. I'm not that asshole anymore."

"Once an asshole, always an asshole. Fuck you, Cole."

She turned and snatched up her basket, brushing past me and taking her groceries to the register. As slow chatter returned to the space around me, a flush ran up my cheeks and I caught more than a few sideways glances from curious onlookers. What must they be thinking about me? And what would they think if they knew the truth?

Everything she'd said was right.

Well, almost everything.

I was no longer that guy. The bully. The asshole. The jock.

I'd have to find a way to prove it to her. I needed to show her I wasn't that guy anymore. It was time for her to meet the real Cole Wallace.

CHAPTER TEN

Mari

Blood rushed through my ears. I could feel everyone's eyes on me, their questioning looks making me retreat inwards. Not that I blamed them. A scene like that was like a car wreck: you couldn't help but stop and look.

What a fitting comparison. My history with Cole truly was a car wreck. Nothing good could come of interacting with him. My breath came in shallow pants. Whatever was missing for dinner, I'd figure out how to do without it because after that scene, I had no intention of continuing to wander the store and chance another encounter with Cole. Sweat beaded on my forehead, and I willed the cashier to move quicker, knowing the adrenaline high wouldn't last much longer. I all but threw the groceries into the trunk of my car, slamming my door much harder than necessary.

Why was he so adamant about talking to me? Hadn't I suffered enough?

I gripped the steering wheel tighter, trying to control my trembling hands, but with that and the fast-paced rhythm of my heart thrumming in my chest, I thought I might be sick.

Today was supposed to be *the* day. No worries, no cares, just signatures on a piece of paper. Butterflies flew around my stomach the entire time. I couldn't wipe the grin from my face. Everything we'd worked hard for had finally fallen into our laps. I didn't have to chase my dreams anymore. They'd found me.

Then I run headfirst into Cole and remember why I'd started chasing them in the first place.

Sawyer's ringtone sounded through the car, the phone vibrating on the passenger seat startling me out of my thoughts. I grabbed it off the seat and hit speaker.

"Hey." My voice trembled slightly. Damn if I didn't know that Sawyer would pick up on that instantly.

"What's wrong?"

I ran a shaky hand through my hair, sucking in a deep breath. "Everything's fine. What's up?" I forced my voice to come out strong and sure, even if it was an octave or two too high.

Sawyer paused and in my mind's eye I could see his brow crinkling while he tried to figure out if I was hiding something from him. "Wanted to see if you would grab some beer on your way home?"

Beer. That I could deal with. "Text me what you want me to get."

"You sure you're okay?"

If only he could have seen me roll my eyes. "Sawyer, I'm driving."

"Fine." He sighed. I knew he didn't want to let it go so before he could argue with me, I disconnected the call and made the turn to stop by the liquor store.

I felt like a damn yo-yo. One minute I refused to let the past get in my way, the next it was causing public meltdowns. I couldn't seem to find a way to break the cycle.

Who knew how long we'd lived in the same city and managed to avoid each other. And now that I'd seen him once, I couldn't seem to shake him. The man did crazy things to my emotions. I had to admit, it felt good standing up to him.

But there was a moment, a split-second, where the hurt I thought I saw in his eyes made me want to believe the things he was saying. Believe in the good in people, and their ability to change. If only the glass half-full part of me hadn't been crushed long ago.

Cole could never change.

Today had been everything. I wouldn't let that asshole and his games ruin it. I went in the store, grabbed what Sawyer requested and added a bottle of champagne. We were going to celebrate.

By the time I got home, Sawyer was pacing a hole in the floor. He took the bags from my hands and carried them into the kitchen. The bags had barely touched the counter before he turned on me.

"What happened?" His gaze was so intent, it was as if he was trying to see inside my skin.

I started to unpack the bags, grateful for something to do with my shaking hands. "Why do you think something happened?"

He quirked a brow at me. "Maybe because when we left the office I'd never seen you smile so big you were walking on the clouds, then not thirty minutes after Monty drops me off, I call and there's a tremor to your voice. So either something happened on the two-hour drive home, or something happened while you were at the store. Which is it?"

I began assembling everything I needed to cook dinner. I knew he knew I was avoiding the question. That was how this friendship thing worked: he knew me almost as well as I knew myself and I, sometimes, hated that fact because it made hiding things from him damn near impossible. Hence the avoidance.

"Mari?"

"Sawyer?"

"You never shut me out. Don't start now."

Ice poured through me, making my muscles rigid. Warm hands landed on my shoulders, massaging out the tension. Slowly, under Sawyer ministrations, I relaxed until my back hit his front.

"Keys?"

I closed my eyes, letting the heat from his body spread through me. "I ran into Cole at the grocery store—or should I say, he ran into me."

"Ran into you?"

"Knocked my basket clean out of my hands. Shit flew everywhere. I didn't realize it was him at first." I cracked one eye open. "Come to think of it, I don't think he knew it was me. At least, not until we were picking everything up."

His hands stopped moving. "And?"

"And I told him to fuck off."

He gripped my shoulders and spun me around, his hands still on my upper arms, holding me away from him. "You did?"

I smiled. "I did and it felt ah-mazing."

His jaw dropped open but he recovered quickly, a large grin spreading across his face. "I knew you had it in you."

I winked. "I know. Now help me unload this shit so I can make dinner."

Between the two of us we worked quickly, although, Sawyer got in my way a lot. I wasn't used to having a shadow in the kitchen. Usually he just sat back and let me do my thing, but with all the excitement of the day he was amped up and wanted to help. It was annoying.

"Yello," a voice called from the front room. The only person who used that phrase was Monty.

Sawyer rolled his eyes. Setting down the spoon he'd been using to stir the sauce, he yelled, "In the kitchen."

We didn't exactly have a dining room table, or any table big enough to seat five people. Sawyer set three plates on the small table in the kitchen and two more on the counter.

"I brought beer," Monty singsonged as he walked into the kitchen, waving around two six-packs.

"So did I." I matched the tone of his voice.

He set them on the counter, pulling out a bottle and twisting off the top, popping the tops off two more bottles and handing them to Sawyer and me.

Monty pointed toward the pot with his beer. "That smells delicious."

He moved toward the stove but I batted him away with the spoon. Sawyer dropped onto one of the stools. "Where are Heath and Jackson?"

He waved his hand in the air. "Fucking around with some new song."

"A new song?" Sawyer asked.

"Yeah. Heath had the words in his head and wanted to get it down before he lost it. Jackson's helping with the melody. I got bored and came over here."

114

I pointed my spoon at him with a raised brow. "You got bored writing songs? I don't think so, that's one of your favorite things to do."

"Not today." He took a sip of his drink. "Today I want to celebrate. We have plenty of time for song writing."

Sawyer shook his head. "You wouldn't be saying that if it was you with the song in your head."

Monty laughed and raised his bottle in a mock toast. "So very true."

About thirty minutes later there was a light knock on the door before, once again, there was yelling from the front room. "Where's the baby?" Jackson stepped into the kitchen, waving a handful of papers.

"Bite me, asshole." Monty flipped them off.

"Shit, Mari, that smells great." Heath stepped into the room, slapping both Jackson and Monty upside the back of their heads. "You two knock it off."

"Is that the new song?" Sawyer asked, holding his hand out.

Jackson handed over some worn pieces of paper. "It is."

"It's not done. The melody needs a few tweaks, but I'm sure we can work in the other pieces as soon as Monty is done with his day off." Heath winked over at him, diving away from Monty's punch.

"If you guys are done fighting, dinner's done." I pulled the chicken from the over, setting it on the counter and drizzling sauce from the pan over the top.

Like a bunch of children, the boys scrambled to get in line, fighting for the front spot. After some pushing and shoving, plus a few pinches to the back of arms, everyone finally had a full plate and a place to sit. The guys dug into their food like they hadn't eaten in days.

Monty made a moaning sound in the back of his throat. "Damn it, Sawyer. I wish you'd told us earlier. How many dinners have we missed out on?"

"Whatever. At least we can celebrate." Sawyer held his beer up. "To record contracts and a long, successful future."

"Cheers."

The sound of clanking glass filled the room. The moment we'd been waiting for had arrived. The contracts were signed and Jaded Ivory was headed to the big leagues.

The feeling when I signed my name on that dotted line was overwhelming. I'd worked hard for things before, but they didn't usually pan out.

This time was different.

There was one thing I still didn't understand, though. "What I can't figure out is why they want us to keep playing the gigs we signed up for?"

Jackson had more knowledge about the industry than the rest of us and took a swig of his beer before answering. "It's simple. We've already built a fan base, which they've seen, and they don't want to chance hurting that by having us cancel. They want to use them to build an even bigger group of fans when we release our first single."

"Actually, that makes a lot of sense. I'd have missed singing to the crowds."

Monty laughed. "This is coming from the girl who almost threw up the first time she sang with us."

"Yep." I winked at him. "Let's just say that you've grown on me."

Chuckles around mouths full of food filled the room. It was nice to finally let myself be part of the group instead of watching from the sidelines; something I'd done for way too long. The guys were too preoccupied with eating to talk anymore so I was allowed a brief moment of solitude as I watched my friends enjoy their food, thinking about the future and what this might mean for all of us.

Two hours later, plates empty, bellies full, we sat around the living room. Empty bottles covered the small tables and the remnants of dinner prep still covered the counters in the kitchen. We didn't have a dishwasher but we were having too much fun for me to harp on Sawyer about getting the dishes done right now. We had a system: I cooked, he cleaned. Worked for me. I hated dishes.

Heath reclined in the chair in the corner, rubbing a hand over his stomach. "Holy shit, Sawyer. You weren't kidding. Mari, you fucking rock. That dinner was amazing."

"Thank you," I said, a warmth spreading through me. The guys seemed to be stuck in food comas, the perfect time to bring up what I'd been thinking about. "I was thinking about getting a guitar of my own again. I haven't played since high school, but I'd love to have one of my own to work on some ideas."

Jackson's brows winged up. "Song ideas?"

I glanced away, not wanting them to see me blush. Most of our songs came from Monty and Heath. Sawyer and Jackson had a few of their own, too, but I usually only made suggestions about what they'd already written, not come up with new stuff on my own. "Yeah, lately I've had these ideas rolling around my head and I want to get them down and see if they'd be worth playing."

"Knowing your talent on a piano, I'd bet they'd be great," Heath said. "I'll go and help you pick one out if you want."

I smiled, his offer doing as much to warm me as his compliments had earlier. "That would be awesome."

"How have we managed to discuss almost nothing about the contract all night?" Monty glanced around the room at all of us. "Isn't that supposed to be what we're celebrating tonight?"

"Yeah." Heath snuck a quick glance at me. "I also think we're celebrating having Mari showing us the real her."

I beamed at him. It felt nice to really be a part of something. "We are. And I have something for us." I stood from my seat on the couch and walked into the kitchen to collect the bottle of champagne I'd bought earlier and a few plastic solo cups. I held them up in my hands for everyone to see. "It's time to toast the contract properly."

Damn, it was like college all over again.

I gave the bottle to Sawyer, who set about opening it. I heard a loud pop and saw the cork fly across the room. Jackson dived for a cup, sticking it under the flowing champagne. Once they'd passed out the cups, I held mine up.

"To our soon-to-be first single."

Everyone raised their cups and downed the contents of their cup. Not really the way champagne was supposed to be drunk, but it worked for us.

"I can't believe this time next week we'll be in the studio recording Runaway Dream. It was the first song I ever wrote," Monty said, almost wistfully.

Jackson nodded. "I remember." Jackson and Monty had been roommates when we were in college. "And about a month after that it'll be hitting the airways."

My hands shook a little as I held out my cup to Sawyer for a refill. "It's surreal to think about hearing ourselves on the radio."

Sawyer laughed. "And you thought our shows were crowded now. I have a pretty good feeling that these places will have to hire extra security for the nights we play. Shit, with the way the guys look at Mari, I almost want to hire private security for her."

"I don't need private security."

And I didn't. Every night I was surrounded by four guys who would never let any jerk touch me.

"Speaking of." Jackson leaned forward resting his arms on his knees. "Do we need to do something about that guy from the other night?"

My hand froze with the cup halfway to my lips. I had no idea how to answer the question. Did I tell them he was a one-night stand who hadn't gotten the hint and let them deal with Cole? Or did I tell them who he was and let them in like I promised to do the other night? Out of the corner of my eye, I saw Sawyer give me a brief nod and I decided to go with the latter.

"No. He's just a guy I went to high school with."

"Yeah, but the look on your face tells me there's more to it than that." Heath's knowing eyes were trained on me.

After my run-in with Cole earlier, I really wanted to forget about him; at least, for one night. I was still a little freaked out by the connection I'd felt when our fingers touched.

"Let's just say that Cole was the popular football player and I was the weird music girl and leave it at that. I'm sure we can all put two and two together." Their eyes all darted away for a moment. Probably thinking about their own rough times in high school. Life was never easy for a teenager who didn't play sports or have friends in the popular crowd. Some people's experiences were worse than others. "It's why I threw the drink in his face, but he didn't recognize me until the other night."

Heath frowned, his brows drawing together. "I don't mean to be a dick, but didn't you go home with him last week?"

Sawyer shot me a look and then crossed his arms over his chest, sitting back in his seat and waiting for my response. He might not have been pissed at me anymore, but I wasn't naïve enough to think he would help me dig myself out of this one. Heat raced to my cheeks. I averted my eyes and took a drink. "I did. It was a really stupid idea."

"Says who? I've done the revenge fuck thing before." My jaw dropped open. I whipped my head around to gape at Monty. "What? It works."

"For fuck's sake." Jackson lifted his eyes skyward.

Monty shrugged and went back to his beer. "The head cheerleader thought she was hot shit. Found her working at the local diner a few years ago when I went home for winter break. Apparently, she'd flunked out of school. She was still hot as fuck, though, so when her shift was over, I fucked her in the back seat of my car and sent her on her way."

There were still times when the stuff that came out of Monty's mouth shocked the shit out of me. This was one of those times.

Sawyer rubbed his fingers over his temples. "Jesus, Monty. I don't think that's the same thing."

"Me neither," Heath mumbled, his eyes trained on me, searching for something.

Silence settled over the room. Not a comfortable silence; one that made you want to say anything to break it.

"So, the Cabet Room on Friday?" Sawyer turned to Jackson.

And just like that, the spell was broken. The conversation changed course, focused solely on our future as a band.

♈♈♈

"Think he'll show up tonight?" Sawyer glanced over at me from the passenger seat of the car.

We were on our way to the gig, the first since we'd signed the contract with LiteStar. News had broken locally about the deal, which meant we could be expecting larger than normal crowds. The studio had already paid for additional security. Not that we were a big draw for anyone outside the area, but they were still concerned about their investment and wanted us to be safe, especially since we'd kept our schedule at their request.

"Probably. I don't know. He's been pretty persistent. I honestly didn't expect him to show up again after I went home with him."

I tapped my thumbs on the steering wheel. It was one thing to sing when Cole had no idea who I was. It was another thing to think about singing if he was in the audience, knowing exactly whose voice he was listening to.

"Mari?"

"Yeah?"

"Can you handle it? Or should I—"

"I slept with him. It won't happen again. I'm a big girl. I'll be fine."

He nodded and said nothing else. There was no way I'd let them start this shit so early in our careers. Unless I became celibate or avoided the public all together, there was no way to avoid moments when someone in the crowd might make me uncomfortable.

If only the lone reason I was uncomfortable had to do with the history I had with Cole.

What I hadn't mentioned to Sawyer were the dreams I'd continued to have. The ones about Cole and the way his lips felt against mine, and I certainly hadn't mentioned the times when I'd woken up breathless, having re-experienced the way he'd touched me. I wouldn't let anyone know that.

Sawyer was silent the rest of the drive, studying me the way Heath had the other night. By the time we reached the venue, I'd had enough and couldn't wait to get out of the car, even more thankful than before that the place had separate changing rooms.

As soon as we stepped through the back entrance, the manager was waiting for us. "Welcome to Cabet Room." He reached out, shaking both of our hands before gesturing down the hall. "The rest of the band arrived a little bit ago. I set them up in one of our waiting rooms." He looked over at me. "They mentioned you might want a separate place to change."

I held up my bag. "If possible. Otherwise, I'll make them wait in the hall." I smiled.

He chuckled. "That's no problem. I put the guys in the room on the left, the room to the right is all yours. Something arrived for you earlier and I put it inside already." He glanced down at his watch. "You have about forty-five minutes. The room is closed for the next half an hour to give you time to set up. The crowd is bigger than we expected so I'm going to head out front to make sure things stay under control. I'll be back to get you when it's time."

"Thank you," I said.

"No, thank you for not canceling. I heard about your deal with LiteStar. Congratulations. Not all bands would have kept their prescheduled commitments."

Sawyer shook his head. "Not our style."

"Good to know," the manager said. "I'll see you in a bit."

The first chance I got, I opened the door to my right and shut myself inside, not wanting to give Sawyer the chance to talk more about Cole when what I really wanted was to let it go.

I heard the door on the other side of the hall close and I knew Sawyer had gone to round up the guys to bring the equipment in and set up. Normally I was all about pulling my weight, but not tonight. It wasn't that I didn't want to help. It more had to do with needing a few minutes to wrap my head around all of it: Sawyer's constant questions, Heath's assessing gaze, Cole's attempt to talk, and the contract. All of it put together made for a very stressful week. A few minutes alone would do me good.

In my need to get away, I'd almost forgotten what the manager said about something being delivered there for me. I glanced around the room. To the right sat a long counter with a mirror, and directly in front of that mirror sat a vase of beautiful flowers in all varieties of colors and types. Would the guys really have gotten me flowers again? They hadn't since the last time I told them I didn't need flowers, but the gesture was lovely. Picking up the card, I took in their sweet-smelling aroma.

Mariella,

Words cannot express how sorry I am for all the hurt I caused you. I know that flowers and apologies aren't enough, but if you would give me a chance to talk, I can prove I'm not the same dumb idiot you knew before.

Cole

I dropped the card as if it had scalded me, but not before I saw his number written on the bottom, letting me know I could call or text whenever. I didn't want to admit to the small flutter of my heart when I saw his name and I did my best to ignore it.

I picked the card back up, sliding it carefully into the envelope and stowing it in my purse. The flowers would go somewhere else. I didn't have it in me to get rid of the card. I might not trust him to sit down and talk, but the apology, sincere or not, was nice to hear.

A soft knock came on the door. "Mari?" Sawyer's voice called from the other side.

"Come in." Time alone hadn't done me any good. Not with flowers from Cole taunting me from the counter.

"Hey," he said, opening the door. "I came to tell you— Oh, who sent you flowers?"

"Cole."

He pursed his lips. "Cole sent you flowers?"

"He did." I tried to paste on a smile, even though I knew he'd see right through it.

"And? What did the card say?" He hadn't moved from the doorway.

I busied myself taking things out of my bag. "That he's sorry and wants to apologize in person."

Sawyer walked forward and wrapped his arms around me, holding my back to his front. "Are you going to meet him?"

"No. There's nothing he could say to make me think that's a good idea."

He held me tighter. "Whatever you want."

"I want to sing and not worry about flowers or apologies. I want to enjoy finally knowing that it was all worth it in the end." I looked up at him in the mirror and watched the smile spread across his face.

"Then that's what we'll do."

"And tomorrow you're coming with me to the tattoo place."

He raised a brow. "Time for a new bird?"

I smiled back. "You got it."

He moved his hands to the top of my shoulders. "You know you're gonna run out of room someday, if you keep it up. You have tiny little shoulders."

"Then I guess I'll need to find another way to mark the occasion."

"I'm sure you'll think of something." He gave a squeeze and met my gaze in the mirror. "Everything is set up and ready to go."

"Yeah, sorry about that," I said, glancing down at the floor.

He rested his head on top of mine. "Don't worry. I could tell you needed a few minutes alone."

"You always know exactly what I need."

"Not always, but I'll take the compliment." He kissed me on the cheek. "We'll be next door if you want to hang out with us."

"Give me a few minutes and I'll be over."

"Okay." Sawyer left, shutting the door behind him.

I paced back and forth across the room trying to shake the nerves that had come over me. My stomach was still tied in knots but my hands were no longer shaking when I left to sit with the guys. It wasn't long after that the manager came to get us.

I walked down the hall biting my nails.

"Mari? Are you okay?" Jackson asked. "I haven't see you this nervous since the first time we sang together."

I quickly dropped my hands. "I'm fine. Just excited for tonight."

He kept his gaze on me. Like with Sawyer and Heath, the intense scrutiny unnerved me. It would appear that letting the guys in came with all sorts of strings.

Finally, he nodded and turned toward the stage door and I took a full breath.

The manager introduced the band and I entered the stage, the guys patting my back or squeezing my fingers on the way past. I couldn't stop my gaze from wandering through the crowd. I told myself I wasn't looking for him. No, I was appreciating the moment.

Liar.

My heart jolted in my chest.

There on a stool at the center of the bar was Cole, his bright green eyes trained on me. I forced myself to look away, but the muscles in my body relaxed at the sight of him and I heard the click of Sawyer counting us in.

Somehow, the guy I'd feared for so long was becoming the one thing that settled me when nothing else worked.

CHAPTER ELEVEN

COLE

Over and over, I sent flowers, apology cards, candy, all with my number attached.

None of it worked.

It wasn't like I was any good at this sort of thing, and I was completely out of ideas. I went to all her shows and watched her sing. She had a beautiful voice. I wanted to kick myself for not paying attention before. My attraction to her had only grown in the weeks since our first encounter. Not that I thought being with her was a possibility, considering the history between us. All I could hope for was a chance to apologize.

The cold beer in my hand did nothing to reduce the heat in my body. Even though I knew I would never have Mari again, the memories of that night had seared themselves in my brain. I'd watch her joke and laugh with the other members of Jaded Ivory and I wanted to punch something.

"Keep squeezing and you're gonna break that bottle."

I glanced out of the corner of my eye to see the keyboard player had taken the seat next to me. I flexed my hand, the skin over my knuckles slowly returning to its natural color.

"Guess you're here to tell me to leave Mari the hell alone." I drained the rest of my bottle and motioned to the bartender for another.

He gestured to the bartender to make it two. "Nope. I'm over here for a different reason."

The bartender set our beers in front of us. I quirked a brow but didn't bother looking at him. "And that would be?" I tipped back the bottle.

"To help you get Mari to listen."

Beer sprayed from my lips and without breaking stride he handed me a napkin and took a swig of his drink.

"I've seen you at every show we play, always watching Mari. A few weeks ago, Mari told us who you were. She didn't mention much of what happened, just that you hadn't made high school a very pleasant experience for her."

I cringed. "And with how protective I've seen you guys of her you *don't* want to kick my ass?"

The keyboard player scoffed. "Oh, I definitely wanted to do that. Mari begged us not to. Then the gifts started arriving."

I rolled the bottle between my hands. I'd thought the gifts might get through to her, and my persistence show her that apologizing really meant something to me. But I'd been wrong. "Which she's ignored. Probably all ended up in the trash before she even read the cards. I know she'd never consider being friends with me. I only want to apologize— show her I'm not the same guy I was back then."

I noticed his gaze had strayed to the far corner of the bar where Mari sat, her back to us, chatting away like she didn't know or care that I was there.

And why should she?

"Sawyer would kick my ass if he knew I was over here, but Jackson, Monty, and I agree that it would be good for her."

Names were swirling all around. Besides Mari, I had no idea who he was talking about. It may not have been important, but it would make the conversation a whole lot less confusing. "Who?"

He laughed. "Shit, I'm sorry. I never introduced myself. I'm Heath." He nodded his head toward the booth with Mari. "That's Jackson. Sawyer's about to take his shot at the table and Monty's watching."

"Cole."

I offered my hand and he smirked, leaving it hanging in midair in favor of tearing at the label of his beer. "Yeah, I kinda knew that already."

"Good point. So besides this Sawyer guy, you all *want* Mari to sit down with me?"

He gestured toward her. "Yep. Monty and Jackson are keeping them busy so we can chat. When we mention you, Sawyer shoots death glares at us. Mari just pretends we haven't said anything."

I set my beer down. Whatever he had to tell me, I wanted to be sober for this conversation. "Can you help me?"

He drained his drink and set the bottle down. "You know she watches you?"

Good thing I wasn't drinking anymore, otherwise I might have spit my beer all over again. "She does?"

"Every gig. You're the first person she looks for. I think she tells herself she's hoping you aren't there, but you can tell that's not the case the minute she gets on stage. Her whole posture relaxes that minute her eyes land on you. One time, I think you must have been in the bathroom or something because she kept looking. Didn't settle until you took your seat at the bar. Deep down, I think there's a part of her that wants you to be different."

His words made my heart thunder in my chest. Could that really be the case? Physically, our chemistry was like an electric current, obliterating everything in its path. I'd wanted her with a vengeance that night. The simple taste of her lips made my dick hard and my head spin. But could there be something emotional there, too?

"What do you think I should do? Like I said, I've sent her a million things and I don't think she's read one of the cards attached."

"Oh, she's read every single one."

Every.

Single.

One.

She *was* reading them. She hadn't bothered to call or even acknowledge my presence at her shows, but she'd read my words. And yet every time, she walked past me without a word, pretending not to see me.

"She read them and still nothing?"

Heath sighed. "How much do you remember about Mari?"

My stomach clenched, the beer threatening to make a reappearance. "Not much. Most of the memories I have, I'm pretty sure she'd rather forget. Then again, so would I."

His eyes narrowed. "I figured. Do you know the last time we bought her flowers?"

"Why would you guys buy her flowers?"

He dropped his elbow onto the bar and rubbed his eyes with his fingers. "Because she sang with us when she didn't have to, but that's . . .

Anyway, we bought her flowers as a thank you. Do you know what she did with them? She took them to a nursing home. Said thank you, but she didn't need them like the elderly in the nursing home did."

The woman had a heart of gold. After everything we'd put her through, she'd still found a way to see the good in people. A way to take care of people.

Maybe she could see that in me?

"Your flowers ended up in the same places, along with the chocolate. The cards, I'm not sure about."

There was a slight pressure behind my eye. So far, he hadn't said anything that would help me get a chance to talk to Mari.

"Okay. Not sure where that leaves me."

"She said you were a jock. You take too many hits to the head or something?"

The label of the beer bottle became dust under my fingernails. "What's that supposed to mean?"

"God, right now I wanna smack you upside the head for being so dense. It means that Mari thinks other people deserve the flowers more than her."

I hung my head, not wanting to see his face when I admitted the truth. "I helped do that to her."

"You did. Which means it's going to take some kind of unique gesture on your part to prove to her you're different. Flowers aren't exactly original."

He pulled his phone out of his pocket, his fingers flying over the keys. "I'm out of time. They're almost done playing pool." He pulled a card out and handed it to me. It was a Jaded Ivory business card. I pulled out my wallet and tucked the card inside. "That's my number. If you need to know where we'll

131

be playing when you think of something, shoot me a text."

He threw some money on the bar and walked back toward the table with Mari and the other guy. He shook his phone in his hand, probably pretending that he'd had to make a call.

Needing to go home and think about everything that had been said, I cashed out my tab and for the first time since I'd figured out who she was, I left the bar before Mari.

Ryan was watching ESPN when I walked in the door. "You're home early. Still no luck?"

I sat down next to him. "Not with Mari, but I had an interesting conversation with one of her band members."

"About what?"

I told him about the whole surreal conversation with Heath, including his advice on how to win Mari over.

He shrugged. "Simple. You knew her for at least four years. What kind of things does she like?"

I closed my eyes, resting my head on the back of the couch. "The shitty thing is, I have no idea. I honestly never paid much attention to her and what she liked and disliked."

He scrubbed a hand over his face. "Fuck. The more you tell me, the more I feel like I don't even know you."

"No, you don't know the old me—and trust me when I say that's a good thing. He was cocky and arrogant. Thought he could do anything he wanted, whenever he wanted."

"What are you going to do then? Sounds to me like the guy's right. Whatever you come up with must be unique to you."

I groaned. "I know, but I have no idea what that could be."

We sat in silence, the TV the only sound in the room as I tried to rack my brain and come up with something. Eventually I got frustrated and stood up. "I have to work in the morning."

He shot me a look, then turned his gaze back to the TV. "Whatever, dude. You've only been torturing me for weeks about this chick and now you're giving up."

My fingers dug into my palms. "I'm not giving up," I growled through clenched teeth. "But I can't think of anything right at this moment, and staying up all night and being useless at work tomorrow won't help me think of anything, either."

I must have missed the twinkle of humor in his eyes, as a smirk rose over his lips. "Good. At least you're not giving up after weeks of work."

My hands and jaw relaxed. "You're an asshole."

"I try."

That night I lay in the dark, staring at the ceiling, my mind blank. What could I possibly do to win her over? So many memories and none of her likes or dislikes. I didn't really know anything about her, except that she liked music.

Like a freight train, the idea hit me.

She liked music.

There was one thing I could do, unique to me, to prove myself to her.

I jumped from the bed and flipped on the light, fishing the card Heath had given me earlier from my wallet. Pulling it out, I sent a text to the number on the front and climbed back into bed. A few minutes later my phone buzzed.

Heath would help. Perfect.

I lay back down and smiled up at the ceiling. I had a plan. Now all I had to do was put it into action.

CHAPTER TWELVE

Mari

"This place is bigger than I expected."

I wasn't kidding. The backstage area alone was twice the size of the stages we'd played on up until now. With the release of our first single coming up in the next two weeks, the studio had started booking additional venues for us to play. Our crowd size continued to grow and they wanted to keep the momentum up, hoping that once it was available, the fans would immediately download the song.

Monty stepped into the room behind me and let out a low whistle.

The B&B Lounge wasn't a bar. While they did serve drinks, this was a concert venue, not a place for people to hang out. It was a place where people paid to get in and see a band.

And tonight that band was Jaded Ivory.

Being on the stage where some of my favorite bands had performed was surreal. I kept wondering if I was going to wake up and realize it was all a dream.

A light tap touched my shoulder.

"Whatcha thinking?" Heath stood behind me, his eyes darting around the space.

I laughed. "I'm actually in awe right now. Think of the bands we love who've played here before us."

He rested his arm over my shoulder. "Unreal, right?"

"You can say that again."

"Unreal, right?" He smiled then jerked his head backward. "Come on, I'll show you where the dressing rooms are."

I quirked my brow. "Already scouting out the place?"

"You bet your ass I have. I was curious."

My cheeks hurt from all the smiling. "Lead the way then."

When I entered the dressing room, I was surprised to find it empty of anything but my stuff. Maybe Cole had given up. It had been weeks and I hadn't tried to talk to him at all, but the gifts had kept coming, and even though the reason behind the gifts caused me heartache, I'd began to look forward to them. I hadn't thrown any of the cards away, choosing instead to keep them hidden in my bedroom, away from Sawyer.

Pushing my disappointment aside, I focused on getting ready. Tonight was too big a night to let my head get in the way.

Almost three hours later, electric energy coursed through me as I left the stage. I'd never felt so alive after a performance. The crowd's excitement was almost tangible. We'd done two encores. I

135

should have been exhausted, instead my body felt light as a feather. Prancing down the hall to the dressing room I knew, even with the risk of losing my voice, I could have sung all night.

The guys had already hustled equipment into the van and were just waiting on me to change, wanting to go out and celebrate our first big performance. I'd argued that I was fine going as I was, but Heath insisted I change, his eyes bright with excitement when he sent me on my way.

The door swung open and my heart leapt into my throat. A brand-new Fender guitar sat on a stand in the middle of the room. A bow attached to the neck of the guitar held a gift tag.

> *Mari,*
> *I believe I owe you this.*
> *Cole*

That was the first time he'd called me Mari since finding out I was Mariella. I hadn't expected him to remember. The room blurred at the thought of my warped guitar bag. It had been my sixteenth birthday present. My parents wanted to throw me a sweet sixteen party but I'd begged them not to, fear of no one showing up, or worse, the popular kids gate-crashing made me not want anything to do with a birthday party. Mom had been a little sad, but said she wouldn't throw me a party if I didn't want one.

On the morning of my birthday, I'd found the guitar of my dreams at the end of my bed.

A brand-new Fender.

The spotlights in my room reflected off the shiny black finish. My parents had decided to spend all their money on the one thing I wanted above all others, but never thought I'd be able to afford.

It had been my most prized possession . . .

Until it wasn't.

That day was etched in my head with vivid clarity. Brian's arm had been resting over my shoulders, and no matter how many times I tried to shrug him off, he'd stayed there, pretending to hit on me. Sam the asshole had already made Maria cry. All I'd wanted was for them to leave us alone for once. His arm had finally moved and I'd been about to get up when the sound of splintering wood filled my ears.

I closed my eyes tight, my hands over my ears to block the sound of my guitar shattering because even though it was just a memory, the pain came as fresh as if it were happening all over again.

Warm arms encircled me in a tight embrace. I buried my face against his chest and let it all go. My entire body jerked under the force of my sobs. It seemed so trivial. A broken guitar. Why cry over that? It wasn't just that, it was everything that broken guitar represented. I hadn't cried this hard since the day I turned around to see Cole sitting on the case.

"Please don't cry," a voice whispered as warm hands rubbed comforting circles across my back. "I'm sorry."

The voice cut through everything and I jumped back out of his embrace.

"Mari," Cole pleaded.

"What are you doing here?" I brushed furiously at my face, hating the fact he'd seen me crying. Mariella cried. Mari didn't.

He lifted his hands palms up and took a step forward. "The same thing I've been doing for weeks. Trying to prove to you I'm not that guy anymore."

"I can't accept that." I pointed at the guitar, relieved that my voice sounded a little stronger than it had a few moments ago.

137

He took another step forward, then another. "Yes, you can."

I shook my head, holding my ground. "No, I can't."

He continued walking until he was right in front of me, close enough to reach out and lightly caress my cheek with his fingers. I just barely controlled the shiver that coursed through me. "Yes, you can. It's a debt I should have paid a long time ago."

I sucked in a breath. His words were like a physical jolt. Never in all my life would I have expected Cole Wallace to speak those words to me. He was standing there, gazing down at me. I had to know and this might be my only chance to ask and see the truth in his eyes. "Why?"

"Break the guitar?"

I nodded, afraid to speak.

"I didn't mean to."

I wanted to slap him. To slap him and to call him a liar and then run.

But something in his eyes stopped me. His gaze never wavered, never moved from mine. Could he be telling the truth?

"What do you mean you didn't mean to?"

"I'd been trying to get Brian and Sam to leave you and your friends alone. I won't lie and say it wasn't for purely selfish reasons. If they'd gotten caught, Coach would have benched them and we needed them for the game."

That admission hurt. Deep down I knew the answers weren't all going to be sunshine and roses. "Sam gave up pretty quickly, but Brian was determined. When I took hold of his arm, I'd expected him to shake me off. What I hadn't expected was for Sam to have moved your guitar behind me, or for Brian to shove me to the floor." He shook his head as if trying to shake off the memory. "I might have been an egotistical dick, but I would never have intentionally destroyed someone else's property."

"Just their self-esteem."

His face fell. "Please, Mari. I know I've made so many mistakes with you, I don't even want to count them. At least let me take you to dinner and I can use the time to grovel for every single one of them."

Something occurred to me and it left a sour taste in my mouth. "How did you get back here? This place isn't like the other ones we've played. You need a pass to get backstage."

"I helped him." Heath stepped around the doorway, followed by Jackson.

My throat closed. I whipped my head around, shooting daggers from my eyes at the two betraying assholes. "I trusted you." My voice was barely above a whisper.

I brushed past Cole and went to do the same to Heath and Jackson when Heath stepped in front of me, wrapping his hands around my upper arms.

"You did and now I'm asking you to keep trusting me."

"Please, Mari. Just listen," Jackson begged.

Heath lifted my chin with his fingers, forcing me to make eye contact. "I never would have helped him if I didn't believe him. Someone that only wants to fuck with you doesn't spend weeks trying to get your attention, buying you things. Buying you a fucking Fender. Someone who wants to fuck with you would have just given up by now."

"You don't know him," I yelled.

"Neither do you." Heath's tone was a hard as mine. "But I can tell you I've watched him sit there, night after night, watching you." I glanced over at

Cole, who stood in the same spot, wringing his hands in front of him. He didn't look like the Cole I knew back then. The Cole back then would have met my gaze without shame. He would have stared me down. And the Mariella I was would have let him.

Maybe we'd both changed?

"Mari?" My attention returned to Heath. "Let him apologize. Let him grovel. Let him beg. You need this more than you realize." He ran his fingers over the tattoos on my shoulder. "Whether you believe him or not."

Sawyer had gone with me to get the first bird on my shoulder, but Heath had been there a few times since then. He knew what they meant to me. Would listening to Cole apologize really help me, or would it just give Cole a reason to alleviate his own conscience?

I didn't even want to think about how readily I'd accepted his comfort earlier. Granted, I hadn't known it was Cole, but his arms had helped me relax enough to let my guard down, the emotions racing to the surface. Sawyer was the only one who usually saw that side of me.

The silence stretched on and on, my heart still in my throat.

"Mari?" Jackson lifted a hand to swipe a tear off my cheek. "Please go. We're not trying to help him. We're trying to help *you*."

The sincerity in their eyes was my undoing. Anger burned through me. Heath and Jackson had no right to interfere in any of this—to help one of the people from my past who most likely didn't deserve it. Rationally, I knew that they wouldn't do anything to hurt me, but that didn't stop me from lashing out, wrenching my arms from Heath's grasp and stepping away.

"Fine. I'll go. But you two can go right to hell for all I care." Without a backward glance, I snapped, "I'm leaving, if you're coming let's go."

I stormed from the room. Cole could follow or not. I wasn't waiting for him.

"Mari." Jackson reached for me. I didn't bother responding, just flipped him off and kept walking.

My fight or flight response had kicked in.

It was time to fight.

I'd learned a long time ago that being meek only made things worse. Cole had seen me cry once tonight, and it sure as shit wasn't going to happen again.

CHAPTER THIRTEEN

COLE

That was not how I'd expected the night to start. Seeing Mari cry the moment I stepped around the corner had been like a vise around my chest. I didn't stop, didn't think about her reaction, I simply held her.

The night we'd spent in my bed had nothing on the sensation of having her seek comfort in my arms. For some reason the gesture was much more intimate. A connection I'd never had with someone before, and not one I deserved. I'd earned anger and hatred, but tears? I had a feeling I caused enough tears to last Mari a lifetime.

As I watched her retreat I stood frozen to my spot, unsure if any of this was a good idea anymore.

"She's never going to forgive us." Jackson rubbed the back of his neck, his eyes on the floor. Heath hadn't taken his eyes off Mari as she stormed down the hall.

"She will. She just needs time to calm down. And listen to what he has to say." He turned to me. "My suggestion is to get your ass on the move. She's not going to wait and if she finds Sawyer, she's outta here."

I didn't bother responding. Grabbing the guitar, I jogged down the hall. It wasn't until I reached the front door that I caught up with Mari, who stood at the exit, arms crossed over her chest, lips flattened into a thin line.

"I don't have my car," she snapped.

I pulled my keys out of my pocket.

It was like a sheet of ice had settled over her, thicker than it had been the last few weeks and I needed to find a way to thaw it. I held the guitar out to her.

When the idea had come to me, I'd thought it genius. But the fact that she'd reacted so severely to just the sight of it made me question whether or not I'd totally missed the mark.

Her breath hitched and she reached out, shaking her head from side to side. Before she could stop me, I flipped her hand over and closed her fingers around the neck. She tried to hand it back.

"It's yours," I said softly.

Mari didn't say anything, just held the guitar tighter and nodded.

"Dinner?"

She sighed. "Fine, but afterward can we stop pretending you give two shits about me?" She pushed her way out the door. I followed, catching up and moving in front. Mari stopped in her tracks to keep from running into me.

"It isn't pretense. I actually do care, which is what I want to show you. It's why I'm here."

"And why should I believe you?"

I gave her a sad smile. "You probably shouldn't. I just really wish you would."

"Where did you park?"

I nodded to the side of the building. "Over here. The guys let me in the side door."

"I still can't believe those fuckers," she mumbled.

We reached the car and I jumped in front to open the door for her. Her eyes widened slightly, but only for a moment before she pulled the mask down she'd been wearing since I'd caught up to her in the hall. She was doing everything she could to keep her emotions in check. I took the guitar from her and lay it carefully on the back seat. I hadn't thought to pick up the case the guy in the store had told me was the best I could buy. It was still in the dressing room. Hopefully the guys would grab it before they left.

Without a word, she got in the car and I shut the door behind her, racing around the driver's side, not wanting to give her a chance to change her mind. As the engine roared to life and I pulled from the lot, Mari kept her gaze focused out the window. It was too dark to see much. She must have been lost in her own head.

"It's too late to go to this little Italian place I like, but there's a great diner about fifteen minutes from here. Is that okay?"

"Wherever is fine." Her eyes remained firmly glued out the window.

The silence was crushing. I thought about turning on the radio, but if Mari decided she wanted to talk I wanted to be able to hear what she had to say. Nothing left her lips the entire ride.

No yelling. No cursing. No screaming.

Nothing.

We pulled into the parking lot at the diner and I breathed a sigh of relief, knowing it would be very hard to escape one another when you were sitting in a booth. Eventually she would have to talk to me.

I hoped.

I stepped out of the car and went around to open her door, only to find her standing there waiting. I gestured for her to go first which was apparently the wrong move because she immediately narrowed her eyes and stormed into the diner.

I tilted my face to the sky and asked for any help anyone would give me. It looked like I'd need it.

I walked through the front door but couldn't see her anywhere. For a brief moment I thought she might have run out the back door, until I spotted her hair over the top of a menu. The waitress had seated her right at the back corner, away from the other couples. Smart move.

The menu blocked her face from my vision when I sat down across from her.

"Mari?"

"What?"

"Mari?" I took hold of the top of the menu and lowered it to the table. "I asked you here to talk. Are you going to put barriers up all night?"

"With you I need four-feet concrete barriers to keep me safe. Besides, I have nothing to say. You're the one who wanted to talk. So talk."

The tone of her voice made it clear she wasn't interested in much of what I had to say, but I'd waited weeks for this opportunity. I couldn't let it go to waste. "I know—"

"Evenin', what can I get you?"

"Coffee," Mari chimed in immediately, her attention solely on the waitress. "Won't be here long enough for anything else," she mumbled under her breath.

"I'll have the same. Plus, can we get two peanut butter pies?"

The waitress nodded and left the table to fill our order.

"Hungry?" Mari asked, scrunching her nose up.

"Maybe." I'd ordered one for each of us, but I had no intention of telling her that. I had a feeling she'd want it when she saw mine. I'd seen her do it at the bar with her band mates. She'd turn down ordering something from the menu, then pick at whatever they got.

She didn't say anything else and I tried to get my thoughts out again. "I know you don't believe me. You think that anything that comes out of my mouth is either completely insincere or that I'm here to take pleasure in torturing you, but that's not the case."

"Why a guitar? How did the guys know about the guitar? I never told them."

Okay. There was something she wanted me to know about her. "I know. Heath only gave me a few hints—like the fact you kept all the cards from the flowers I sent." Her cheeks grew pink and her sleeve suddenly became very interesting. "He also told me that flowers weren't enough, that I needed to make a grand gesture, unique to me, if I wanted to win you over."

"And he told you to buy me a guitar since I'd been talking about getting one?" she snapped.

"Is that what you think? That I got the guitar because Heath told me to?"

"That's exactly how it is."

I reached out and covered her hand with mine, only to have her snatch hers away. "That's not how it is. When Heath suggested I needed something unique to me, he didn't tell me anything else. It took a few days to realize that breaking your guitar was

146

my biggest crime against you. Not the only one, but the one I needed to make up for over all the others."

Mari watched me, her eyes assessing, boring deep down, searching for something. "So you spent a couple hundred dollars on me, a girl you barely knew and one you didn't care about at all when you could have had a chance to know me, and expected it to be all forgotten?"

"That might have been true when I was a dumb, self-absorbed asshole—"

"And you're no longer a self-absorbed asshole?" she scoffed, picking at the corner of the menu. "History makes it hard for me to believe that."

My stomach soured, like it always did at the thought of what I'd lost. "Let's just say I learned a lot about myself and my life in college."

With a roll of her eyes, she stood and pulled her phone out. "We all learned a lot about ourselves in college. Wanna know what I learned? To not put up with people's bullshit anymore." She started to walk away from the booth but I grabbed her hand and pulled her around to face me.

"Cole, get your fucking hands off me. I did what the guys wanted. I came, I listened, but nothing's changed. Keep the guitar."

She tried to pull away again, but I just couldn't let her go. I wanted her to see the real me; the man I'd become. And yeah, it might have taken climbing a mountain of problems for me to get there, but I'd still gotten to the peak and found my way back to the bottom. It was probably the dumbest thing I'd done all night.

That didn't stop me from pulling her closer and capturing her lips with mine, silencing any other protests she might have made. Her body stiffened, her lips unmoving beneath mine but I kept the connection, my heart pounding in my chest as I braced for her to push me away. Her hands lifted and landed on my chest. Surprisingly enough, she didn't push me away. She slipped her fingers up around my neck, sinking them into my hair.

The moment her mouth opened, I slid my tongue inside and the fire that had ignited the night we were together lit up like an inferno. I cupped her ass, bringing her lower body tight against mine, knowing she could feel how hard a simple touch from her made me. I couldn't get enough and almost whimpered when she tore her mouth away and dropped down into a seat, the breath coming from her in pants.

Her eyes were glassy with a faraway look in them. Afraid of scaring her off, I sat back in my seat and waited until my legs were under the table to adjust myself out of her sight. She didn't speak a word. The realization of where we were finally hit. I glanced around to see a bunch of eyes trained on us, some looking away when they saw me staring back. Even the waitress had stopped dead in her tracks, the tray of coffee and pies in her hand. She started forward again, an overly bright smile on her face.

"Here ya go. Do you need anything else?" She glanced back and forth between us.

"No, thank you," I answered, watching Mari, who was still staring off into space.

I grabbed two packets of sugar and poured them into my cup while I waited for Mari to do more than just sit there, anything to distract myself from the taste of her on my lips. Whatever was going through her head, I hoped she'd share and talk to me instead of trying to run again.

I wasn't stupid. I knew sexual attraction wouldn't erase all the shit I'd put Mari through. She had every right to hate me, even though I wanted things to be different. But she couldn't deny our connection, and that had to count for something.

Right?

Slowly, she moved her legs back under the table and turned to me, her eyes firmly locked on the table. Her hands wrapped around the mug like it would anchor her. "Why?" she whispered. "Why now?"

I may not have known her very well, but her real meaning wasn't lost on me.

"Your voice."

That brought her eyes up fast. "My voice? You'd never heard me sing a note until a few months ago."

"Exactly. I hadn't been facing the stage when you started to sing. The sound of your voice made me turn around. I may have been stupid and blind before, but trust me when I tell you my eyes are wide open now. You're fucking gorgeous."

She opened her mouth to say something. I held up a hand and continued. "I know that doesn't mean shit under the circumstances. But it's all tied together. I wanted to get to know you from that first night. It wasn't until I figured out who you were that I understood why you'd given me the cold shoulder. I thought about all the hurt I caused you and wanted to find a way to make up for it. To try and heal some of the pain . . . if I could."

"How did you figure out it was me?"

Her asking questions was a good sign. At least I knew she was listening.

"Something that happened in the hallway a few weeks ago. Two of the football players were harassing one of the girls. After I reamed their asses for treating someone that way and benched them for the next game, I couldn't get the moment out of my head. How I wished someone had put an end to my

149

shit. One game on the bench would have been enough to get me to see." She narrowed her eyes. "Maybe it shouldn't have needed to come to that, but my only defense is that I was a dumbass back then. It wasn't until I was on my way to see you that everything fell into place." I glanced down at her neck, where the same pendant hung. "I remembered your necklace."

Her hand shot to her throat, her fingers touching the cool metal of the flower. "My necklace?"

"Yeah, for some reason it stood out to me. I notice you play with it whenever you're nervous. You used to do the same thing in high school." I didn't take my eyes off her for one second. Mari might say she didn't want to speak to me, but her body language spoke volumes.

She ran her finger around the rim of the mug, her lips drawn into a tight line. She didn't look up, didn't move except for that one finger. When I was almost positive she was going to bolt again, she lifted her eyes from the glass and pinned me in her gaze. "Did you say you benched two football players for giving a girl a hard time?"

"Yeah?" Where was she going with this?

She gave her head a brief shake. "I'm confused. Weren't you supposed to be some big NFL player? I remember it being in all the papers before I left."

My breath caught for a moment. Even though she'd hated me, she'd still paid attention to what I was doing. "Let's just say things didn't work out the way they were supposed to."

She lifted a brow. "Then what do you do?"

"I'm a teacher."

CHAPTER FOURTEEN

Mari

My mouth fell open. A warning. A red flag. Some kind of advanced notice still wouldn't have been enough to hide my shock.

The guy in front of me had defied teachers and rules at every turn. He'd done whatever he wanted, whenever he wanted to. He probably would have done a lot more had there not been consequences to his actions—like losing his scholarship. And even after everything I'd learned in the last few minutes, I still couldn't quite equate the idea of this Cole and the one I knew being the same person.

"That surprises you." He picked up the mug and took a sip of the coffee, his eyes on me through the steam.

"It does. You didn't just make my life a living hell." He winced, but I refused to take the words back. "You did everything you weren't supposed to, damn the consequences."

And yet, that didn't seem to be him anymore. This Cole worried about the ramifications of his actions and seemed to understand that he deserved them for his behavior. But it hadn't been until Cole mentioned benching the two kids for harassing another student that my anxiety at being there with him had started to ebb. The Cole I knew would have laughed with them, made a few comments of his own, and sent the boys back to class without any consequences.

Let him apologize. Let him grovel. Let him beg. You need this more than you realize.

Heath's words rang out in my head and I finally realized how right he was. Cole's story created a lightness in my chest that hadn't been there since I was a child.

"I've learned a lot over the last few years. There are consequences, and I'm answerable to them as much as anyone else." He glanced down at the table, absently playing with the fork.

"I'll be honest, part of me wants to forgive you, while another part is screaming at me to get up and storm away."

He brought his eyes up, bracing for whatever I might say. "Which side are you going to listen to?"

"Neither."

He narrowed his eyes. "Neither?"

I sighed. "Honestly, a guitar and some flowers aren't enough for me to forgive you completely. It took a long time for me to get to this point. A point where I can look in the mirror and love the person I see there. A few small gestures don't make up for all the hard work and tears it took for me to get there." The corners of his mouth turned down. "But . . . I am willing to give you a chance to prove you're not that guy anymore. One chance. That's what I can give."

His shoulders relaxed and a smile touched the corners of his lips. "One chance is all I need."

He picked up a fork and handed it to me, along with the second piece of peanut butter pie, one of my favorites. "What makes you think I like peanut butter pie?"

"I can't imagine anyone who doesn't like peanut butter." His hand froze with his fork halfway to his mouth. "Shit, you aren't allergic, are you?"

"No, it's actually one of my favorites, too." I speared the first piece and lifted it to my lips.

He winked. "See. Who doesn't like peanut butter pie?"

"Why did you order two if you weren't going to eat both? Not that I'm not grateful that you did."

A light blush tinted his cheeks. Okay. Weird. I honestly never thought I'd see Cole blush. "What's the big deal?"

"It's just that . . . I've spent a lot of time watching you over the last few weeks. I've learned a lot about you." He ran a hand over his face. "Now it almost sounds stalkerish. After every show, I stayed and watched you at the bar. I wanted to know more about you. A hint about what I could do to reach you."

"You watched me?"

He looked away.

Now I was intrigued. He'd watched me for weeks. God only knew what he'd seen. "And?"

"You're not a fan of beer, or making decisions about food. Usually when the guys in the band order, you end up tasting theirs and ordering the same. So I ordered two pieces of pie to save you the trouble."

It was sweet, in a weird, roundabout way. Knowing that he was paying attention made me feel a little self-conscious, but I pushed it to the side and we ate our dessert in silence, until Cole spoke up again.

"Tell me about yourself. About the band."

My gut reaction was to shut down but I buried that quickly. Talking to Cole would be good practice for the interviews the label wanted to do after our first single was released. If I couldn't tell someone I knew my story, how would I tell a complete stranger? And it gave me the chance to be totally honest with Cole about what happened after I left, a chance to see if he could truly handle hearing about the fallout of his actions.

"Let's see. I guess I'd have to start when I left for college. I met Sawyer in Freshman Seminar. Honestly, I was a mess. Afraid to trust anyone." The corners of his mouth turned down. Reality might have been worse than his memories from school. "When he found out we were both music majors, he was determined we should be friends. I wasn't all that keen on having friends but some way, somehow, he pushed his way in. He spent years helping me rebuild my self-esteem, freeing the person I'd buried way down deep to keep her safe."

"Mari," he whispered, but I shook my head, needing to continue.

"Sawyer has been my rock. He's shown me the world in a new light. Helped me find the courage to change."

He'd stopped eating but still held the fork in his hand. He pointed it toward my hair. "So he's the reason for the short hair and tattoos?"

"Not really." I lifted my hand, absently twirling my fingers in my hair. "I'd always wanted to cut my hair, I just didn't want to add any more fuel to the fire. I figured the less I changed about myself, the more I could blend into the background." I shrugged. "Keep people from noticing me."

"I really like it shorter."

The simple compliment was worth a whole room full of flowers. Same as when he mentioned my voice. Cole had never paid *me* a compliment in my entire life and it was nice to hear the words from his lips. My face heated. "Thank you."

"How did you start singing with the band?"

"It was supposed to be a one-time thing. Jackson lost his voice and they had a gig they'd had to call in a lot of favors to get."

He stopped playing with the pie on his plate. "Why would you guys have to call in favors to play? I've seen your crowds. There's no way a bar owner is going to turn down the kind of money you'd bring in. I see them begging you to play."

I fidgeted in my seat. "Well, most of that happened afterward. Sawyer asked me to sing for them one night. They practiced in my basement, so I knew all the songs and Sawyer knew I could sing. There was no way I could tell him no. And the rest is history. Our popularity skyrocketed, and here we are today."

It seemed weird to sit there and talk to Cole. He was genuinely interested in the story I had to tell. I'd thought he might want to know to earn brownie points, but the focus in his eyes said that most certainly wasn't the case. For some reason, Cole Wallace wanted to know more about *me*.

I took another forkful of the pie and noticed my phone light up on the table.

Sawyer.

I reached my hand over, then a voice in the back of my head screamed that was probably a bad idea. I snatched my hand away. When I glanced up, Cole was watching me.

"Everything okay?"

I glanced over at my phone and back at him. "Yeah, everything's fine."

I put the bite of pie in my mouth and my phone went off again. Ignoring it, I turned to Cole. "So, tell me, what do you teach?"

"I'm a phys ed teacher." He shrugged. "Guess that's no surprise."

I laughed. "Not really." Again, my phone lit up. I tried ignoring the messages, but they kept coming in.

"Do you need to get that?" He nodded his head toward the phone.

"No, but we should probably finish our pie and get going."

His eyes dropped to the table. "Okay."

I shook my head. "It's not that I'm blowing you off. I listened and I'm willing to give you a chance to prove you're a different person. Maybe, just maybe we can be friends." I shot my eyes over to the phone, which had lit up with three more messages. "But right now, I'm pretty sure Sawyer is pissed and if you want to help me save Heath, Jackson, and Monty from his wrath, we should probably go."

Cole glanced up then and nodded.

He motioned to the waitress for the check. I tried to give him some money, but he shook his head and dropped some cash on the table. Once he stood, he held out a hand to help me from the booth.

And, god help me, I took it.

The Cole in front of me was so different from the one I knew in high school, it was hard not to notice how gorgeous he was, or his sweet gestures. Not that I was anywhere close to letting my guard down completely, but little cracks were starting to form in the wall I'd built around myself.

He helped me up and smiled. "I hope I can see you again soon."

I returned his smile with one of my own. "I think that can be arranged."

Cole led me out to the car. I gave him the directions back to my place, my phone burning a hole in my pocket as I continued to ignore the messages from Sawyer. Whatever he had to say could be said in person. It wasn't worth a text war with him.

My stomach fluttered when we pulled into the driveway. Cole hopped out and ran around to open my door. Another surprise.

"Thanks for—" Cole started when a slamming door brought both our attentions around to the angry man storming across the front yard.

"Get the fuck away from her, you worthless piece of shit. How dare you force her to go with you?"

"Jesus Christ, Sawyer." I shut the door and rolled my eyes.

Heath and Jackson tried to pull Sawyer back in the middle of his advance, but anger fueled him and he shook them off as if they were an annoying fleck of dirt on his sleeve. He stepped right up into Cole's face.

"I told you to get the fuck out of here," Sawyer snarled, his hands balled into fists. I didn't want them fighting. Whether or not I forgave Cole was up to me. Lines of strain formed on Cole's brow, the muscles in his shoulders tightening as he held himself back from Sawyer. The rest of the guys were waiting to see what would happen. Sawyer was usually the level-headed one. Calm.

Today he wasn't.

I moved between the two of them, forcing them to take a few steps back. I glanced up at

157

Sawyer, hoping he'd see that I was fine and chill out. "He didn't drag me out kicking and screaming."

He pinned me with a glare that damn near knocked me over. "That fucker made your life a living hell. Now you're having coffee? Jesus, fuck, Keys."

I felt the heat race up my cheeks. Cole took hold of my arm and pulled me behind him.

Protection.

Not exactly where I expected it to come from. Sawyer was usually my knight in shining armor, yet somehow in the twilight zone that was my life, the devil had become the prince who swooped in to save me.

"You want to be pissed at someone, be pissed at me." Cole held out his hands. "Go ahead. Want to hit me, be my guest. Just leave Mari out of it. She doesn't deserve it."

"Like you know what she deserves." Sawyer's voice was coated in distain. "You're the one who made her scared of the world, but what did you care? You were off to your big NFL career. Didn't matter what you left behind. But you see, big shot, I met her. I spent time with her. I picked up the pieces of what you broke, and I won't let you come back now and break her all over again."

"Sawyer," I cried, my eyes burning.

Monty jumped in and shoved Sawyer back. Heath jumped in and they dragged him to the other side of the yard. Blinking away the tears, I turned to Cole.

"You better go. It's only gonna get worse if you stay, and I don't want you two fighting."

Cole shook his head. "I'm not going to leave you to deal with him."

158

I placed my hand on his arm. "I'll be fine. You've already done more than I expected you to by coming to my defense."

His shoulders dropped. "I told you, I'm not the same guy. I wish I could find a way to prove that to you."

The voices behind me grew louder. "Tonight was a good start. Trust me, I'll be okay."

Jackson wrapped an arm around my shoulders. "I got this, but she's right. You two fighting isn't going to fix shit."

Cole's eyes moved warily around to everyone. He stopped on Sawyer and nodded, then climbed in the car and pulled from the driveway.

"What the fuck is his problem?" I snapped at Jackson. He'd been in on this and until that moment, I'd forgotten I was supposed to be pissed at him, too. Sawyer happened to be taking up all that part of my brain.

"He's pissed at us for setting this up, and the fact that you're not flipping shit on Cole only pisses him off more. Plus he's been drinking."

I brushed furiously at my face to catch a few escaping tears. "I'm pissed at you, too."

Jackson sighed and took hold of my shoulders, turning me to face him. "You can't tell me what he had to say hasn't helped. Until Sawyer started with all his shit, I hadn't seen you that relaxed in months."

I thought back on the conversation in the diner. Everything Cole had said and done since I'd gotten into the car with him. Jackson was right. Even though I hated admitting it.

"It was hard to talk to him, but you're right, I needed to hear him apologize. Not that I can forgive him yet."

Jackson gave me his trademark crooked smile, the one all the girls fell for. "I wouldn't expect you to. He needs to prove that he's different."

"That's what I told him."

I glanced up to see Sawyer stalking away from Monty and Heath, who caught my eyes and shook their heads. Whatever they'd tried to tell him, Sawyer wasn't listening. He stormed over to Jackson and me, giving Jackson a small shove away.

"What the fuck, man?" Jackson caught himself.

I rubbed my fingers over my temples. "Let it go, Sawyer, he's gone."

Sawyer threw his hands in the air, his eyes wild, his hair in disarray. "Why aren't you pissed?"

"I was pissed earlier. But they were right." I looked over at the guys. "Hearing Cole apologizing was a good thing for me."

Sawyer put his hand out and started counting off things as he said them, the scent of alcohol coming off him in waves. "You revenge fuck him, he apologizes, and then everything is A-okay?"

Heath told Sawyer not to be an ass the same time my hand came forward and his head snapped sideways. Jackson slung an arm around my waist and whispered in my ear, "Don't do something you'll regret later."

I struggled against Jackson's hold as my gaze locked onto Sawyer's, a handprint visible on his left cheek. "And right now, what makes him any different from Cole?"

Sawyer's eyes darkened, but now I was too pissed and too hurt to care. I finally struggled out of Jackson's hold and stormed into the house, slamming both the front door and my bedroom door behind me.

My throat burned. Tears streamed down my face. Sawyer had said too much and pushed too hard. When Cole treated me like shit, he'd been the enemy. Sawyer had done it when he was *supposed* to be my friend. My best friend.

I went to the closet and grabbed the box where I kept the cards Cole sent me. They all had his number on them. I sent him a quick message. Two wrongs didn't make a right.

Me: It's Mari. I'm sorry about Sawyer.

I stripped out of my jeans and shirt. Yanking a tank top on, I grabbed a pair of pajama shorts and climbed into bed. I didn't want to deal with anyone at the moment. My phone buzzed.

Cole: It's okay. Some of what he said was true.

My fingers flew over the keys, refusing to give Sawyer the easy way out.

Me: Doesn't mean any of this is his business. It's between you and me.

A few seconds later my phone lit up again.

Cole: I hope we can hang out again. Besides, I still have your guitar.

Shit.

In all the chaos, I completely forgot about it.

Me: We will. Good-night.

I watched the phone, waiting. I so didn't want to analyze what that meant.

Cole: Night.

My body ached as if I'd run a marathon, the emotional upheaval more than what I wanted to handle for the day. I felt the tears coming on again. Instead of trying to fight them, I closed my eyes and cried myself to sleep.

"I'm so sorry, Mari."

I jumped. Sawyer had crawled into bed with me and wrapped his arm around my waist. I tried to pull away, but he held me tighter. "Please stay. I don't know what came over me. All I've ever wanted to do is protect you. And tonight all I did was hurt you."

I bit hard into my cheek. I wouldn't cry again tonight.

"You needed a friend and I wasn't there to support you. I was so pissed at the guys. I almost beat the shit out of Heath. Then I tried texting you to make sure you were okay and when you didn't answer it sent me over the edge."

I sat there in silence. Cole's apology hadn't been enough earlier, and Sawyer's wasn't now. And being drunk wasn't an excuse.

"Talk to me, Mari. Please." The pleading in his voice caught my attention. He pressed a soft kiss to the back of my shoulder. "We don't talk anymore. At least not in the last few weeks. Ever since the flowers and gifts started coming. It's not an excuse for my behavior. I guess . . . I guess . . . shit, I don't know."

Sawyer was right. We hadn't talked much lately, and even though it wasn't a good reason for him to be such a bastard, it was mainly because I'd been avoiding any conversations about Cole.

Even after everything that had happened tonight, I still wasn't sure how I felt about Cole, but I knew that the only way to be the person I wanted to be was to give him a chance to prove himself. Somehow I needed to explain that to Sawyer.

I rolled over to face him. "You need to realize that I'm not the same girl you first met."

He brushed a few wayward strands of hair from my face. "I know. I have to remember you can handle things yourself. If you need help you'll ask. There's just something about knowing what he did that makes me want to beat his ass into the ground."

"Did you even bother listening to Heath?"

"Heath's an asshole," he growled.

Forget this.

I turned back over. "I'm tired and I don't feel like arguing."

He caressed my shoulder with his thumb. "Me neither. That's why I came in here. I'd blame it on the alcohol, but that's not fair when I was just being a dick."

I glanced over my shoulder at him. "A dick? No, that's a guy in the audience who keeps screaming obscenities while we sing. You mean a twatwaffle? Nothing like making me feel like a cheap whore who will jump into any guy's bed even if they've treated me like shit, hey, Sawyer?" My voice grew raspy with each word and I bit the inside of my cheek so hard I tasted blood.

Sawyer groaned and brought me around to face him. He pulled me into his arms, holding me tight to his chest. "Oh, Keys, how can I make it up to you?"

I sucked in a shuddered breath. "I'm not sure."

"Please don't shut me out."

Looking up, I saw the way Sawyer's eyes pleaded with me. "Fine. But you better not pull that shit again."

He shook his head. "I won't, I swear."

Being mad at Sawyer wouldn't get me anywhere. Sure, he'd gone way too far with his words, but deep down I knew it was him lashing out because he cared about me. It was easy for my head to realize it, not so easy for my heart. Still, Sawyer was the one person I could always talk things out with, no matter what. This was one of those times.

"I swear to god I won't." Sawyer lay his hand over his heart.

I placed my head back down on his chest, the sound of his heartbeat bringing me a sense of comfort. It took me a few seconds to put my thoughts into words.

"Do you want to hear what happened tonight?

He released a breath. "Tell me. The guys wouldn't tell me anything except who you were with. I think they were afraid of making things worse."

I nodded against his chest. "I can imagine, but I have a feeling it might have calmed you down."

"What happened?" There was a tightness to his voice, almost like he was trying to keep his cool, but everything about Cole pissed him off.

"After the show, I went to the dressing room to change. I thought we were going out to celebrate. When I walked inside, a brand-new Fender was on a stand in the middle of the room."

Sawyer sat up so fast, I had no time to brace myself and found myself being dropped back onto the bed. At least it was soft. His eyes were wide, his jaw practically sitting on the bed. "A Fender? He bought you a fucking Fender?"

"I was as shocked as you are when I saw it."

He glanced around the room. "Which one? Where is it?"

"In all the chaos, I forgot it. It's in his car, though. He wants to meet up again to give it to me."

He narrowed his eyes as he stared down at me. "And how do you feel about that?"

I shrugged. Sawyer watched me for another moment, before lying down and pulling me back into his arms. "I'm not sure, honestly. But most of that has to do with the rest of what happened tonight."

He nodded for me to continue. I started with the story about my guitar, finishing with what happened at the diner, including the kiss. The kiss that grabbed hold of me and refused to let go.

"Do you believe him?" I could hear the hesitation in his voice.

"I don't know what to believe. But if he really has changed, what kind of person does it make me if I don't at least give him a chance to prove himself?"

Sawyer placed a finger under my chin and lifted my face to his. "I think you need to be careful." I opened my mouth to speak but he covered my lips with his finger. He tapped my temple gently. "In here you know you should keep him at arm's length until you're sure about his motivations, but"—he moved his hand over my heart—"the way you described that kiss, your heart isn't listening to what your head is telling you."

"I'm not falling—"

Sawyer shook his head. "I didn't say you were falling for him. What I'm saying is your heart may be more willing to forgive him than your head thinks you should be."

Deep down, I knew what Sawyer meant. One kiss and I promptly sat my ass down, ready to listen, even if it had taken me a few minutes to get my mind off the tingling in my lips.

I sighed and dropped my head back down, my breathing becoming slower as Sawyer lightly caressed my back. My eyelids dropped.

"Sleep, Keys. We can look for answers in the morning."

The exhaustion of the day combined with his light touch pushed me toward sleep.

What possible answers could I find in the morning?

CHAPTER FIFTEEN

COLE

We will. Good-night.

Mari's text stayed with me all week. Even the disaster at the end of the night with Sawyer hadn't diminished how I felt about my conversation with Mari. Only time and actions could prove to her that my apology was sincere, but it was a better start than I expected.

And it was a start.

The start of something. I'd be lying if I said that I only wanted to prove that I'm a different guy and that's it. Mari was like no other woman I'd met. Mystery surrounded her. I wanted to unravel it. And her.

Ever since our talk, Mari and I had traded text messages. What started with her apologizing for Sawyer's behavior—which I'd told her she didn't need to do. After all, I'd put her in that position. If anyone were to apologize, it should be me—became a series of messages ranging from "How are you?" to "What are you doing?" The texts came randomly throughout the day. Whenever I had a break from the students, I'd check my phone. If there weren't any messages from her, I'd send one of my own. The quick chats gave me more insight into Mari and the woman she'd become, and I found myself addicted to the contact. We had yet to find time for me to get her the guitar so I'd put it in the case, thankfully Heath had grabbed the night we ran out, and placed it in the corner of my room to keep it safe. I wouldn't risk anything happening to it again.

The last bell blasted through the room, yanking me from my thoughts. The students bolted for the door as if it was the only path to freedom. Not that I could blame them.

Mari had agreed to meet me when she was done doing something for the band. She hadn't told me what exactly she was doing, just that she had about a two-hour drive before she got back. We agreed she'd text me on the way home. I hope she liked what I'd planned.

There was an open mic night every Thursday at one of my favorite coffee shops. I had no idea if she'd want to sing, but I figured she'd enjoy the music anyway. Plus, it would be a great buffer if we ran out of things to talk about. Not that I thought that might happen. The conversations between us had run smoothly over text, but I knew that didn't necessarily translate into anything. I'd had more than my fair share of dates where things had gone great over text beforehand only to fall flat on their face when we met.

When I'd arrived, there were still a few booths open along the wall. Wanting to keep the door in my sights so I could see when she got here, I took the seat with my back to the main stage, tucking

167

the guitar in next to me. If she decided to sing, at least she'd have an instrument to play.

Less than fifteen minutes later, I saw her walking along the sidewalk outside the window. My eyes darted to the door, waiting for that first glance of her—the moment she'd step into the room and be too busy looking for me to remember to keep up her walls. The moment where I'd see her how everyone else did.

The door opened and I practically swallowed my tongue.

Mari was sexy as fuck.

Her hair was in messy curls that framed her face, which only accentuated her blue eyes. The way she held her shoulders straight allowed a few of the bird tattoos to peek out from the neckline of her shirt, her confident stance belied by the way she bit the side of her bottom lip. Every part of her called to me. My dick perked up.

Down boy. She's not interested in me like that.

Karma was an absolute bitch. Of course I had to want the one person who I'd pretty much guaranteed wouldn't want a goddamn thing to do with me. High school me had fucked everything up. I'd been too stupid to realize how many mistakes I'd been making, but I was sure paying for them now.

Her eyes connected with mine and her step faltered when she realized that I'd been watching her. Eventually she caught herself, taking a step forward and walking to the table with all the grace of a ballerina.

"Hi." She dropped into the seat across from me, tucking a loose strand of hair behind her ear. I couldn't take my eyes off her.

"You look absolutely gorgeous."

A light pink tinted her cheeks. "Thanks."

Silence descended over the table. For the first time in my life, I was out with a woman and I had absolutely no idea what to say to her. My hands began to tremble, so I dropped them into my lap because, no matter what happened, I didn't want her to see that she made me nervous.

The corners of her lips turned up in a shy smile and she glanced around the room, her eyes sweeping over everything as her smile grew in size. "I've never been here before."

I gestured toward the stage. "It's open mic night. I thought you'd enjoy the music."

Her entire face lit up. "I love live music." Almost immediately she looked away, the blush on her cheeks returning with renewed force.

"I figured you would." I did nothing to hide the smile in my voice. "Do you know what you want? I wasn't sure what you drank so I waited for you to order."

"I'll have a caramel mocha."

"You got it. Give me a minute and I'll be right back." I stood from the table, careful not to knock the guitar, and made my way to the counter where I could order our drinks.

"What can I get you?" the barista asked, not looking up from her computer.

"I'll have a caramel mocha and a coffee, black." Call it intuition, but I had a feeling Mari hadn't eaten much all day.

The barista glanced up, her eyes widening. She blinked rapidly, her hand coming up to tuck her hair behind her ear as she said, "Umm . . . hi."

I handed her the cash, noticing her fingers caressing mine as she took the money from my hand. I sensed eyes on me from behind and glanced over my shoulder.

Mari was watching the barista intently, a frown making her eyes narrow and cute wrinkles had appeared between her brows. When she noticed me looking, Mari quickly glanced away, pulling out her phone. For some reason, it gave me a bit of pleasure to know that Mari seemed to be a bit jealous of the woman behind the counter talking to me.

I watched her until our drink order was called, her eyes never leaving the phone. Whether there was something very interesting on the screen in front of her or she was just avoiding catching my eye again. I wasn't sure, but the fact that I might just have witnessed jealousy, even in the most fleeting of moments, was a boost to my floundering ego.

When I heard my name called, I turned away from her and took the cups from the outstretched hands of the barista.

"Too bad you're taken." She nodded her head toward Mari. "I'd have loved to get a drink with you."

Taken.

It had a nice ring to it, even if it was a pipe dream.

I smiled to let the girl know I'd caught her meaning, but turned away before she read too much into it. The only woman I was interested in was physically on the same page as me. Her body definitely enjoyed being touched by mine but emotionally she was way out of reach.

I set the cups on the table and took my seat. Mari's eyes were still on her phone, the frown lines on her forehead deeper set now than they had been minutes earlier.

"Everything okay?"

Her eyes snapped up from her phone. "Yeah, just Sawyer." She sighed.

170

I took a sip of my too hot coffee and burned my tongue, simply to avoid saying something that might piss her off.

"He's worried about me."

That caught me off guard. I set my cup on the table and in a move that I wasn't entirely sure wouldn't earn me a slap to the face, I put my hand over hers. She looked down at our connected hands, but said nothing.

Score one for Cole.

"I promise I won't do anything to hurt you."

"I'm trying to believe you." With her free hand, she gripped the pendant around her neck.

"Sorry, I didn't mean to make you nervous."

"I'm not nervous."

I looked down at her neck, then back to her eyes. "You're playing with your pendant again."

She pulled her hand out from under mine and dropped the necklace, like it burned her. "How would you know that?"

Hopefully she didn't find my answer to be as stalkerish as it sounded in my head. When the hell had I become a creeper? "Remember I was watching you. Every time you'd look at me across the bar, you'd reach up and your fingers would rub over the metal."

She glanced down at the table. "Oh."

"Like I said, I don't want you to be nervous around me."

Mari wrapped both hands around her cup, her fingers tapping idly against the top. Her eyes moved up to meet mine. "You don't . . ."

I cocked a brow, waiting for her to say I didn't make her nervous. It was written in every fidget, every movement, even in her eyes.

171

"It's not you as a person that makes me nervous," she explained. "It's more about this." She pointed back and forth between the two of us.

My heart thundered in my chest. "What *this*?" I made the same movement with my finger as she had.

"What this is supposed to be."

Her words were exciting. I wanted Mari, but she couldn't really mean us together. As a couple.

At this point, I was happier leaving things undefined. I didn't want to force anything on her, and that included a friendship, if she didn't want it. It would suck if she couldn't handle at least being friends, but I understood that whatever relationship she chose to have with me was exactly that—*her* choice. And however that choice made me feel, I had to be okay with that. At least, on the outside.

It might have been a reckless and crazy notion, but I hoped for much more. She was like a magnet; an unseen force, connecting two people. There was no one I'd rather be connected with.

"So we just go from being enemies to friends?"

Friends.

It was better than nothing, but the whole idea of her thinking of us as enemies? It bothered me. "I've never thought of you as the enemy."

She hesitated a moment. "Trust me when I tell you, I've thought of you as the enemy plenty of times. I don't know why I figured you'd think the same. Honestly, you probably never thought of me at all."

I was at war with my own mind. If I lied to her, she'd walk away without another glance. But thinking about telling her the truth made my stomach roll. I sucked in a breath and weighed up my options. Some things were more important than others.

"I promised earlier that I wouldn't hurt you, and now I'm caught between that and lying to you."

She pinned me with a glare. "Lying is definitely worse."

I sighed. "The truth is that, until a few years ago, I never consciously thought about you. I went day to day not worrying about anything but what was in front of me." I rubbed the back of my neck, trying to release the tension the conversation was bringing. "I made *a lot* of mistakes. Later things changed."

When I glanced up at Mari again, her eyes had welled up. My gut clenched. The last thing I wanted to do was make her cry.

"How?" Her gaze never faltered.

"When I changed schools, and had to reevaluate the plans I'd had for my life."

I leaned forward and brushed the lone tear from her cheek. The gesture was simple, but it helped me avoid a topic that made my head pound and my chest tighten.

"Why would you switch schools?"

I shifted around in my seat, unsure if I wanted to go there now, if ever. "That story is a little longer and definitely not a high point in my life."

My gaze focused on the cup in my hand when a soft caress made me look up to see Mari's hand on my arm. It was the first time since the night she'd come home with me that she had consciously touched me.

"Tell me," she whispered.

The light blue of her irises held understanding; sincerity. She truly wanted to hear the story. Maybe it was to gloat. I wouldn't blame her, but I didn't know if I could hear that from her lips. I'd lost everything after I'd cost her enough.

"It was a game in the middle of junior year of college. Different NFL teams had contacted me, wanting to know if I planned to skip senior year to enter the draft. Honestly, I hadn't decided. My dad thought that was my best choice. I'd go first round. Which team would take me was the question.

"Mom wanted me to finish my degree first. She wanted me to have something to fall back on when football was over. I just never thought it would be over so soon." A lump formed in my throat, and I had to force the rest of my words over it. "That game, I leaped for a catch I knew I shouldn't have. Something about the way it was coming down seemed off, plus, the defense from the opposing team was barreling down on me. We were three points down at the end of the fourth quarter. A good catch would give us the first down and put us in position to make a field goal, tying the game. I came down with the ball in my hands but at an awkward angle, which under normal circumstances wouldn't be a big deal."

When I paused for a breath, she nodded for me to continue. "Two of the defenders hit me before I had a chance to move my leg. My knee went into the ground first. Their weight plus mine left me with a broken tibia, right behind my knee cap."

Shame washed over me like it did every time I thought about that night. Deep down, I knew it had been a freak accident, but the what ifs always screwed with my head for days.

"There isn't anything they can do? I haven't noticed you limping."

"No." I shook my head sadly. "Even with physical therapy my knee is only about ninety-seven percent. No team will risk millions of dollars on a wide receiver with a risk of reinjury. The plate they put over the break can only hold so much, but my knee is weakened. Any hard hit to the ground could leave me in the same boat."

I looked up into her eyes and saw it. The pity. Pity for me, the one person in the world who didn't deserve it.

"I'm so sorry." She leaned toward me, her tone sweet and gentle. "I hate that they wouldn't take a risk on you."

Silence descended over the table as I attempted to digest her words. Her defense of me against the big, bad NFL teams. Not that I could blame them for their decision. I still could have put myself in for the draft, but then I'd have to hope a team would grab me and play me, and not simply leave me sitting on the bench.

"Okay, so you moved schools. Why choose to be a teacher?"

I shrugged. "It was the only thing that felt right at the time. My head was a mess when I showed up here. My roommate, Ryan, helped a lot. I was skipping classes, not eating. Forget the freshman fifteen—by the end of junior year, I'd lost fifteen and then some. Throughout my senior year, Ryan pushed even harder to get to know me. Eventually, I could see what good I could do." I covered her hand, which still rested on my arm, with my own, rubbing light circles across the back of it.

"I realized that, as a teacher, I could protect any kid in your situation from assholes like I used to be. Plus, it gave me a chance to be a part of football. Until recently, I never imagined coaching anywhere but high school or youth league."

Mari picked up her coffee, taking a sip. "What happened recently?"

"The head coach at my school pulled me aside to tell me about colleges who'd been looking at me for their offense coaching positions."

Her brows shot up into her hairline. "Colleges? Really?"

The discomfort that had taken hold of me at the beginning of the conversation seemed to loosen and fall away the longer I talked to Mari. Besides a handful of people, I didn't usually open up about what had happened. It was actually a relief to let Mari in. Not that anyone who wanted to know couldn't find the answers on any sports website, but it was different telling someone than having them read a news story that you had no input into.

"I guess. None of them have ever contacted me."

She tilted her head to the side. "Would you want to coach a college team?"

I shrugged. "Not sure. I only started really thinking about it when Coach mentioned it to me. But yeah, I think I would."

"Sounds like it could be a good option for you."

The concern she had for me was a bit overwhelming given our situation, but I hadn't asked her here to talk about my sad past.

"Maybe. What about you? Do you work outside of singing for the band?"

There was a moment where she paused, staring at me, before she refocused. "Nothing besides the band. About a year ago we all left our jobs to focus on the music. Up until then, I did the whole random retailer thing because being a music major doesn't always pay the bills, not unless you make it big or play as often as we did."

I nodded. "I did notice that you guys played four nights a week pretty often."

"It was the easiest way to only work on the music."

"Good evening, everyone."

I glanced up at the stage to see the manager standing at the mic. "Welcome to the weekly open mic night at Avenue A Cafe. Some of the slots are already filled, but we do still have a few open so if you'd like to participate, you can sign up at the table next to the counter." He pointed along the wall. "Our first singer tonight is all ready to go. Please give a warm welcome to Dennis Weeks."

Mari turned her shoulder to focus on the stage and we both applauded as a man took the stage, a guitar strap slung over his shoulder. The music filtered through the room for a decent cover of Bruno Mars.

"It makes sense, especially with the size of your crowds. Who wouldn't want to book Jaded Ivory?"

The blush that I was starting to find endearing pinkened her cheeks once again. She tucked a piece of hair behind her ear. "Yeah. They're pretty good."

"So are you. You're just as much a part of the band as the guys are."

She nodded, but didn't say anything else about it. We continued to talk about her college years and what it was like being a music major. It was interesting to hear. Being a physical education major was so far removed from what she'd done.

Every once in a while, I'd catch Mari glance longingly at the stage, her fingers tapping out a beat on the coffee cup. I had a feeling she wanted to sing but something was stopping her.

"Do you want to sing?"

She looked quickly at the stage and back at me. "I wouldn't know what to sing. Besides, I don't have any music with me."

I reached behind me and pulled out the guitar, placing it gently on the table.

177

"How about you make your own?"

CHAPTER SIXTEEN

Mari

The guitar.

I'd been so pissed when I found out Heath and Jackson had helped Cole, I never bothered to really look at it. With shaking fingers I reached for the zipper, slowly pulling it around to open the case. Inside happened to be one of the most beautiful guitars ever made, the finish still as shiny as I remembered.

A Fender acoustic.

The Fender I'd lost to the bullshit in high school was nowhere near the level of the guitar that sat in front of me. As I stared my eyes began to water, but I was afraid that if I blinked it would disappear.

"I still can't believe you spent this kind of money on a guitar for me."

Cole placed a finger under my chin and lifted my gaze. "To see your smile, it was worth every penny."

My heart took off like a racehorse. It was a wonder he hadn't heard it from across the table. I took deep, even breaths to get myself under control. I ran my hands over the strings reverently. "I'd need to have it tuned."

Cole shook his head. "Already made sure the guy tuned it before I left the store. Said it might need a small adjustment from travel, but that's it."

"You did?"

Now, on top of his sweet words sending my mind into a frenzy, my stomach churned with the idea of playing and singing alone. Since the first moment I'd stepped on stage with Jaded Ivory, it had always been all of us. I'd never been up there alone.

"Mari?"

I looked up into the softest, ocean-blue eyes ever. "I was a jackass in the past and missed all my chances to hear your voice back then. But I've heard you now and you're amazing. Please sing for me."

Something about the way he asked, combined with the irrational need to prove myself, had my legs moving of their own volition until I found myself putting my name on the sign-up sheet.

Can I do this alone?

Realistically, I knew I shouldn't feel that way. Cole had given me no reason up until then to think that I needed to prove my abilities, but that didn't stop me from needing the validation for myself.

"I can't do this," I whispered to my friend Jennifer. "What if I sound terrible?"

It was our in-school performance for the choir concert. Every year we'd put it all out there on the line, praying that the popular kids either

180

skipped school that day or would be on their best behavior, which wasn't likely. This year it was my turn to sing the solo, and as I waited in the wings of the stage I wondered what they had planned.

Jennifer narrowed her eyes. "You have to be kidding me. You have one of the best voices in the entire choir. You are not going to mess up. When you get out there, you're going to show all the assholes in the audience how good you really are."

She meant well, but with my luck, whatever happened it would be worse than normal. I walked out on stage pretty sure I was going to puke in front of everyone. The rest of the choir took their places on the risers and I moved to the front where the microphone stood. My knees felt like they were going to buckle beneath me, so I tried to keep my focus on Mrs. Mathews, the choir director.

She gestured to the piano player and the music picked up in volume. At first, I ignored the whole room of kids, focusing on the lights or the wall at the back.

Then the murmuring hit my ears. I looked down.

There in the front row was Sam holding a poster that said, "Will you go to prom with me?"

I almost missed my words, doing a double take at the poster. He couldn't possibly mean me. I kept singing and glanced back again. The poster definitely said it, and he held up another sign with my picture from the yearbook. I brought my hand to my chest. Deep down, I knew nothing good could come of this. Heads were starting to swivel back and forth between Sam and me.

Keep singing, *I told myself.*

Laughter started to build in the room. When I glanced over, I found out exactly why. Sam had turned the sign around. Now it read, "The perfect prom dates" and my yearbook picture had been replaced by the one from the day they threw the gum in my hair. Next to it was the creepy janitor, holding a scraper, using it to clean gum off the desks. Tears leaked down my face, my voice cracking as I tried to finish the song.

As the laughter grew and grew until I could barely follow the music, I ran from the stage. In the background, I heard the principal yelling at the students for their behavior, but the damage was done. My phone began buzzing in my pocket. It hadn't even been five minutes but already the whole thing was all over social media, along with a picture of Sam talking to the principal, still holding the "Will you go to prom with me?" sign.

After that, I'd refused to audition for any solos, even though Mrs. Mathews begged me to. I swore to myself on that day that I'd never leave myself that vulnerable again.

Until now.

I did this for a living and I wanted to prove to everyone in the room that I was a good singer, not so they knew . . .

So I believed it.

There were three people in front of me. They seemed to be taking a few minutes in between each performance. I went back to the table on legs that felt like rubber. Sitting down, I noticed two pieces of cake on the table; one chocolate, one red velvet, my favorite. Not that I could have eaten it if I wanted to.

Besides choir performances, I'd never sung solo. And it had been a while since that happened. Tonight I was all on my own.

Twirling my pendant in my fingers, I asked my grandmother for strength. I also found Cole making light conversation to distract me. It was sweet and unexpected at the same time. Even as I tried to keep up with what he was saying, I caught myself glancing at the stage. Eventually, my name was called and I stood from the table, smoothing the invisible creases from my clothes and picking at non-existent lint.

"Mari?"

I glanced up from the guitar in my hand and got caught in Cole's gaze.

"Yeah?"

He smiled. "You're gonna be great."

I gave him a nod, unsure whether I could get my voice to work. As I walked up to the stage it felt like the first night I sang with Jaded Ivory. I took a seat on the stool, placing the guitar on my lap and every song I'd ever known floated from my mind.

How was I supposed to sing if I suddenly couldn't remember a single song?

Sweat began to form on my brow and I caught myself fidgeting with the strings on the guitar. Needing to gain perspective, I glanced up and found Cole watching every move I made. His gaze sent a wave of comfort through me and, just like that, the lyrics I needed popped into my head.

My fingers hit all the notes, the words bringing to the surface all the pain I'd done my best to hide. I hadn't intended it to be that way, but one look at Cole, the way his skin paled and the haunted look in his eyes, and it was obvious he knew the lyrics referred to him.

I finished the song and the audience went crazy, clapping and cheering. Cole was on his feet, fingers at his lips, whistling. They were the same reactions I got singing with Jaded Ivory, but the accomplishment was more meaningful having faced my fears and done it on my own. I stepped down from the stage and received high fives and words of encouragement and congratulations all the way back through the crowd as I skipped between the tables. A sense of contentment filled me.

I'd done it.

Me.

Alone!

The moment I reached the table, Cole pulled me into a hug.

"No matter how many times I hear you sing, your talent astounds me," he whispered in my ear.

"Thank you."

Cole's words were everything I needed to hear, the deep satisfaction like a balm to my soul. The Band-Aid had been ripped off the first night I saw Cole, and each moment I spent with this new grown-up, mature Cole healed the pain and heartache a little bit more.

The cake was still on the table and Cole caught me eyeing the red velvet the moment I sat down. He winked and pushed the piece across the table, stabbing it with a fork and smiling. We stayed for the rest of the open mic list and this time I was able to pay attention to the music. At the end of the night, Cole walked me to my car.

"How did you know I liked red velvet cake?"

He chuckled. "I didn't. Lucky guess."

We reached my car and I hit the unlock button. Before I could reach out, Cole opened the door. "I had fun tonight. Thank you for agreeing to hang out with me."

"Thanks for asking me."

Silence fell over us like a blanket, the sounds of the night growing in volume. Laughter of friends and couples leaving the café cut through the quiet and my teeth dug into the skin of my lip. I wasn't sure what to say, and instead of sounding like an idiot, I figured I would let him speak first.

He shuffled his feet, kicking a rock with his shoe. "Look, Mari, I like spending time with you, but I know you have a hard time trusting me. I'm really trying to prove that I'm different. Do you think we can get together again?"

The first word on my tongue was *no*, it would only make all of this more complicated. Then I thought about why he'd become a teacher and how he'd defended the girl from the jock bullies. Plus, I couldn't deny that I'd had fun hanging out with Cole. He was smart and funny, and he had a way of making me feel settled even when I thought I should be pacing a hole in the floor. Tonight, I came out of my shell and did something I would never have considered doing without the rest of the band. And the man standing in front of me had made that happen.

"Okay."

Even in the dim light of the parking lot I could see Cole's eyes widen. "Okay? Wait . . . really?"

I nodded.

Cole held out a hand to help me into the car. "Okay then, I'll text you later this week."

I shook my head. He'd done something for me and I wanted to return the favor. I wanted to trust him, and maybe letting him into my world would help with that.

"No, this time, I'll make the plans."

The corners of his mouth lifted. "I like that idea."

"Good-night, Cole."

"'Night, Mari."

He shut the door and I pulled out of the lot, watching him in my rearview mirror as I drove away.

When I put the car in park in my driveway, I noticed the living room light on. When he was home alone, Sawyer usually ended up in his room watching

Netflix and working on music, so the only reason that light would be on was if he was waiting up for me. As I walked inside and shut the door behind me, Sawyer looked up from the book in his hands, marking his page before putting it to one side.

"How did it go?"

I took the seat next to him, stealing a cushion and hugging it to my chest. "Better than I expected it to, that's for sure. He took me to an open mic night and convinced me to play."

Sawyer's jaw dropped. "Wait . . . you played the guitar and sang in a room full of people, by yourself?"

"I did."

Sawyer cupped my cheek. "I'm so proud of you."

"I think I'm going to hang out with him again."

His hand dropped but he didn't take his gaze from mine, nor did he say anything.

"I know it sounds stupid and you think I'm out of my mind for wanting to spend time with him, but the more I do, the more it feels like the weight of all those years is being lifted from my shoulders."

He nodded and a look passed over his face, but just a quickly he covered it up by changing the subject. "Now let me see this guitar. Heath and Jackson have been talking about it nonstop."

I pulled the bag onto my lap, unzipping the fabric. The instrument came into view and Sawyer gasped. "*This* is the Fender he bought you?"

"I know. I think I had the same reaction as you. It's miles above the guitar he broke, which it turns out really wasn't his fault at all."

Sawyer whistled his appreciation, running his fingers along it. He struck a couple of chords and handed it back to me. "That's one helluva guitar. The

186

way a Fender sounds beats any other guitar, any day of the week." He closed his eyes, like he was savoring the sound in his head.

"I'm glad you approve. Although, I have a feeling he had no idea what he was picking out and let the salesperson in the shop talk him into this one." I carefully placed the instrument back into the case. "Which is fine with me."

Sawyer was quiet for a moment, glancing around the room as if he had something else to say, but wasn't sure how to say it.

"Just spit it out."

His eye darted to mine. "It's just . . . Did you tell him about the contract?"

"No."

My answer was firm and immediate. I wanted to trust Cole after all he'd done recently, but there was too much history there to simply lay everything at his feet. I didn't want someone spending time with me for what I could do for them. If we were going to hang out and be friends, it would be because he was genuinely interested in that friendship.

"Probably a smart idea."

I stood, picking up the guitar and having every intention of locking myself in my room for the rest of the night. Sawyer's hand latched on to mine, bringing me back down to the couch.

"Stop jumping to the conclusion that I'm being an asshole. I know *you*. And you would never want someone to be around you and spend time with you because of who you are."

"You're right. Sorry for assuming the worst." I leaned the case on the couch and snuggled into Sawyer's arms. We never used to fight. I needed to stop thinking the worst and remember that this was Sawyer—the guy who'd saved me and helped me embrace a new image of myself. He'd always been there for me. He was also the one I could share any secret with. "What's strange is I think he and I could actually be friends."

He traced circles over my back, relaxing me even further. "You know better than anyone that people can change."

"I know. It's why I wanted to give him the benefit of the doubt."

He squeezed me tighter. "And I wouldn't expect anything less."

I giggled. "I can't breathe."

Sawyer loosened his grip chuckling in my ear. The sounds made goose bumps rise on my arms.

"The thing is, I don't know if I'm making a colossally bad decision by letting him in."

"Go with your gut. It hasn't been wrong before."

There was a sadness to Sawyer's voice. I held him tighter, knowing that Sawyer had regrets about not listening to himself. Deep down he worried about the choices he made. I wanted to lighten the mood for him.

"You're right. After all, my gut led me to you." I leaned up and gave him a quick kiss on the cheek.

"Thanks, Mari. I'm not sure what my life would be like here without you."

I sat in the quiet for a bit longer with Sawyer. When a yawn escaped my mouth even though I tried to disguise it with my hand, he laughed and pushed me to my feet. "You need to head to bed. It was a long day for all of us. And don't forget, we need to head back to the studio tomorrow."

I stopped, bent over reaching for the guitar, and glanced up at him. "Tomorrow?" On a Saturday?"

He nodded. "Yeah. They want Runaway Dream recorded by Monday to start on edits in case we need to rerecord parts of it. They're determined to release it sooner rather than later."

I sucked in a breath.

"Don't stress," he said. "They wouldn't be releasing it if they didn't think it would do well."

"I know. Doesn't make it any less scary."

He took hold of my shoulders, rubbing them with his thumbs as he squatted down to lock eyes with me. "Just remember we're all as nervous about this as you are. Don't push us away. We'll get through it together."

"We will." He let me go and I smiled. "I'll see you in the morning."

I climbed into bed, thoughts of releasing the single to the world still running through my head. I still couldn't fathom thousands of people hearing me sing. Each time I closed my eyes, they'd pop open again.

Great. How was I supposed to record tomorrow when I couldn't sleep? I let my thoughts wander to Cole, the other anomaly in my life. Instead of getting more worked up, I found thinking about him settled something deep inside me.

And as I finally let my eyes slide shut, it was with the memory of pride etched in every feature of Cole's face when I'd finished playing.

CHAPTER SEVENTEEN

Mari

I was pretty sure I was going to pace a hole in the cement outside of the movie theater. No matter how many pep talks I'd given myself, I couldn't shake the nerves. I knew I was being stupid, it was just a movie for crying out loud. But it meant revealing more of myself. I was usually the girl who went along with what everyone else wanted to see. Choosing something that I loved and sharing it with someone else was big for me. I never wanted to give anyone the chance to make fun of me again.

I was so stuck in my head, I didn't see Cole until he was almost toe to toe with me.

"Hi." He glanced around at our surroundings. "Ready to tell me what we're doing here?"

I'd given him no indication on the phone. I'd really wanted to see his reaction to my suggestion in person. My fingers wrapped around my pendant, moving it side to side.

"Umm . . . a movie. Is that okay?"

Cole stepped forward and removed my fingers from the necklace. "It's great. What are we seeing?"

"The Princess Bride. It's only in theaters for this weekend," I said in a small voice. Shit, why was I questioning myself all of a sudden? I braced for his reaction.

A smile curved his lips. "You want to take me to see the six-fingered man, or maybe challenge me to a battle of wits?"

I smirked, feeling relief flood through me. "If you're not careful, I'll take you to the fire swamp."

His booming laugh filled the air and when he leaned closer, I shivered. "As you wish," he whispered, his impression damn near perfect.

I grabbed his hand and pulled him toward the box office. The second I realized what I'd done, I dropped his hand like it was on fire. A corner of his mouth lifted. He reached down, took my hand again, and purchased the tickets, even though I tried to argue with him about paying for myself.

Once we had the popcorn, with extra butter, and he'd found us seats in the back of the theater, the movie began. It was lucky I'd seen the movie enough times to practically have it memorized because if Cole would have asked my favorite part I wouldn't have been able to tell him otherwise. The scent of his cologne enveloped me, taking hold and making my head spin.

Near the end of the movie I peeked at Cole and saw his eyes on me. I turned to face him, leaning across the armrest that separated us until our lips were only inches apart.

My breathing sped up. Cole stared at my lips, his tongue darting out, making my heart race. The theater that had seemed cold only seconds ago, now felt like an inferno. Cole started to lean in.

Closer.

Closer.

I turned my face away. I couldn't go down that road with him again. Above the noise of the movie I heard his sigh, and my seat shook as he turned back to the screen.

The second the credits started to roll, I leapt from my seat like my ass was on fire. I needed fresh air. His proximity was messing with my head.

But even outside, the air between us felt charged. Ever the gentleman, Cole leaned forward to open my car door and something distinctly . . . *Cole* assaulted my senses. I swallowed in deep gulps of air, trying to get my wayward body under control. My hormones and my brain needed to get on the same wavelength.

Cole helped me into the car, caressing my palm as I took my seat. "I had fun tonight."

"I did, too."

"Thank you for giving me a chance to earn your trust."

I gestured at myself with my free hand. "Everyone has it in them to change."

"That they do." He placed a kiss on my hand. It was the kind of gesture you only see in movies and on TV, and it almost stopped my heart with its sweetness.

"'Night, Mari."

"Good-night."

As I drove off, watching him from my rearview mirror until I lost sight of him, I wondered whether I would ever be able to let go and just enjoy his company. But there was the question of where to draw the line. From the time I'd spent with him, I knew we could be friends, except there was a part of me that screamed it could be something more, if only I could open myself up to the possibility.

$$\gamma\gamma\gamma$$

"It's on the fucking radio!"

What the hell? I threw the covers off and walked to the door. Opening it a crack, Jackson's excited voice traveled down the hall.

"I can't believe it's out already. Or that anyone agreed to play it."

There were whoops and the slap of high fives and I had the immediate desire to lock myself in my room and hide. But the guys would never go for it.

Deciding that going out to the living room on my own was better than them coming in and jumping on my bed if I pretended I was sleeping. I threw on yoga pants and a T-shirt. No way in hell was I going out there in my skimpy pajama bottoms.

I finger-combed my hair on the way down the hall, the noise getting more raucous as I moved through the house. "What's all the yelling about?"

Four sets of excited eyes turned to me. "Runaway Dream is on the fucking radio."

I swallowed hard. "They released it?"

Heath smiled. "Yes. Way sooner than we expected."

Jackson pulled out his phone, pulling up our Twitter feed. Hundreds of tweets tagging us stared back at me. People begging for more.

Love her voice @JadedIvory

New release from @JadedIvory. We need more from this band

Awesome debut from @JadedIvory

Runaway Dream needs the number 1 spot @JadedIvory

My jaw was practically sitting on the floor. People's reactions were way beyond even the wildest of my dreams. I ran and jumped into Sawyer's arms, wrapping my legs around his waist, squeezing him as tightly as I could.

"We did it, Keys."

"Thank you for asking me to sing that night."

Monty pressed up against my back, hugging Sawyer and me. "We couldn't have done it without you."

Jackson and Heath joined in with our Jaded Ivory group hug, making the weight too much for Sawyer and we all went crashing to the floor. Laughter pealed from us, filling the room until, slowly, we got ourselves under control. Jackson was the first to make it to his feet. That's when I noticed they were all wearing their pajamas.

"At least I had the decency to change."

Monty winked. "Hey, we were excited. Now we need to go and celebrate."

I glanced at the clock on the microwave in the kitchen. "We are not going out drinking at ten in the morning, and I'm not going anywhere with you guys dressed liked *that*." I pointed at their clothing.

Monty struck a ridiculous pose, like something you'd see on the runway. "What are you talking about? I make this look good."

"Uh-huh." I smirked. "I have a better idea. How about you guys head back to your place, make yourself somewhat more presentable, and Sawyer and I will make brunch. Then after we eat, we can go out and celebrate."

"Deal." Heath had his hand on the doorknob before Jackson or Monty even made it to the door. With all eyes on him, he shrugged. "What? We're talking about Mari's cooking here."

"Good point. We'll be back," Monty yelled, shoving Jackson out the door.

Sawyer wrapped an arm around my shoulder. "Brunch, huh?"

I shrugged. "Yeah. It'll give me time to process everything. You're forgetting that everyone in the area knows who we are now. If we go out, people are going to recognize us. Things might get crazy. Better to start later, on full stomachs."

"Always thinking." He nodded his head toward the hall. "Go shower. You take longer than me."

I flipped him off and was just turning to head for the bathroom when his hand landed firmly on my ass. I squealed and raced down the hall, glancing over my shoulder right before I stepped out of sight. "Now I'm gonna use all of the hot water."

He groaned and I laughed, amazed at how much lighter I felt. This was happening. It was really happening.

I showered quickly, unable to slow myself down even though I would have loved to have messed with Sawyer more. I was just too damn excited to keep still.

I opened the door with my towel wrapped tightly around me and ran into a wall of solid muscle. Sawyer's eyes connected with mine and I couldn't help but smile up at him. The moment held as if we were in a trance until a shiver raced down my body. He smirked and once again smacked my ass.

"Go get dressed." He stepped into the bathroom and I narrowed my eyes at him as the door closed. Once I was dressed in a pair of jeans, a black tank, and leather jacket, I went to the kitchen to get breakfast started.

"We're back," I heard Monty call. I'd finished everything but the waffles.

"Grab a plate."

"Holy shit." Jackson's eyes were wide, taking in the counters covered in food. "You're quick."

"Damn, Sawyer. Why haven't you scooped Mari up yet? She's fucking perfect." Monty's plate was already piled high with food, all of it balanced precariously.

I glanced over at Sawyer who shared a look with Heath. Apparently, Heath also knew about everything that had happened. "I'm perfect? Have you met me?"

Monty busted out laughing. "Okay, fair enough."

Crisis averted.

I turned off the waffle iron and filled my own plate. "How do you think LiteStar is going to react to the release?"

"I have a feeling we're going to hear from Tom pretty soon, about more than a debut single. But you know that's probably going to mean a lot more time in the studio." Jackson shoved another forkful of food into his mouth.

"About that," Heath said, his tone somber. "Depending on how things continue, I wonder if it's time for us to start considering moving closer to the city."

Groans sounded throughout the room.

"I know, I know." Heath raised his hands. "But we can't keep driving back and forth two hours each way. We only stayed here because it was close to our normal spots. With those shows ending, it's something to consider."

As much as I hated the idea of moving, Heath had a point.

Then I thought about Cole and my stomach soured. Moving closer to the city meant moving farther from him. We'd spent a lot of time with each other over the last few weeks, but that shouldn't have any bearing on a decision to move. My life was with the band. That was what I needed to focus on. Besides, it was only something to think about. It wasn't as if we were packing up and leaving tomorrow.

"It's something to think about," Jackson said. "But I don't think we need to worry about it yet. The song just debuted today."

"It would have been nice if Tom would have given us more notice." Sawyer set his empty plate on the coffee table.

I laughed. "Yeah, I doubt we're at that level yet. We're just lucky it *got* released."

"Ain't that the truth." Monty oinked at his piece of bacon before shoving it into his mouth.

I couldn't stop the snort that escaped. Monty had a way of taking any serious situation and turning it around. It was one of the few talents in his arsenal I was grateful for.

"You guys have dish duty," I said, holding my plate out to whoever was going to take it. The guys had attacked all the food until there was nothing but a few rogue pieces of waffle left. A harmony of groans hit my ears. "I cook, you clean. It's the rule."

"Fine," Sawyer grumbled, taking my plate.

The four of them piled into the kitchen, coming back a little while later.

"Everything's done." Jackson shoved his hands into his pockets.

I stood from the couch. "All right, boys, then take me out to celebrate."

"That's what I'm talking about." Monty bent, throwing me over his shoulder and carried me out the door, tossing me into the back seat of the car.

And off we went to celebrate our first single. For a moment, I thought about texting Cole. Then I shoved the phone into my back pocket, deciding against it. He could wait. It startled me that I thought of calling Cole even before my parents. They were my go-to people. I had to tell them first.

I'd talk to Cole later.

CHAPTER EIGHTEEN

COLE

Bus duty.

Besides lunch duty, it had to be the worst job in the school; constantly dealing with attitude and dirty looks when you asked students to put their phones away until they were off the bus. With modern technology, we had to be super vigilant about cyber bullying. Kids taking pictures of other kids in school and using it against them was, unfortunately, not a rare occurrence, and I had firsthand knowledge of how much damage that could do to someone. Mari had suffered enough from the decisions my friends and I had made. Honestly, looking back, I think I knew what a bastard Sam was. Someone as fucked as that in the head probably wouldn't bother trying to change.

No wonder it had taken Mari so long to trust me. We'd spent more and more time together and each day I'd started to notice her opening up. I couldn't blame her for wanting to be sure that I'd really changed because she'd only seen the way she'd

199

been treated. She probably didn't realize that I'd been on the sideline for most of it. Not that it excused my behavior. I should have stood up for her.

Another student stepped out the door, headphones in, staring at his phone. I stepped into his path, he practically ran into me before he looked up and noticed I was there.

"Mr. Wallace?"

I crossed my arms over my chest, glancing down at his phone and back at him. He yanked the earbuds out, the music so loud I opened my mouth to tell him to put it away, when her voice hit me like a ton of bricks.

"What are you listening to?"

The kid narrowed his eyes at me. "Umm . . . I think their name is Jaded Ivory."

"Where did you find that song?"

He took a step back. "I swear, Mr. Wallace, there's nothing bad."

His reaction made much more sense now. He was afraid to get in trouble for breaking the principal's new rule about inappropriate music being played in school. She wasn't messing around. I'd already seen two students suspended.

"Relax, I was just curious. I think I've heard that band before."

"Oh." His features instantly relaxed. "The song is epic. It's been all over Twitter today."

Twitter.

I needed to get to my phone.

"Just put it away until you're off the bus."

"Got it." He shoved it in his pocket and climbed onto the bus.

I tapped my foot, waiting for the buses to leave. Could Mari and the guys have really released a single? Why hadn't she told me?

The moment the buses pulled out of the drive, I ran down the hall to my office, yanking my keys out of my pocket and unlocking the top drawer where I kept it. I hadn't been big on social media after everything that happened, but I kept my accounts for when the few times I wanted to see a feed.

I pulled up Twitter and searched for the hashtag #JadedIvory. Apparently, they were trending. Their name was everywhere. Tags. Hashtags. All relating to their debut single, Runaway Dream.

The reviews praised the band and the talent of the lead singer.

That's my girl.

My girl.

Oh fuck.

I'd fallen deeper into the hole than I expected to. Mari wasn't mine, even if my subconscious wanted her to be. But while we might not ever be *that*, I would consider Mari to be a friend. A good friend. Ryan had joked the other night that he felt like he was being replaced. I'd laughed, but Mari had become more important to me than I expected. I'd gone into this whole thing hoping she'd be able to forgive me for the past. Never in a million years did I think we'd come this far.

But she never mentioned that they'd be releasing a song on the radio—something I knew they had to be hoping for. Who in their situation wouldn't? My best guess, with everything I'd learned about Mari over the last few months, was that she wouldn't want me hanging out with her because of that. Nothing like that would ever cross my mind. It was Mari herself who drew me in. Yes, her voice was beautiful and I enjoyed listening to her sing, but that wasn't all she was. There were many more layers to

Mari. Layers that I was starting to care about way more than I should.

I dialed Mari's number. She needed to know she didn't have to keep this from me. I wanted to take her out to celebrate her success, not boost myself from it. It would have been the same had I made the NFL. I wouldn't have wanted a cleat chaser who was only after fame and money.

The phone rang a few times before her soft voice answered, making a chill run down my spine. The noise in the background was deafening.

"Hey, Cole."

A chorus of, "Hey, Cole," sounded in the background. It was a little after three in the afternoon and they were already wasted. They had to be out celebrating their release.

"Hey. I just heard your new release. Congratulations."

"Thanks. Hold on a second." The sound became muffled, but I heard her tell one of the guys to move so she could go somewhere to talk. When she spoke again, there was less noise. I could hear her better. "Sorry, I went out front."

"No problem. You could have told me you guys were releasing a song. I would have blasted that shit all over social media."

She laughed. "You hate social media."

"I would have done it for you."

The line went silent.

"Mari?" I said a few moments later, wondering if she'd hung up. My grip on the phone tightened.

"I'm here," she whispered.

"I'd love to take you out to celebrate. And this has nothing to do with me, I want to celebrate you. What you've accomplished."

She sighed. "I'd like that, but I don't want to ditch the guys right now."

"I wouldn't expect you to."

"I know." I could hear the smile in her voice. "How about I text you tomorrow? There's somewhere I want you to come with me."

"You name it, I'll be there."

"I'll hold you to that." There was a rustling over the line. "Look, I gotta—"

"Go. I'll talk to you tomorrow."

We disconnected the call and I immediately found myself looking forward to tomorrow. Every piece Mari shared with me gave me a little more insight into who she was. The downfall was that it made it harder and harder to keep my hands to myself. The night she'd come home with me was burned into my memory, my mind taunting me with it, over and over in my dreams.

By the time I walked in the door Ryan was already home, head in the fridge, looking for a snack.

"Hey." He straightened up, a slice of cold pizza in his hand.

I dropped my duffel on the floor. While I loved football, getting home before the sunset was nice. "Did you hear Jaded Ivory released a single today?"

"No shit. Did you talk to Mari?"

"A little bit ago. They're out celebrating, but she wants me to go somewhere with her tomorrow."

He dropped onto the couch, resting his feet on the coffee table, his tie hanging over his shoulders, already tugged loose. He glanced over at me. "Damn, I envy you. I'm tired of the shirt and tie. I wanna where gym clothes to teach in."

I raised a brow at him. "You could always go get a phys ed certification."

"Oh hell no. No more school. I'm just gonna sit here and be jealous."

"I'm going to change and go for a run." I stood to head to my bedroom.

He rolled his eyes. "Who wants to exercise?"

"You will in about an hour when I get back. Just like you always do."

"Probably. Get in a couple of extra miles for me," he said, patting his stomach like there was an ounce of fat on it. Ryan may joke about being lazy, but some days I wondered if he spent more time in the gym than I did.

My feet pounded the sidewalk. Mile after mile, I tried to stop worrying about where Mari wanted to take me. She'd sounded nervous asking, which raised the hairs on the back of my neck because there was absolutely no reason for her to be nervous. I would never judge her. I hoped she knew that by now.

After ten miles, I called it a day and headed home. I walked through the door and dropped on the couch. Ryan was nowhere to bc found. The running sneakers that normally sat by the door were gone, exactly like I'd said they would be.

After taking a quick shower and grabbing something to eat, I went to my room to listen to Jaded Ivory's debut song. The only part I'd heard was the small bit from the kid's phone and I was curious to hear more.

Finding it was simple; the song was tagged everywhere. The moment her sultry voice filled the room my dick ached. Memories of her on my bed, crying out as she came assaulted my mind and I couldn't stop myself from getting rock-hard.

The music held me, but it was Mari's voice that truly sucked me in. Maybe I was biased, but for me it wasn't hard to see how the band had grown more popular with Mari singing lead; although, after watching the band interact off the stage, the true leader of the group was probably Heath. He seemed to keep the balance between the serious and the crazy.

But whether she liked it or not, Mari was about to become the face of Jaded Ivory.

ᐱ ᐱ ᐱ

The next day moved at a snail's pace. Between each period, I ran to my desk to check my phone. They couldn't have been out that late considering their level of intoxication at three, unless they'd stayed out all night.

Finally, during my lunch, my phone buzzed on my desk.

Mari: Can you pick me up at my place tonight?

My fingers flew over the keys, anticipation making me spell words wrong. Thank god for autocorrect.

Me: Sure, what time do you want me there?

Her answer was almost immediate.

Mari: Any time after 7.

Me: Gonna give me any hint where we're going?

Mari: Nope, not until you get here.

Me: Tease.

The banter with Mari was refreshingly easy, but it wasn't long before I had to go back to class and lock my phone up again. Thankfully it was a running day. All I had to do was sit with a stopwatch. I didn't think I could have paid much more attention if I tried. As the kids lapped me over and over, I tried to guess where we could be going. Nothing came to mind.

The last two classes were torturous. When I got home, things weren't any better. Even though I'd taken a long run the night before, I went out again—anything to distract myself from pacing a hole in the living room rug. I should have been exhausted when I got back, but it was the exact opposite; I was practically bouncing on the balls of my feet throughout the shower.

Wearing a button-down shirt and cargo shorts, I pulled into Mari's driveway. Before I could even step out of the car, she was out the front door and on her way to the passenger side. She climbed up into the SUV with a huge smile on her face, but it didn't reach her eyes. On top of that, she was playing with her necklace again.

I knew the easiest way to fix that. I covered her hand with mine. "Relax, Mari. It's me."

"I know. That's the part I'm worried about."

It was like a shot to the gut to hear her say that, but instead of dwelling on it, I wanted to learn the reason behind it. "Will you feel better once we get there?"

She shrugged. "Maybe."

Maybe. I could work with that. "Okay, then tell me where we're going and I'll get you there."

She let go of the pendant and flipped her hand around in mine, threading our fingers together. "Lakeside Tattoo."

Unwilling to let go of her hand to put the car in gear, I reached over with my left hand, which caused a smirk to lift her lips.

The ride wasn't far, thank god. Mari got more and more agitated the closer we got, her hand beginning to tremble in mine. I drove into the parking lot and turned to her. She was still looking out the front window at the building.

"I'm guessing we're here to get you a new tattoo. What I don't get is why you're so nervous. You have tattoos covering both arms. You don't get ink that size if you're afraid."

She shook her head. "It's not the tattoo I'm afraid of. It's the meaning behind it."

"Do you want to tell me what it means?"

"Yeah, but only part of it. The rest I'll tell you when it's done."

I couldn't stop myself from running my thumb over her bottom lip. The reward was a shuddered breath. "So tell me."

"You've seen the birds on my shoulder."

I wanted to answer "intimately," but I had a feeling that wouldn't get me the rest of the story. "I have."

"I started that tattoo not long after meeting Sawyer. Actually, he took me to get it right after I cut my hair the first time. It was to celebrate doing something new—something I'd never done before. Ever since then, every time something new happens in my life, I add a new bird." She glanced at her shoulder. "Every day when I look in the mirror, they remind me of all the things I can do, no matter how hard the road is to get there."

Suddenly everything was making sense. With the new release, it was time to add another bird to her shoulder. Fuck. I'd played a part in making that road harder. Not anymore. I'd clear every bit of debris to give her the straightest, smoothest path possible. "Well, let's go get that bird. It's time to celebrate the release of your new song."

She sucked in a deep breath. The smile on her lips still felt off but I ignored it, thinking that maybe she did have a small fear of needles that she didn't want to talk about. She climbed from the car and took my hand as we walked into the shop.

The artist by the door immediately stood from his seat. "Mari. Long time. Adding more birds?"

"I am."

As if just realizing I was there, he turned to me. "Hey, I'm Carter."

"Cole. Nice to meet you." I glanced around the room, taking in all the art hanging from the walls. His work was gorgeous. Some of the best I'd ever seen. "All these yours?" I asked, gesturing around the room.

"They are." He glanced down at my arms. My tattoos covered by the sleeve of my shirt. "Interested in getting some of your own work done?"

A conversation from long ago popped into my head. "Actually, I might be. I'd been asking around about a good artist to add to what I already have, but I couldn't seem to get an answer."

Mari's eyes snapped up to mine. I gave her a wink and was rewarded with her warm smile. When I looked back, Carter was watching the two of us, his eyes darting back and forth, trying to figure out the puzzle. Well, good luck, buddy. I'd like to figure it out myself.

"We'll have to sit down and talk about your ideas."

"That would be great."

Carter gestured toward his chair. "Have a seat, Mari. It'll only take me a sec."

Mari took off the leather jacket she wore, revealing a skimpy tank top underneath. I wanted to groan at the sight, the top of her breasts practically on full display above the fabric. It made sense she'd wear something to expose where she wanted the tattoo, but a man could only take so much.

208

Carter took a seat on the rolling stool next to the chair. "Where are we putting this one?"

She held up two fingers. "Two. I want two birds today. One here and here," she said pointing with her finger to two different places on her shoulder.

Two? What was the second one for?

Carter smiled. "Good for you."

He dipped the needle in the black and moved toward Mari's shoulder. "No pattern?" I asked, my eyes glued to the gun in his hand.

He shook his head. "Nah, I've done enough of these for her. It's easier to do it freehand."

Mari peered up at me through her lashes. "Besides, that makes each bird unique."

"Good point."

I watched her flinch as the needle first touched her skin. It was irrational, but I wanted to punch the guy for hurting her. Luckily, the reasonable part of my brain was working and reminded the rest that tattoos hurt. The large tribal band around my arm was a testament to how well I knew that.

Each time the needle touched her skin, she'd make the same face. Not once did a sound leave her lips. Her hand balled into a fist, her nails digging into her palm. I took a step forward and wrapped my hand around hers, prying her fingers loose from their tight grip and taking her hand in mine. I leaned down and whispered, "Squeeze my hand instead. I don't want you to hurt yourself."

When I moved back, her eyes shimmered under the light, the teal color looking more like the ocean.

Then her grip tightened and I saw Carter had moved on to the second bird. The outline and fill were complete in no time. Mari's grasp loosened and

I flexed my hand, shooting her a wink as I helped her from the chair to the mirror on the side of the room. The banging of equipment as Carter cleaned up was drowned out by the ringing in my ears at what I saw in the mirror. Mari stood directly in front of me. The top of her blond head barely reaching my chin. But what caught my attention was how perfect we looked together. A pipe dream it might have been, it didn't stop me from wondering.

"It's perfect," she whispered.

And for one split second I wasn't sure if she was talking about the tattoos or the picture we made. Our gazes locked in the mirror and I froze, afraid to break the spell.

"Looking good, Mari," Carter called, startling us both.

With a slight blush, Mari stepped out of my arms and let Carter cover her new ink. She quickly pulled on her coat and paid.

"Thanks." Carter smiled and looked over at me. "Come by anytime. We'll see what we can do for you."

"I will."

Mari took my hand and pulled me out the door, waving to Carter. She didn't stop moving until we reached the car. I'd been so focused on the pain she was in, I almost forgot about the extra bird. I turned to face her.

"Why two birds? I thought this was to celebrate your new single?"

Her eyes fell to the pavement below. "One is."

"And the other?" It bothered me that she thought she couldn't look me in the eye while she told me what was going on. I only had myself to blame for that one.

"Remember in the car I said I would tell you the other thing about the bird tattoos after they were done?"

"Yeah?" I drew out the word, completely confused by the conversation. I couldn't imagine what else there would be to tell.

She shuffled from foot to foot. "Well, one of the birds was to celebrate the release of the single. The other bird." She paused. "Well, the other is to . . . umm . . . celebrate you coming into my life."

CHAPTER NINETEEN

COLE

Me?

Celebrating me?

Any response I might have had died in my chest as my lips parted, a rush of desire burning through me, my hand trembling as I tucked it under her chin and lifted her face to mine. Her chest rose and fell with rapid pants. My eyes zeroed in on her lips.

Fuck it.

I slid my free hand into her hair and brought my mouth down on hers. Her lips parted the moment they touched and I groaned at the taste of her tongue against mine. Mari was fire and passion and beauty. My body surged with a hunger to be near her. But like that first night, the feel of her mouth on mine made my head spin. I wouldn't push. Yes, I'd kissed her; now it was up to her to set the pace.

Should I stop? Should I keep going?

I waited for some kind of signal. My head was a mess. The smell of vanilla and jasmine wrapped around me like a vine, holding me to her.

The moment she pressed her body tighter to mine, I was lost to her. Backing her up against the car, I took possession of the kiss, pushing my hips into hers, letting her see exactly how she made me feel.

A heartbeat later and she tore her mouth from mine. The sense of loss was strong, like a piece of me had been taken and given to her. I wanted my hands on every part of her body.

"Let's take this back to my place," she said against my lips.

My brain practically melted at the heat in her eyes. I needed to be rational. I didn't want my ass kicked later for it. "What about Sawyer?"

She leaned in even closer, placing kisses at the base of my neck. "He went to his parents' place for a few nights."

I captured her lips again, leading her around to the passenger side of the car. Without breaking the connection, I opened her door and maneuvered her into the seat. She reached down and caressed my aching erection through my pants.

God, I fucking wanted her.

I tore my mouth from hers. "Stay there."

I shut the door and ran around to my side of the car. *Focus*, I told myself. I needed to get us back to her house in one piece. Throwing the car in reverse, I backed out of the space. The second the car was in drive, I slammed my foot on the gas sending little pebbles from the pavement flying behind me as Mari's warm hand made its way up my thigh.

"I'm trying to get us home safely," I said, glancing over at her from the corner of my eye. "I'm not sure we'll make it if you keep doing that."

"This?" She did it again.

"I hope there are no cops on this road," I muttered to myself as I watched the speedometer needle creep up and up.

We pulled into her driveway and I breathed a sigh of relief.

We'd made it.

Without the road to concentrate on, I became fully aware of the heat scorching my body from the inside. I jumped out of the car and was shocked to find Mari already on her porch, keys in her hand as she fumbled with them, trying to get them in the lock. They slipped from her fingers. I bent at the waist and scooped them into my hand before they hit the ground. My experience as a wide receiver had its perks, after all. I slid the key in the lock and opened the door.

Mari yanked the keys from the knob and slammed the door shut behind us, tossing the keys onto a table by the door. Her leather jacket followed them down onto the couch as she stalked toward me, eyes dark, her shoulders back.

I'd made a lot of mistakes in the past. I didn't want to make anymore. Before this went any further, I needed to know exactly what Mari wanted. I wouldn't take her to bed just hoping I was doing the right thing.

She ran her hands over my chest and I ground my teeth together, closing my eyes and taking a deep breath through my nose. "Mari, please. Wait."

Her hands froze and her gaze snapped to mine, the color draining from her face. Damn, when was I going to stop being an asshole where she was concerned? She tried to take a step back, her chin trembling, but I clutched at her wrists, holding them against me. I couldn't let her get away from me.

Not again.

She wouldn't look at me as I pulled her flush against my chest. A shuddered breath left her. I felt it.

"Believe me, I want you so badly my whole body is on fire. But I've wronged you in so many ways in the past, I just want to slow down and make sure this is what you really want."

Her whole body relaxed momentarily, and then she held me tighter. "The fact that you're worried is exactly why I know it's what I want."

I tipped her face up to mine, needing to taste her again. She nipped at my bottom lip and leaned back to scan my face. "Now stop stalling and take me back to my room."

"Lead the way."

She dragged me down the hall, which I didn't mind in the least. Shit, if I'd known where her room was, I would have hefted her onto my shoulder and carried her there myself.

As she walked backward down the hall she grabbed the hem of her tank and yanked it over her head, revealing a blue lace bra that left little to the imagination. She pushed open the door and flicked on the light, backing up until her knees hit the bed. I dropped down in front of her, kissing my way up her stomach as I undid the button of her jeans, slowly sliding them down before caressing the inside of her legs, all the way up to her thighs. Shivers rocked her. I helped her slip off her boots and tossed the jeans aside. She was sexier than I remembered, my dreams not doing her justice.

I stood up and ran my finger lightly over the bandage that still covered her shoulder, the implications of everything the simple bird meant hitting me all at once. My throat closed and I struggled to form words.

"I'm not sure I know what to say."

"Don't say anything. Just kiss me."

That I could handle. I cupped her face in my hands, devouring her lips as if they were my lifeline. Gently, I laid her on the bed covering her body with mine. She tugged at the buttons on my shirt. "I think you have too many clothes on."

I peered down her body and smirked. "So do you."

I divested her of her bra and panties before bringing my mouth down to lave her nipple with my tongue, sucking it into my mouth as her hips pumped beneath me.

"Please, Cole. Touch me."

My lips wrapped around her breast and she squirmed on the bed as I snaked a hand down her body. I slipped one finger inside her, loving the way her hips thrust in time with my hand. Our first time had been quick and dirty and fucking hot. This time, I wanted to savor every moment. Hear her moans, watch her squirm.

She sank her hands into the hair on the back of my head, holding my mouth to her chest, arching her back so I could pull her other nipple into my mouth, my finger still slowly moving in and out of her body. I stroked her with my thumb, adding to the sensations she was already feeling.

"I can't take it anymore. Please," she begged again.

I kissed my way up her jaw, loving the softness under my lips. "No," I whispered against her lips. "Tonight, I'm savoring every part of you."

"I'm gonna go up in flames here."

I leaned my elbows on either side of her. "Trust me when I tell you, you are already on fire."

I kissed her, thrusting my body against hers, the fabric of my shorts creating friction against my

216

rock-hard shaft. The noises that left Mari made my cock twitch. The more I tortured her, the more I tortured myself.

I licked a hot, wet path down her neck, over one breast then the other, before traveling lower. She moaned when I dipped it into her belly button but still I went lower, curling my tongue around her clit. Her hips punched off the bed. Taking her hips in my hands, I held her flat to the mattress. Her legs began to quiver with each flick of my tongue.

"Oh fuck," Mari cried.

Then I began to fuck her with my tongue, her body moving in time until her muscles began to stiffen and I knew she was close. Moving my mouth, I sucked hard on her clit and her back bowed off the bed, her whole body trembling.

As she writhed on the sheets I stood and tore off the rest of my clothing, my dick leaking in anticipation of sliding inside her. Pulling a condom from my wallet, I slipped it on and crawled over her. She pushed me to my back, straddling my waist, bending to take my lips at the same time she brought her body up and slid down on my cock.

She lifted her head. "My turn," she said, her eyes alight with mischief.

She rocked forward, slamming her hips down on me. My eyes rolled into the back of my head, pleasure coursing through me. She felt fucking fantastic. Not wanting to miss out on my chance to touch her, I cupped her breasts in my hands as they bounced above me. I climbed higher and higher the harder she rode me, my balls pulling tight to my body. She cried out when I pinched her nipples. Her body squeezed tightly on mine. I couldn't hold back any longer.

"Mari." The sound echoed around a room filled with only the sound of our heavy breaths.

She collapsed on top of me, the weight of her welcome. My limbs felt like jelly, but that didn't stop me from banding my arms around her and holding her tight to me. The scent of vanilla filled my nose and I was in heaven.

Wow. Just . . . wow.

As much as I enjoyed having her there, I knew we needed to get cleaned up. Then I could hold her in my arms the entire night, exactly like I'd wanted to that first time.

I brushed her hair from her face. "I'll be right back."

I stopped at the door, looking first left, then right. She giggled. "Bathroom's down the hall on the right."

I winked and walked down the hall.

After discarding the condom, I washed up quickly, wanting to get back to Mari as fast as possible. Memories of the night I'd found my bed empty the next morning taunted me. I couldn't do that again. Not after all this. This woman turned me inside out and I wouldn't have it any other way.

I jogged back down the hallway to find her sitting with her back against the headboard, the sheet pulled up to her chest, her hair was tousled from my fingers. The Neanderthal in me beat his chest that the half-lidded, just-fucked look on her face was thanks to me.

She patted the bed next to her. I climbed back in and sealed our lips together.

When I moved back, her eyes fluttered open. Once again, I ran my fingers over the bandage on her shoulder. "I still can't believe you did this."

I'd never tire of seeing her blush. "Speaking of that, let me go take it off and put some cream on them. I'll be right back."

I stole another kiss, massaging her breasts before she stood from the bed and walked out of the room. It gave me the opportunity to study her room. I'd learned a lot about Mari over the last few months by simply watching her. Damn, that still sounded so stalkerish. Not that I was even remotely sad with how things turned out.

The room was simple. White dresser and headboard, the blankets and sheets a light shade of green. There wasn't a single thing on the floor, except the Fender, which stood on a stand next to a chair. On the chair sat a notebook.

I had a feeling the notebook contained the songs she'd talked about, but there was no way I'd invade her privacy by looking inside.

Her dresser was littered with pictures, none of them from high school. Some of them were from her childhood, others more recent, but those four years were missing.

She stepped back into the room, gloriously naked and fucking sexy as hell. For a moment, I thought she'd seen me studying the pictures on her dresser. Then fire lit her eyes when she realized my gaze was completely glued to the creamy skin and long shapely legs.

"See something you like?" She swayed every part of her body as she walked into the room.

How the fuck did women do that and make it look sexy? If a guy tried, they'd be calling for an ambulance, thinking they were having a seizure.

"Very much."

Mari flipped off the light and slipped beneath the covers. I moved to lie down, giving Mari the chance to curl into my arms and place her head on my chest. I roved my fingers over her arm while I listened to her breathing settle. I couldn't stop touching her.

"Thank you," I whispered into the dark. Never once in all those months of dreaming about her could I ever have predicted this outcome. I honestly thought I'd always have to watch her from afar, maybe hang out with her as friends, if I was lucky. This was so much more than I could ever have asked for.

"For what?" And even in the darkness I could imagine the way her brows were drawn together, including the little crease between them.

"Giving me a chance."

The smile was in her voice. "Everyone can change."

I kept stroking her arm until I was sure she was sound asleep. The alarm on my phone should wake me in time to get home to get ready for work, but that was the last thing on my mind. What I really wondered was how it would feel to wake up with Mari in my arms, and I was more than a little excited to find out.

Mari

The soft press of lips against my forehead tugged me from sleep. I felt warm and safe. My eyes opened.

Wait, what?

My bed feels too small.

There was a man's bare chest below me. Outside I could see it was mostly still dark.

"Mari?"

I moved my face up to see his, and for a second I wanted to drown in the liquid green of his eyes.

"Cole," I said, my voice breathy.

He kissed my forehead again. "While I would love to stay here with you all day, I have to go if I'm gonna make it to work on time."

I snuggled closer, reluctant to let him out of my sight again. "I know, but I wish you could stay. I like having you here."

"Trust me, this is the best morning I've had in a long time."

I sat up, grabbing a set of pajamas from the drawer. The least I could do was walk him to the door. I watched as Cole pulled on his clothes, all his bronze skin on display. The way those fingers . . .

I shook my head. There was no time for that. Thinking about it would only get me worked up and horny.

"You don't have to get up." His eyes were focused below my neck.

"Up here, sexy." I gestured upward with my fingers. "We don't have time for that unless you plan on being late."

He groaned, pulling me against him. "Don't I wish."

"So do I. Now it's time for you to get going." I stepped back, taking his hand, leading him to the door because I had a feeling if we stayed in here another second, neither of us would have clothes on anymore.

"I'll call you later," he said, reaching for the doorknob.

"I expect it."

He smirked and walked out into the cool morning air. I felt the early morning rush inside and I closed the door, locking it behind me. It was way too early to be out of bed. I had no idea how Cole did it every morning. But since I didn't have anywhere to be, I went back to my room and crawled between the sheets, which now held the scent of something uniquely Cole. I buried my face in the pillow he'd slept on and let myself drift off into dreams of the night before.

The next thing I knew someone was crawling in bed with me. I opened my eyes to see Sawyer, lying in my bed, facing me. The room was filled with light, the sun risen. I rubbed the sleep from my eyes.

"What time is it?"

The corner of his lip pulled up. "Past noon, but I take it by the mussed-up sex hair you're rocking, you had a long night."

I ran my hand through my hair trying to control the mess. "How do you know it's not bed hair?"

He leaned his head on his hand. "I've seen your bed head. That," he pointed at me, "is straight-up sex hair."

I buried my face in the pillow. The man was fucking Sherlock Holmes; never missed a thing. "Whatever."

"I knew you wouldn't be able to resist him."

I looked up and his eyes dared me to deny it. Instead of confirming what he already knew, I shoved his shoulder. "Shut up."

"Why does everyone always hit me?"

"Because you have a big mouth."

I followed his gaze and realized he was looking at my shoulder. His mouth dropped. "You got a new bird without me?"

It had been our tradition ever since he'd taken me to get the first one. Not that Sawyer didn't mean as much to me as he did now, but this time it was something I needed to share with Cole.

"*Birds*. Plural."

"How many did you get?"

I glanced down. Sawyer still wasn't Cole's biggest fan and I really didn't want to give him a reason to hate him even more.

"Two."

"I don't get it. I know one is for the release, but what's the other for? Did you go by yourself?"

"Cole went with me." I traced circles on the blanket, trying to distract myself. "I got the other one for him. Even if it doesn't work out with him, I know that I faced another fear." I rushed the words out, trying to convince him before he got upset about it.

Sawyer titled my chin up. "I'll admit I'm still worried about him, but you're right. Good for you."

I narrowed my eyes. "He's done nothing to give you that impression."

He tucked a piece of hair behind my ear. "You have to remember, I knew about Cole and his friends before you ran into him again, even if I didn't know his name."

"He's not the same guy," I argued. It had taken me months to come to that conclusion, otherwise I would have never let him in.

"I hope you're right. I've made a lot of mistakes and I don't want you to follow in my footsteps."

"But you ran instead of facing your problems."

It was a low blow and I should have felt guilty, but it was the truth. His eyes dropped from mine. "And maybe I should have stayed and talked to Reagan. At least you're strong enough to face this head-on. I'm proud of you. I just want you to be careful."

I could see his problem. Sawyer had a lot of regrets about things that happened before he'd left home. I did, too. Sometimes I wondered what life would be like if I'd stood up for myself instead of being like a ragdoll dragged through the mud. Things weren't as easy for Sawyer. While I'd had a chance to face my fears and prove I was stronger, he hadn't had the same opportunity; at least, not yet.

"What are you doing back already, anyway?"

His lips turned down and he sat up facing away from me. "I couldn't find what I was looking for."

Something more was going on. As well as Sawyer could read me, I could read him, too.

I also knew that, even if I asked, Sawyer wouldn't tell me. When he was ready to talk, he would. I just had to be there for him when that happened.

I kneeled behind him, placing my hands on his shoulders, trying to rub out the tension that now resided there. "I'm sorry. Hopefully you'll find it when you really need it."

He was quiet for a few minutes, slowly leaning more and more into the ministrations of my fingers. Eventually whatever trance he was in was broken.

"What do you want to do today?"

I leaned around to face him. "I wanna finish that song in my head."

"New inspiration?"

Heat crept into my cheeks. "Maybe."

"Well, grab that guitar of yours and let's get to work."

I hugged him, then rummaged around my room for my notebook. I grabbed my guitar and went to the living room where Sawyer already had his own guitar settled over his lap. He nodded his head at the notebook in my hand. "Let's see what you got."

I opened the book and settled the Fender on my lap. I strummed the first few notes and looked at Sawyer, who gestured for me to play again and then picked up with me.

And that's how we worked; jot down a lyric, pick out a tune, put them together.

Lather.

Rinse.

Repeat.

Sawyer stretched his arms up above his head, twisting until I heard the crack of his elbows. "Break time?" he asked.

"Break? I think it's time to call it a night. We've been at this for hours."

The screen of my phone lit up with a text.

Cole: Dinner?

An idea formed.

Me: What would you think about having dinner with the guys? I want you to get to know them.

My phone dinged less than a minute later.

Cole: I'm game, what about them?

I looked over at Sawyer, who was reading through the lyrics one more time. "How would you feel about having dinner with Cole and me tonight? The others, too."

He shrugged without looking up. "Sure."

Not encouraging, but not a no, either. I sent a text to Heath who I knew would be in my corner on this one. Sawyer picked his guitar back up and started playing again, turning so that his back was to me. What was his problem?

Heath: Sure. Need me to pick up cranky on our way?

How did he know Sawyer was in a mood?

Me: Yes, please. I'll let you know where we're going.

I picked up the guitar. "I'm going to get changed and head over to Cole's. Heath will be by later to pick you up."

"Sounds good."

I wanted to wrap my hands around his neck and choke the life out of him, but I bit my tongue and said nothing. It wasn't worth another fight.

226

At least he was willing to go.

γ γ γ

My foot kept a steady rhythm on the floor of Cole's car, my fingers up and around my pendant. If Cole and I were going to make this work, being able to hang out with the guys was a must. Thus far Sawyer had been cordial, but it was clear to everyone he still didn't trust Cole. Or maybe it was just that he was worried about me.

Either way, both men were staples in my life at the moment, and I really hoped they'd find some common ground because otherwise things were going to get really awkward. I'd thought about bringing Cole to our place to spend some time just with me and Sawyer; that was, until I realized Cole still talked to Heath. Having that buffer might help soften Sawyer a bit more. He could be one stubborn man when he wanted to.

"What's wrong?" Cole glanced at me out of the corner of his eye.

As if it burned me, I dropped the pendant from my hand. *Shit*. If I was ever going to find a way to keep people from knowing I was freaking out, I really needed to stop doing it. I was so used to hiding my feelings from anyone but Sawyer, it still threw me how easily Cole could read me.

"I'm hoping Sawyer isn't a dick tonight."

He picked my hand up from my lap and placed a kiss on the back of it. "He won't be. You can't really blame him for not trusting me. Shit, there are days I'm still surprised *you* trust me."

I gripped his hand tighter. "No. Since we met again, you haven't given me any reason not to."

"Yeah, but I'm guessing Sawyer knew about me long before we met up again. You can't tell me you didn't talk to him about high school." He gave me a pointed look. "I've seen how close you two are."

I nodded. "I've told Sawyer a lot of things over the years."

"See. Don't give him such a hard time for worrying about me. I know I'm different. *You* know I'm different. That's all that should really matter."

I opened my mouth to speak, but he continued.

"But, I plan on proving to him just how much you mean to me."

A warmth settled over me. Hearing someone say those words to me was like a balm to my soul. For so long I'd worried I'd never trust anyone besides Sawyer, and yet here I was, letting someone in. There was a lot to be said for facing your fears.

"I think I like the sound of that."

We pulled into the restaurant parking lot. I'd picked a restaurant over a bar because I figured it was the best place to talk . . . and no one would get wasted. If we'd gone to a bar, there were no guarantees.

I took a few deep breaths and, straightening my shoulders, I stepped out of the car.

CHAPTER TWENTY ONE

COLE

The way she continued to fidget even after we reached the restaurant worried me. It was clear she wanted Sawyer and me to get along, but I hadn't been lying in the car; I couldn't really blame him for thinking the worst of me.

Wanting to relax her before we walked inside, I slid my hand into hers, entwining our fingers. She offered me a small smile and as we walked hand in hand into the restaurant, we spotted the guys, already seated in a large round booth in the corner. Heath waved us over. He and I'd talked after a few of their shows. He'd done me a solid by setting everything up with Mari. We wouldn't have been here if he hadn't stepped in. I owed him.

"Hey, guys."

Heath stepped out of the booth to let us sit down. Mari immediately climbed in, taking the seat next to Sawyer, leaving me on her other side with Heath next to me.

Mari nodded her head at me. "Guys, this is Cole. Cole, you've already met Sawyer and Heath." She pointed at the guy sitting next to Sawyer. "That's Jackson, and the goofball next to him is Monty."

"I'm not a goofball," Monty said, attempting to balance a toothpick on his tongue.

Heath lifted a brow at him. "Seriously?"

He let the toothpick fall to the table. "Fine, I'll behave."

"You don't have to behave for me. It's nice to meet you guys." I actually remembered Jackson from that night in Mari's dressing room, but seeing as her fingers were still wrapped around her necklace, there was no reason to bring it up and fluster her further.

Heath punched my shoulder. "Looks like things are working out for the two of you."

I took Mari's hand in mine. "They are."

The words were assertive, but that didn't mean I didn't still feel like I was walking on thin ice with Mari. It had been less than a week since she'd finally let me in. I wasn't ready to let her go. I had this irrational need to keep her close, worried that the more time she had, the more she might believe I could hurt her again.

Damn.

Too many regrets.

"Wait." Monty turned to face me fully. "I've heard of you. You're that wide receiver. Buckeyes, right?"

I shifted in my seat. It wasn't like that information was hard to come by, and neither was the story about the injury that ended my career before it started, but if I could avoid the subject, I usually did. People could read about it all they wanted. I didn't feel like recounting every detail.

This time it was Mari squeezing my hand.

"He's coaching the local high school team."

"You're a teacher?" Jackson asked.

I nodded. "Yeah. This is my second year. But I'm not the head coach, just the offensive one."

Monty smiled. "I saw you play. Man, you could catch anything that came your way."

Mari leaned in closer. "I bet he still can."

"I guess I could. Haven't really played in a long time." I really hoped that would be the end of the conversation; the end of the one topic I really didn't want to be on the table.

Heath gave me an understanding nod. "That's right. Your knee."

The guys all glanced in different directions, avoiding eye contact. "Sorry, man," Jackson said.

I looked over at Mari, wondering for the first time how different things might have been if I'd made it to the NFL. I definitely wouldn't be sitting here.

"Don't worry about it. Things happen for a reason, right?"

"Yeah, they do."

The waitress chose that moment to take our orders and, thankfully, the topic of conversation changed after she left, most of it revolving around stories of the band; how they met, crazy things they'd done.

"Crazy bastard jumped the fence and climbed to the top of the slide." Heath laughed and I glanced between him and Monty. Most of our plates were empty, waiting for the server to return and take them away.

"Was the water on?"

Heath shook his head. "Nope, that shit was dry as the desert. Didn't stop numbnuts here from sliding down it anyway."

My ass and legs hurt simply thinking about them rubbing against the plastic as I went down. "Shit, didn't that hurt?"

Monty smirked. "Road rash took weeks to clear up. Totally worth it, though."

I couldn't stop the laughter. I'd known some crazy assholes in college, but none crazy enough to pull that shit.

Jackson spoke up. "You forgot the part where he got chased by the cops. Spent the night hiding under cars and in dumpsters to avoid them."

My jaw dropped and I watched Monty twirl a spoon through his fingers. "Dude, there's something seriously wrong with you."

Monty laughed, his eyes on the spoon. "I know. Isn't it great?"

The rest of the table burst into laughter and Mari buried her face in Sawyer's shoulder. It hadn't been the first time that night. I had a feeling she didn't even know she was doing it. It was hard for me not to notice how much they touched, either. Nothing major, just a hand on the shoulder here, or an arm over the shoulder there. But that was normal. They were friends. Close friends.

At least, that's what I kept telling myself.

Afraid I might say something to piss everyone off, I bit the inside of my cheek and wrapped my arm around her shoulders. The tension flowed from my muscles when she snuggled closer.

Sawyer glanced at us out of the corner of his eye, careful not to turn his head. I still noticed. I noticed everything to do with Mari. I really didn't want to be jealous of Sawyer, but he was making it fucking hard.

I forced the thought from my head. With Mari sitting close to me, it was easier to listen to their stories and keep the green-eyed monster at bay. The waitress brought the check. Heath grabbed it before Mari could get her hands on it.

"Not again," she groaned.

I glanced over at Heath "I've got me and Mari."

She turned in my arms. "You don't have to buy me dinner."

Unable to resist touching her, I ran my thumb over her bottom lip. "I don't have to, but I want to."

I glanced up to see Sawyer watching me. "She always fights us when we try to pay."

I looked back down at Mari. "This gonna be an all-the-time fight with you?"

Sawyer chuckled. "All the time."

"Good to know."

Mari crossed her arms over her chest, but the corners of her lips twitched as she fought a smile.

"Just remember, we never let her win that argument." Sawyer winked.

"Thanks, I'll keep that in mind."

That was a relief. It seemed like we were finally on the same page with Mari. Maybe Sawyer and I could become friends; that was, if I could find a way to keep the touching to a minimum. Next time, I'd make sure my ass was planted next to Sawyer instead of Mari. Easy fix.

"You realize that I'm sitting right here."

I pressed a quick kiss to her lips and as the waitress cleared the rest of the plates, Heath threw his money into the black folder and handed it to me. "We need to hang out more often."

I put my own money in and handed it over Mari's head where she couldn't reach it to Sawyer.

"Come watch the Final Four with us," he said.

I peeked at Mari. These were her friends. I didn't want to step on any toes. She had a wide grin on her face. "Sure. Think Kansas is gonna take it all?"

"Nah." Jackson shook his head. "Connecticut will put up a helluva fight."

Mari's eyes glazed over. I'd learned the other night she wasn't a fan of basketball, but it was good to know I could find common ground with the guys other than her.

With dinner over, Heath moved out of the booth. I followed suit, taking Mari with me.

"Are you coming back to my place or am I taking you back to yours?" I whispered in her ear, low enough so no one else could hear.

She looked around at the guys. "Definitely yours."

I had a feeling she knew the rest of them would end up at her house. During dinner they'd mentioned working on a few songs for the label and with their basement, meaning no complaints from the neighbors about the noise, Mari and Sawyer had the most viable place to work.

We said good-night to the guys and I took Mari's arm and led her to the car. On the way back to my place, I noticed she was much calmer.

"See, that wasn't so bad."

I swallowed the rest on the tip of my tongue. There was no reason to mention the way she and Sawyer behaved around each other. I had a feeling neither of them—well, at least Mari—didn't realize it was happening.

"Not at all. I had a lot of fun tonight. I knew Monty was a little crazy, but even I'd never heard some of those stories. You fit in really well."

I narrowed my eyes. "Did you expect me not to? I've chatted with Heath at a few of your shows."

She shrugged. "Yeah, but that was different. Besides, the jocks and the music geeks don't always get along. You know that."

The insinuation that I was still "the jock" was like a punch to the gut. Choosing to make light of it I placed my hand over her thigh, stroking my thumb over the fabric. "This jock happens to enjoy every moment he spends with this hot-as-fuck, smarter-than-everyone-he-knows, music chick."

There was no way I'd call her a geek. She might have said it, and really it was just a word, but with our history it wasn't a good choice.

As soon as we got back to my place, Mari settled herself on the couch. I grabbed two beers from the fridge and climbed behind her, her back to my chest, my thighs either side of hers. I hit play on the DVD.

She looked over her shoulder at me. "The Breakfast Club?"

"I figured you'd like it."

"It's one of my favorites."

I caressed her cheek with my fingertips. "Look how well I know you already."

She placed a soft kiss on my lips and turned back to the screen. The scent of her was intoxicating. I ran my nose along her neck, placing kisses along the same path. She shivered under my touch. When she bent her head to give me better access, I ran my hands up her shirt to caress her breasts. Even through the fabric of her bra, I felt her nipples rise up proudly against my hand.

She moaned and turned into my arms, my tongue plunging into her mouth the same way I wanted to plunge into her warm body. Our bodies entwined, the heat of her calling to me.

"Oh for fuck's sake," Ryan groaned. "The bedroom is like five feet down the hall."

I broke the kiss and peered up at Ryan, who stood in the doorway, hands over his eyes. At least we both still had our clothes on. A few minutes later and I was sure that wouldn't have been the case.

Mari's face was flushed with desire and I stood from the couch, offering my hand to her, not really wanting Ryan to see her like this. This was for my eyes only. She sunk her teeth into her lower lip, placing her hand in mine. I walked Mari toward the hallway and glanced over my shoulder. Ryan caught my eye and my wink and rubbed his fingers over his temples. "Shit, am I going to need earplugs?"

"Probably." I smirked, and left him in the hallway.

Mari

Cole kept glancing over his shoulder.

"I think you have some admirers."

We'd chosen a restaurant a few towns over to avoid being recognized. With the popularity of our first single, people had begun asking us for autographs. It was happening at the grocery store, the gas station, even at the post office. People had no problem approaching us. Nothing out of hand, but for once I wanted to have dinner out with my boyfriend without worrying about people bothering us. It wasn't like we were a household name. I figured an hour away from our homes we'd be safe.

Apparently not.

"What are you talking about?"

"Two tables to your left."

I didn't want to glance over and give them any indication that I'd seen them. Cole had been

237

great about the interruptions closer to home. Not once had he complained, but for me, this was starting to get old very quickly.

I pushed the food around my plate, my appetite completely gone.

"Hey," he whispered. "Look at me."

I brought my gaze up to his. "Sorry about this." I moved my eyes in the direction of the table.

"Don't be sorry. Your song is killin' it. It comes with the territory."

I set my fork down. "You didn't sign up for this."

Cole reached across the table to cover my hand with his. "If I have you, I couldn't give two shits if people stop us to get your autograph. If it makes you happy, it makes me happy."

"Are you sure?"

He laughed. "You forget that I was supposed to play in the NFL. I've had my fair share of people stopping me on the street. Some of them would even ask in my classes, probably hoping it would be worth something someday."

His eyes dropped and although I knew he was attempting humor, I could see from the way his shoulders slumped that it still hurt him to think about what might have been. I ran my fingers up his arm. "Don't do that. I still think they should have taken the risk on you."

"Maybe." He shrugged. He moved his hand away to wipe his napkin across his lips. Was it ridiculous for me to be a little jealous of that napkin? With people watching, I wouldn't give them any photo opportunities by kissing Cole in the restaurant.

"Speaking of taking a chance on people, I got a call the other day from Hayward about me coaching for them."

Cole's eyes were on the tablecloth as he spoke. Was he embarrassed?

"As in the university?"

"Yeah." It was his turn to push his food around his plate. "They're looking for someone for the fall season."

I watched him, trying to pick up any clues. But while I was an open book, Cole was good at giving away nothing.

"Excuse me?" a quiet female voice said.

Even without looking, I knew who had to be standing next to our table. The same ones Cole mentioned earlier. All I wanted was to dig deeper into my boyfriend's reaction to being offered the job of a lifetime, but I found myself having to paste a smile on my face. I turned to face the two girls idling by our table, mobile phones clutched in their hands.

"You're Mari from Jaded Ivory, right?" The girl's voice was so high-pitched, it made my ears ring.

"That's me." I kept the smile in place, leaving my shiny, white teeth on display.

"We're so sorry to bother you," the other girl said in a much calmer voice, "but we absolutely love your song Runaway Dream, and we were wondering if we could get your autograph?"

I nodded. Not to be a bitch, but the sooner I signed whatever they wanted, the sooner I could get back to figuring out what was bothering Cole.

"Sure. What do you want me to sign?"

The first girl pulled out a sharpie and her phone, flipping so I could sign the case. The other one asked me to sign the top of her Chucks. Squealing, the girls said thank you and bounded back to their table.

"Nice fake smile." Cole's trademark smirk was there, visible even behind his glass. Okay, so he was feeling better.

Or trying to change the subject.

"It's good that you're the only one who notices. Besides, it might have been a real smile if my boyfriend hadn't dropped his new job offer in my lap with a look like he was heading to the gallows."

Cole put his drink down and rolled his eyes. "The gallows? Really?"

"You looked like you were being led to your death. What's the deal? I thought you were excited by the idea of coaching a college team?"

"I am. I mean, I was . . . No, I am. It's just—" He ran a hand through his hair. "It's not the only call I got. Cambria called me about a week ago."

I gave his arm a shove. "Why didn't you tell me?"

His gaze roamed around the room. "You were stressed about the new song."

"Doesn't mean I wouldn't want to know something that exciting. Remember this"—I wagged my finger between the two of us—"is a partnership, which means we share things with each other. The only reason you knew I was stressed about the new song was because I told you. You need to talk to me when something's bothering you. Then we can figure it out together."

"I know." He sighed. "But how was I supposed to tell you that I was excited about a job two hours from where we live? And that's if I take the coaching position at Hayward. Cambria is five hours."

Two hours? *Five* hours?

We'd fallen so easily into a routine that worked for both of us that the possibility of him having to move cities for his job never once crossed my mind. "I never thought of that."

"I figured as much. It's not that I don't want the job, but the thought of moving that far from you doesn't sit very well. When Harrison mentioned it, I didn't really believe they would actually call me."

There was a cough next to us and I looked up to see the waiter. "Can I get you anything else?"

"No, just the check please." Cole reached for his wallet.

I took my purse from the back of my chair. "Please, let me get it tonight. It's kind of my fault the dinner went to shit."

He shook his head. "Nope. Let me pay and then we can talk in the car on the way home. Lots of ears listening in."

He glanced over my shoulder and I just knew the two girls from before were hanging on every word that came out of our mouths. "Okay."

Cole put his card in the folder and handed it to the waiter. A few minutes later he returned, Cole signed the slip and we were on the road home. I waited until we hit the highway to start with my questions.

"Taking distance out of the equation, do you want either of the jobs?"

Even in the dark of the car I could see his hands tighten on the steering wheel. "Yes, but I don't want to leave you."

"Cole?"

He kept his eyes forward.

"I need you to really listen to me. Do you promise to actually hear what I'm saying?"

"I always listen to you," he said solemnly.

"I don't want you to give up your dreams for me. You've already had them ripped away from you

241

once. Now you're getting a second chance. Don't waste that chance on me."

The car jerked, throwing me forward as he pulled over onto the side of the road. He put the car in park and turned to face me. Cars whizzed by us, but I ignored them for the man in front of me. "I listened, and now I need you to hear what I'm saying. I may have lost the NFL and, yeah, it really sucked. But the one thing I remind myself is that if I hadn't lost that dream, I may not have found you." He leaned forward and took my lips in the sweetest, softest kiss. "I don't want the other dream if it means giving you up."

"That's the thing, Cole, it doesn't mean giving me up. The studio said by the summer they want us to start as the opening act for a few different bands. Which means we could be on the road quite often. It won't matter if you're two hours away, or need to travel for an away game. We'd figure it out, and spend the time together when we could."

His brow rose. "Now who's been keeping secrets? You never told me about becoming an opening act."

I glanced away, knowing he'd caught me there. "Sorry. I wasn't sure how to tell you."

"Well I guess I'll have to figure out how to sneak into your dressing room." He waggled his brows at me.

"I think I'll help you sneak in." I kissed him, pushing my tongue between his lips. He groaned and pulled away.

"As much as I'd like to continue this, I also would rather not get arrested for having sex on the shoulder of the highway, which is exactly what's going to happen if you keep that up."

I leaned up once again, running my tongue along the shell of his ear. "Then I guess you better find a place to pull over where we won't get caught."

Cole reached down to adjust himself. With my eyes on him, I popped the button on my jeans and slid them down my legs. I let out a squeal as my back pressed against the seat and stones were thrown from the back tires as Cole sped back onto the road.

Exit after exit passed and for one moment, I thought he wouldn't pull over. I thought about taunting him some more, at least until he put his blinker on for an exit that definitely wasn't ours. He took us down a few more streets before he turned down a trail, hidden from sight by the trees.

"Where are we?"

"I used to come here to hike when I needed to burn off extra energy."

I pushed my jeans to the floor and climbed over the center console to straddle his lap, his erection hard as it pressed into me through his jeans. "Let's burn off some energy then."

I slipped my hand under his shirt, tracing my fingers over the crease of his abs. He ran his hands around my hips to cup my ass. "You're playing with fire."

"I really want to play with something else."

Sweat formed on his brow as I reached between us, running my hand over him. He gripped the fabric of my panties and gave it a tug. "Then you better get rid of these."

In a flash, I had them off and tossed them onto the floor with my jeans. In all my teasing I'd gotten myself more than a little worked up, and the sight of Cole pushing his pants down his legs, freeing his dick, had me clenching my legs together. He slipped a condom on and I moved back into position, slowly sliding down on him.

"Mari," he moaned.

I covered his lips with mine, swallowing the rest of the sound. His tongue slipped into my mouth as I lifted up, only to slam back down again. The car was hot, the windows fogging from our panting breaths. And it still wasn't enough.

"Take me," I whispered against his lips.

He wasted no time grabbing hold of my hips, hard enough to leave a mark, and held me above him as he started to thrust. My heart pounded in my chest as Cole took me higher and higher. Our tongues tangled, our bodies joined. All I needed was him. Each powerful stroke pushed me closer to the edge. So close I could almost feel it.

The fear of getting caught and the ways he moved was enough to make my muscles begin to quiver and tighten. And suddenly I was falling. Pleasure pulsed through me, taking over. Cole held me to him as he reached his own climax. Panting filled the air and I opened my eyes to see his green ones illuminated by the dashboard light. One after another, emotions passed through his eyes, until wonder finally settled in.

"I'm not sure how I got you, but I'm never letting you go." He kissed me one more time and my heart soared.

I wasn't sure when it happened, or how for that matter, but each day I found myself falling a little more for Cole. He was the breath in my lungs, my light on a cloudy day. Thoughts of "I love yous" filled my head.

But while I might have been feeling it, I wasn't ready to put my heart on the line just yet. Maybe it was wrong, but I needed to hear the words from his lips first.

Rebecca Brooke

"I have a surprise for you."

Mari plunked her hands on her hips as I stepped inside her front door. "And what would that be?"

Sawyer was bent over the table, guitar in hand, filling in sheet music. "New song?" I asked, nodding to the paper.

"Been working on it all night."

He wasn't kidding. The bags under his eyes looked full enough to travel around Europe for a few months. "Do you need Mari? I know you guys have a day off today."

"I tried to help him last night but he wasn't having it and sent me to bed." She held her hand out toward him. "I found him in exactly the same spot this morning."

"Whatever, Mari. Like you haven't done the same." He put the pencil behind his ear and glanced at me. "And no, I don't need her. I have three more bars to write then I'm heading to bed to sleep until tomorrow."

I wrapped my arm around her waist and brought her flush against my body. "That means you're all mine today."

"Mmm, I like the sound of that."

Sawyer stuck his fingers in his ears and closed his eyes. "Not in front of me. Take that shit elsewhere, I'm trying to concentrate."

Laughing, I followed Mari down the hall to her room. As soon as she shut the door behind us, she jumped into my arms, her perfect ass in my hands and legs wrapped around my waist almost making me forget all my plans for the day. I captured her lips with mine, loving the electricity that came every time our lips touched. Every day I fell a little harder for the woman in my arms. It was like being on a runaway train. I knew there was no way to slow down or stop, but I was too afraid to even try. After the rocky start to our relationship, all I could hope for was a clear and easy track to follow. Nothing to crash into along the way.

I disentangled her legs from my waist and set her feet on the floor. "Not interested?" The flirt knew she was messing with my head, especially when she ran her hand along my already straining erection. My pants felt a little too tight, but I wouldn't be deterred.

"Oh, I'm interested, but we'll have plenty of time for that later. Right now, I want to take you somewhere."

"You won't tell me where?"

"Nope. Now get ready." I crossed my arms over my chest and watched her eyes move down to my biceps. She stared for a moment before looking back up.

ROCK ME

When she realized that I wasn't going to budge, she blew out a breath and went to her closet to pull out something to wear. Not that she didn't look sexy as fuck in the sleek, black yoga pants, but I knew she'd never leave the house like that.

"Any suggestions on what I should wear?" she called over her shoulder, digging through the mountain of clothes she owned.

"Not really." I gestured at my jeans and Henley pullover.

She examined my outfit for a moment, then went back into the closet. How would I know what she should wear? Guys clothes included a few common staples: button-down shirt, jeans, pullover, and, if you're really lucky, dress pants. Other than that, most of us didn't worry about clothes, as long as we were comfortable.

She emerged a few minutes later, dumping the contents of her arms onto the bed. She stared for a few minutes more before pulling on a pair of black leggings, boots, and a tunic-style shirt.

"Give me a minute to fix my hair."

She already looked perfect to me, but I knew she wouldn't hear it. "I'm gonna wait in the living room with Sawyer."

Watching them create new music was fascinating. I loved seeing how their minds worked. The more I examined it, the more I understood it wasn't much different than creating plays for the field. Both the play and the song had its own beat, and if anything was out of rhythm, things wouldn't work. The receiver wouldn't catch the ball and the music would sound like shit.

"Is it weird switching instruments?" I asked Sawyer, who was scribbling something down on a piece of paper when I walked back into the living room, tucking the pencil behind his ear before picking the guitar up again. I took the seat next to him on the couch. I didn't know much about the creative process, but it was amazing to me that a drummer could just pick up a guitar and play.

He lifted a shoulder. "A little, but creating the melody is impossible on skins. At least I learned how to play the guitar. Some drummers never learn anything outside percussion."

Ahh. That made sense.

"So the more instruments you can play the better?"

"It's kind of like learning how to catch the ball but never learning how to block the defense for another receiver." It still amazed me how well he understood the game I loved. Then again, there was nothing to say someone couldn't love football just because they were good with music.

I nodded. "Fair enough. You'd lose the game if you never bothered to block for any other receiver."

He pulled the pencil from behind his ear, pointing it at me. "Exactly. And without learning another instrument, a drummer can never create their own songs."

"You like writing your own songs?"

He jotted something down in his notebook. "I do. Not as much as Monty does, though. The guy may be a fucking nut, but the way his mind wraps around music stuns me. And yeah, there's nothing like hearing your song played."

That was exactly how I felt when the kids pulled off some crazy-ass play I'd come up with. And when it led to a touchdown? Even better.

"Where are you stealing Mari away to today?"

I peeked over at the hall to make sure she wasn't trying to listen in. "I got tickets to the new rock exhibit at the History of Music Museum?"

Hi eyes went wide. "Fuck, that's awesome. She's gonna flip her shit."

"I hope so. They were a bitch to get. Apparently, the exhibit's been sold out every day since it opened."

He set the guitar on the table, leaning back into the couch. "That's what I heard. Damn, to think about the band being included in something like that." He closed his eyes, probably imagining what the exhibit would look like.

"Ready?" Mari stood at the end of the hall, hands on her hips. When she spotted Sawyer she winced. She lowered her voice and asked, "Did he fall asleep while you guys were talking?"

"I'm not asleep," he mumbled.

She walked over and taking his hands in hers, pulled him up to standing. "Come on, off to bed for you." She wrapped an arm around his waist. "I'll be right back. If I don't get him to bed, he'll end up sleeping on the couch then bitching about his neck hurting for the next week."

It still bothered me with how touchy-feely the two of them were together. I don't think I'd ever seen two people find so many ways to touch each other when they weren't in some sort of relationship. I bit my tongue and waited.

A few minutes later, Mari came back into the living room. "Ready?"

"Yeah." The excitement I'd had when I showed up was gone. I told myself to stop being a dick, but always seeing Sawyer's hands on Mari or vice versa was getting to me. Not for the first time, I wondered if Sawyer actually wanted to be more than friends with Mari.

She ran her small hands up my chest and around my neck. "Everything okay?"

Taking her hips in my hands, I held her body close. I gave my head a brief shake, trying to push the negative thoughts creeping up on me out of my head. "Yeah, sorry I zoned out for a minute."

Her discerning eyes stayed on me for a minute, most likely attempting to figure out what I was hiding. But nothing good would come of me showing her that deep down was a jealous asshole, which meant hiding it.

"Okay," she said, dragging out the word, then smiled. "Then let's go. Since you won't tell me where we're going, I want to get on the road."

That made me chuckle. "Antsy?"

"Yes, now let's go."

Mari practically shoved me out the door and into my truck. About halfway to the end of the road, she moved in her seat to lean her back against the door and face me. "You really won't tell me where we're going?"

"Nope," I said, popping the "p." "But how about you tell me how your conversation went with your mom."

Mari hadn't talked to her mom since the release of the record. She knew nothing about me. Well, that wasn't true. I was pretty sure she knew plenty about me. We didn't grow up in a small town, but someone making it to the pros from our area was a big deal. My name had been plastered everywhere at one point. But that wasn't what worried me. I had no idea how much Mrs. Cosmann knew about the me from high school. The last thing I needed was for Mari's mom to convince her to kick my ass to the curb.

I knew how lucky I was to get a second chance at knowing the woman next to me.

Considering our history, I knew not everyone would see it that way. Mari shifted in her seat.

"Umm . . ."

"You didn't tell her," I muttered.

She held her hands up. "No, but it's not my fault. I only got to talk to my mom for like five minutes before she passed the phone around to her entire office for everyone to tell me congratulations."

"And you haven't called her back?"

She leaned over the center console, her warm breath tickling my ear. "No, because I've spent every moment outside of the studio or practice with you."

The weight of her words settled the annoyance bubbling up. She *had* been with me; both literally and figuratively. There really hadn't been another time for her to talk to her mom. "Sorry, I'm just worried she'll convince you I'm not worth the time."

"I told you. I didn't talk to my mom a lot about what went on in school. She obviously knew about the guitar, but I told her it was an accident. My grandmother, on the other hand, knew some of what happened. I'm pretty sure if she saw you now, she'd understand exactly what I see when I look at you."

"And what's that?" Even guys needed an ego boost every once in a while.

"A sexy piece of arm candy." She barely got the words out before she doubled over in mirth.

"Very funny."

I kept my eyes on the road while she got herself under control. This was one of my favorite sides of Mari; the one that let her inhibitions go and just was. Outlandish things came out of her mouth, and for those few minutes she was simply Mari, not the girl who had the weight of the world on her shoulders.

Her laughter subsided. "I see a guy who's gone out of his way to prove how much I mean to him. Who still does his best to show how much he cares. He's fun and charming, not to mention sexy. And for some reason, he wants me."

I couldn't help glancing at her, words on the tip of my tongue I didn't think she was ready to hear. "That guy wants you more than you can imagine and he's lucky as fuck that you want him back."

Mari wrapped her fingers through mine, silence descending over the car. It wasn't an uncomfortable one, either. For a brief moment, we were enjoying simply being together. No words needed to be said.

I turned into the lot for the museum and Mari squealed, grabbing my arm. "The Rock exhibit?" She pleaded with her eyes for it to be true.

"Yep. I got tickets."

"Holy shit. How? Those tickets have been sold out for like a month. I can't believe you did this." The rambling continued, her ass bouncing up and down in the seat.

"The how doesn't matter. Do you want to go in or not?"

She leapt out of the car and I had to scramble to keep up with her. I'd had a feeling she'd like it, but I didn't realize just how excited she'd be. Good thing my legs were longer than hers, otherwise I'd never have been able to keep up. I brought the tickets up on my phone, letting the guy scan us into the museum. After that, I let Mari lead the way.

She oohed and ahhed at each display. Every once in a while I noticed someone watching her. Whether her enjoyment of the exhibit was contagious or they recognized her, I wasn't sure, but either way, no one bothered us as we strolled through the museum.

As we made our way through the exhibit, Mari taught me a ton about music. It was hard not to embrace her excitement. The idea that someday someone could, one day, be screeching and jumping up and down over Mari's guitar or the outfit she'd worn on stage was humbling. I thought with my experience I knew what to expect, but this was a whole new level. She was on her way to great things, and I was happy to encourage her from the sidelines. This was all about Mari. Anything she wanted or needed I would give her.

We stepped out into the setting sun, when Mari's small hand slipped into mine bringing my step to a halt.

"Thank you for bringing me here." She leaned up on her toes and pressed a soft kiss to my lips. The feel was dizzying. "It was perfect."

"You're welcome. I'm just glad I got to experience it with you. I have a whole new appreciation for what you guys do. I knew you all worked hard, but the creativity to create the stuff you do astounds me."

The lights in the parking lot flickered on. I hadn't realized how much time we'd spent inside. Time had passed in the blink of an eye, like every moment I spent with Mari. Alone time was at a premium, and with more and more of her hours being spent at the studio, the job coaching at Hayward seemed more and more appealing every day.

CHAPTER Twenty-Four

COLE

Lesson planning sucked. I'd never figure out why I couldn't do my job without scheduling each part of my day on a piece of paper and turning it in. The damn things never stayed the same. If the students enjoyed a sport, I refused to move on just because my plans said I was supposed to, which made the whole document nothing more than a torture tactic.

A loud knock on the door brought my attention away from my computer. "Come in," I called.

A mane of dark-brown hair peered around the door. "Do you have a minute, Coach?"

"Sure, Chris, come on in." I gestured with my hand to the chair in front of the desk.

He pushed the door open and I was a little shocked to see him lead Kristen inside. Her hands trembled, her eyes darting around the office like she was looking for an escape route.

"Kristen." I nodded at her. "What can I do for you two today?"

Obviously something had happened. It had taken a lot of courage for her to come back, even though I'd promised I would handle anything else the guys dished out. What I really wanted to know was why Chris had come in with her?

"Coach, we have a problem with Jarrod."

No shit. Kid's a complete asshole. "Okay, want to tell me what happened?"

Kristen looked at Chris, her eyes welling up. "I got a text message."

I waited but she said nothing else. I stayed silent, watching on as she took the phone out of her bag, her hands shaking so badly she had a hard time unlocking it. She handed it over to me and I wanted to crush it in my hand. There were about twenty messages. The first being a dick pic.

Fucking hell.

Below that the message read, *My cock is too big for a virgin pussy like yours.*

Kristen had responded, *Chris?*

Of course. Being in art class make you forget how to read?

My stomach churned as I continued to read the messages. *Chris, what's wrong with you?*

Just waking up from the horrible dream I might have fake dated you.

Kristen's messages stopped for a bit, but the insults kept coming. At some point in the conversation, Kristen must have figured out it wasn't Chris. Then the tone of the messages changed. My guess was that Chris had taken over responding. *Who the fuck are you, and how did you get my phone?*

The sender responds with a video of a life-size picture of Kristen's face, a hole cut out where her mouth was supposed to be and Jarrod shoving his dick into that hole. He'd added to the horrifying scene by screeching, "Fuck my mouth, Jarrod," and, "You're so much bigger than Chris," in a girl's voice. The video was captioned *Gonna do this to your girl after school at her house.*

I closed my eyes, trying to suck in a full breath and not throw the phone. How could anyone think that shit was okay? Once I knew I could ask them questions without completely losing my shit, I opened my eyes to the two of them watching me. I never ratted on Sam when I should have more times than I could count, but this little shit?

He was done.

I wasn't worried about being the popular kid or the NFL star anymore. I knew how much this kind of thing could hurt someone. I'd seen the pain in Mari's eyes the first night I'd figured out who she was.

"Chris, I have to ask. Where's your phone?"

"I have no idea. You can search my bag, my locker, whatever you want. I haven't seen it since this morning when I got off the bus." He reached for his bag to hand it over.

"No, that's okay, although, the police may have to search it. This goes well beyond cyber bullying. Jarrod's now stepped into sexual harassment and sexting. Before we take this to the principal, I need to hear the story from both of you."

God, give me the patience to sit through this shit and not hunt the little bastard down.

Kristen swallowed hard. "I got the first text at the beginning of third period. I know my phone is supposed to be in my locker, but too many have been stolen recently. I figured it was safer with me."

"What happened after you got the text?"

"I knew it came from Chris's number but the texts didn't sound like Chris. I couldn't stop myself from responding. I wanted to know who was sending those texts."

Tears began to spill from her eyes. "They kept coming. Even when I ignored them, they wouldn't stop. I knew I'd lose it if I stayed in class, so I shoved my phone in my back pocket and asked to go to the bathroom."

Kristen shook her head and looked pleadingly at Chris. He took her hand and turned to me. My eyes zeroed in on that simple gesture. For a split second, it made me wish I could have been Mari's Chris.

"I ran into Kristen in the hall. I wanted to know why she was so upset. She yelled at me about some text I'd sent but I told her I had no idea what she was talking about. She showed me and I wanted to punch something. I'd already gotten one detention for my phone and really didn't need another so I'd started leaving it in my locker. We checked my locker but it was gone. I thought about going after Jarrod, but Kristen convinced me to come talk to you."

I looked over at Kristen, whose eyes were puffy and red. "Good. I need to keep your phone for now. We're going to take it to Mrs. Sloane's office. She'll handle everything from here." Their entwined hands drew my focus once again. "She'll need to call the police and you'll both have to answer some questions. For now, Chris, I wouldn't go anywhere near your locker and keep your bag with you. Let Jarrod do with your phone whatever he's gonna do and let the police deal with the fall out."

"Okay." He clenched the fist of his free hand tight, his teeth grinding together.

I could see he was near losing it, not to mention, Kristen looked like she wanted to cry again.

"Kristen?" She peered up at me. "I'm gonna let you into the girls' locker room, give you a few minutes to yourself while I talk to Chris. Is that okay?"

Her eyes shot to Chris, who smiled and gave her a nod of encouragement. "We'll fix this," he said.

"All right."

"You wait here," I told Chris. I walked with Kristen a little way down the hall and let her into the locker room. On my way back, I gave the girls' gym teacher a heads-up that Kristen was in there, telling her I was taking care of everything and Kristen just needed a moment. By the time I got back to my office, Chris was wearing a path in the carpet.

He rounded on me the moment the door shut. "That asshole stole my phone and thinks it's fun to torture my girlfriend? I'm gonna kill him."

"Sit down." The tone of my voice left no room for argument. He took the seat and I continued. "I'm guessing you dating Kristen is what set him off."

He slouched in the chair. "Yes and no. After our talk in the fall, I really started to watch how he treated people. I saw what a total dick he was." His eyes snapped to mine. "Sorry about the language."

I waved him off. "I'd rather you be in here with every curse word in the book than out there putting your hands on Jarrod, but get it out of your system now because Mrs. Sloan won't appreciate it."

"Thanks, Coach. Anyway, after that, I tried to stay away from him, so did a couple of other guys on the team. We were tired of getting shit for his crap. One day I sat down with Kristen at lunch to apologize to her. Jarrod called me every name in the book, but I didn't give two shits what he said to me." He stopped and rubbed the back of his neck. "Kristen and I became friends and things shifted. Some of my friends began sitting with some of her friends. Things were fun again. Jarrod started targeting us for 'ditching him.' Like I said, I didn't care as long as he left her alone. And he did. Until today."

So many parallels. Except Chris had learned much sooner than I had.

Another regret.

Could Mari and I have gone to college as high school sweethearts? Maybe, maybe not. Something told me that Mari had to take the path she did. I focused on Chris. "I'm really proud of you. Not just for coming to me today, but for taking my advice all those months ago. It's not easy to walk away from the people we think are our friends." I stood and walked over, clasping him on the shoulder. "You did good. Now let's go get Kristen and get this phone up to Mrs. Sloan."

He beamed as he stood, the first true smile I'd seen from Chris since he stepped into my office. We got Kristen from the locker room and I took them both to the main office where they waited while I explained the whole story to the principal. Her eyes darkened with each word. After showing her the phone, she called the school's resource officer then brought Kristen and Chris into her office. I had a class to teach, but Mrs. Sloan promised to come see me at the end of the day with an update.

Turned out, I didn't need to wait until the end of the day. Gossip burned through the school like wildfire. Parents had been called in. After a search of Jarrod's locker, they were able to find Chris's phone, all the messages still on there. Jarrod was taken out of the building in handcuffs. While it was sad to see someone so young ruin their life over petty bullshit, there was a lightness in my chest as I drove to Mari's later than night. I'd put a stop to it.

I'd saved someone the heartache Mari went through. Every day I thought about how I should have done something sooner.

Sawyer was already gone by the time I arrived and even though I'd offered to take Mari out for the night, she voted to stay in. We'd settled for pizza and binge-watching Netflix. It still amazed me how much we had in common and for the hundredth time I wondered how things would have been different if I'd bothered to get to know her before. Then, I thought about Chris and part of me wished I could turn back time.

Mari was lying with her head resting on my chest, her arm slung across my waist, while I played with her hair. "Remember that girl I told you about months ago? The one the football players were messing with?"

Her whole body stiffened. "Yeah?"

"She came to me today."

"Assholes," she spat.

I ran my fingers along the skin of her back hoping to settle her. "Actually, only one asshole. One of the kids listened to what I said to him and stopped hanging out with the other one."

I told her the whole story, from the time Chris and Kristen walked into my office until I heard what happened to Jarrod. Wetness splattered on my chest. I tucked a finger under her chin and lifted her face to mine. "Please don't cry."

"That little shit deserved to be arrested for what he did."

I brushed a tear from her face. We both knew she was talking about more than Jarrod. Sam deserved a whole lot more than what he got. "Yes, he did. Today made me regret not stopping the bullshit for you."

"That's not your fault."

"But it really is. I could've stood up to him at any time."

She shook her head, brushing her cheek against my chest. "Let's not live in the past."

It was hard not to sometimes, but it wasn't fair of me to force her to dwell on it when she obviously didn't want to. It was my guilt to live with. She lay her head back on my chest and was quiet for another moment.

I ran my hand over her back in a soft caress, stealing my nerves. The worst she could say is no, but I hated the thought of her reliving all the shit she went through again. "I got Kristen's email. Would you mind talking to her? I think it would do her good to hear from someone else who has been there."

Mari lifted her head once again to stare at me. "You really think I could help?"

"More than you know." I brushed my thumb across her bottom lip.

"I would love to talk to her. Thank you for standing up for her today. The world needs more people like you and Chris in it."

Sometimes I wondered if Mari put me on a pedestal I didn't deserve.

CHAPTER TWENTY-FIVE

COLE

The music in the car cut out, my phone ringing over the speakers. Seeing Mari's name pop up on the screen, I hit talk.

"Hey, sweetheart, I thought you were at the studio today?"

"We are." Her voice was a few octaves higher than normal. "But I had to call you."

I turned into my driveway and shut the car off. "Well, you know I love hearing your voice. This mean you're gonna sing for me?"

She giggled. "Tonight. The studio asked us to be the opening act for one of their bands. One of the original band members has the flu and can't perform so we're on."

"Oh my god. That's fantastic!" Fuck, I loved seeing her succeed at what she loved.

"Will you come with us?"

"I'd love to, but don't I need a ticket?"

"You would if you were sitting in the audience, but I want you backstage with us."

I ran a hand through my hair. "Are you sure I won't make you nervous? I know you've never played to a crowd that size. I wouldn't want to do anything to distract you."

Her voice lowered to a whisper. "Please. You won't make me nervous. Knowing you're there will settle me."

My chest swelled, the idea that me being there would help her making me feel like I could fly. "Then I'll be there. What do you need me to do?"

"I already have a badge ready for you. Do you think you could stop by my place and grab the black tank top from my closet?"

All the time I'd spent watching her perform was paying off. I knew exactly which one she meant. I knew it was her go-to shirt when she sang for an audience. Luckily we'd traded keys to make it easier to meet each other after work, so I could just swing by without having to get a key from her. Our relationship was moving forward. Yes, it was slow, but I was just happy to be with her. I'd take anything I could get.

"I can. What time should I be there?"

"Can you get here by six?"

I glanced at the time on the dash. That was a little over two hours away. "Yeah, but I have to go if I'm gonna make it there in time."

"I can't wait to see you."

"Me, too."

I disconnected the call and ran into the house to change. Ryan lifted a brow in my direction as I raced around. I didn't have time to stop and explain so I promised to text him later.

After a quick stop at Mari's, I was on my way toward the venue. With time to spare, I pulled into the parking garage of the address she'd texted me and went to the side door. After presenting ID, I was given an all-access backstage pass and shown the way to her dressing room.

The moment I stepped into the room, she launched herself at me. "Can you believe it?"

Her ass firmly cradled in my hands, I carried her over to the couch that sat along one wall of the room. An entire counter of cosmetics and a mirror large enough to give any hair salon a run for its money filled the other wall. The rest of the room held a rack full of clothes and table with all kinds of drinks and snack foods.

I sat down, placing her so she was straddling my lap, and gazed up into her eyes. "I'm so proud of you." I brought her lips to mine, savoring the taste of vanilla that lingered there.

"Thank you for coming," she whispered against my lips.

Sometimes I wondered if she still didn't get it. If not, I'd keep saying it until she did. "I told you, anything for you."

"I know." She smirked. "I just like hearing you say it."

I reached around her hips, tickling along her ribs. She jumped out of my lap and across the room, laughter pealing from her lips. I stood advancing on her, waggling my fingers. "Aww, what's wrong, sweetheart? Everything okay?"

"Don't you dare." She hid behind the clothing rack, using it as a shield.

"Don't I dare what?"

She stepped out from behind the rack, hands on her hips. "You know what."

The mirth in her eyes, the sexy way one hip jutted out to the side . . . I didn't bother trying to control myself. I stalked her step for step, moving backward until she ran into the wall. I bent my head and devoured her lips like I needed her to survive.

Her hand slid up my chest and fisted in my hair, pulling the strands until the sharp pain combined with the sensation of her breasts pressed tight against my chest broke what little control I had and I snapped my hips forward, letting her know exactly what she was doing to me.

I slipped my hands up under her shirt, gliding along her ribs until I reached the underside of her breasts. Thumbing under the bottom of her bra, I heard a groan in the back of her throat.

A knock sounded at the door. "Twenty minutes," a voice called.

I dropped my forehead to hers, my breath coming in pants. "Why do we always seem to get interrupted?"

She nipped at my bottom lip. "After the show tonight, there won't be any interruptions."

I stepped back, knowing she needed to get ready. The heat in her eyes and the flush to her cheeks had me reaching down to adjust my straining erection.

"Get ready," I begged. "I'm not sure how long I can control myself, otherwise."

The corner of her mouth pulled up as she picked up the tank top from where I discarded it on the couch. She whipped her other shirt off over her head, taking entirely too long. I growled, slamming my eyes shut. "You're such a tease."

"Only for you. You can open your eyes now, I'm dressed."

I cracked one eye open to make sure. Mari was in a mood to be a tease and I had no doubt she'd tell me she was dressed just to see my reaction when I realized she wasn't. A mixture of relief and disappointment filled me when I saw her tank top-covered back as she looked in the mirror, fixing her hair and makeup. I opened the other eye and sat back down on the couch to watch.

Another knock came. "Five minutes."

She held out a hand to me. "Ready for this?"

"Better question is, are you?"

"With you here, I am."

She pressed a brief kiss to my lips and led me out the door, navigating the maze-like hallways until we reached the rest of the guys.

"Hey, Cole. Glad you could join us." Heath clasped me on the shoulder.

"Thanks. This is pretty amazing."

Sawyer twirled a drumstick in his one hand, his eyes zeroing on Mari. "Good?" he asked.

She grabbed his arm, squeezing his bicep. "Good."

She winked and he beamed at her. I placed my hands on her shoulders, massaging the muscles there. Just a little reminder to Sawyer. We'd gotten along great since that first dinner, but there were still times where it was hard to ignore the relationship that existed between them. Mari leaned into my touch. "You're going to be great," I said against her hair.

The door opened. "Jaded Ivory?"

"That's us," Jackson answered.

He held the door open. "You're up."

The guys led the way, Mari following behind, bringing me with her. The guy glanced down at my badge and tilted his head, giving me a strange look, probably wondering what I was going backstage for. I ignored it.

Mari squeezed my hand and walked onto the stage.

The crowd went crazy. Cheering, screaming. When I peered around the corner and into the audience there were people holding signs up. *We missed you, Jaded Ivory* and *We love Mari.* Word sure as shit traveled fast. They'd only found out a few hours ago they'd be playing. Their loyal fans must have scooped up any available tickets when Heath updated the website and social media pages.

The smile Mari gave the audience was brighter than the sun. "Fuck yeah," she called into the mic. "We missed you, too. For those of you who don't know us, we're Jaded Ivory."

Sawyer started the beat and the music flowed in behind it. It was different watching them from backstage. The way Mari swayed, the music seemed to take over her whole body. The crowd grew rowdier with each song they played, and that was before they played the single the studio had released to the radio.

When they closed out the set with Runaway Dream, the crowd was jumping. Hearing them sing along with Mari made my heart flutter in my chest. I was close enough to see her eyes fill with tears at the sound, but she kept singing beautifully. I'd never tire of hearing the way her sultry voice settled over the lyrics of a song.

Mari stepped forward. "Thanks for having us." She pointed to each band member. "This is Jackson, Monty, Heath, Sawyer, I'm Mari, and we're Jaded Ivory."

The sound in the place was deafening. Mari walked off the stage and right into my arms, our lips pressed tight. "You were phenomenal," I said when I lifted my mouth from hers.

Her eyes sparkled. "That was absolutely unreal."

"Time to celebrate?" I whispered, nipping the lobe of her ear.

"Don't you know it." She took my hand and led me to the stage door. The same guy from earlier stood there with his clipboard.

His gaze locked with mine. "Are you Cole Wallace?"

An uneasiness settled into the pit of my stomach. "Yeah, that's me." I'd been out of the spotlight for almost four years. It wasn't often I was recognized anymore. Usually they didn't remember my face, just the sad story of what could have been. Mari gave me a questioning look, but I shrugged it off and let her lead me into the hall.

She turned to me. "Let's go celebrate back at your place. I'm pretty sure I promised you a night with no interruptions." She winked and began walking down the hall, her ass swaying with every step she took.

A shove came from behind. "Wake up, dude," Monty said. "The sooner you stop staring, the sooner you can start touching."

"Great show tonight," I called over my shoulder, all the guys except Sawyer giving me a knowing grin.

CHAPTER TWENTY-SIX

Mari

I ignored the ringing and cuddled into Cole's warmth, too comfortable to bother with the outside world. A few seconds after it stopped ringing, it went off again.

"What the fuck?" I sat up and reached for the bag I'd dropped on the floor the night before. Clothes were everywhere. In our defense, getting naked had been more important than where things landed.

Cole's arm wrapped around my waist. "Where are you going? Come back to bed." His voice was rough with sleep.

"Checking my phone real fast. Whoever keeps calling won't give up."

"Fine," he mumbled. "I'll be back." He got up and pulled on a pair of boxers. It was hard not to appreciate the way his muscles rippled as he walked from the room. I heard the bathroom door shut and my phone buzzed in my hand again.

"Keep your pants on," I said, opening the screen. Twenty-two missed calls and at least a dozen texts. *What the fuck?* I opened the first text thread to find a bunch from Sawyer.

> *Mari, pick up.*
> *Where are you?*
> *Answer your goddamn phone already.*
> *For fuck's sake, call me.*
> *Read this.*

Below the last message was a link to a gossip blog. The hair on the back of my neck rose. I didn't bother listening to the messages or reading the other texts. Instead, throwing caution and good sense to the wind, I clicked on the link. What I saw made my heart drop.

Former NFL prospect sitting pretty with singer from up-and-coming Jaded Ivory.

Underneath that was a picture of Cole and me kissing. The caption had both our names with it.

"Oh fuck."

"What's wrong?" Cole stood in the doorway, running his hand over his very impressive abs, but even that wasn't enough to distract me from my phone.

I held out my phone and he took it from my hand, his face taking on a range of emotions as he scanned the article.

"Cole Wallace, supposed first-round draft pick who disappeared four years ago after a career-ending injury to his knee, reemerged last night, found backstage with Mari Cosmann, the lead singer for Jaded Ivory. Jaded Ivory released their first single a few months ago. The two looked awfully cozy wrapped in each other's arms after an incredible debut show. This writer is pretty sure hearts are breaking everywhere to see these two off the market."

Cole looked up from my phone, amusement in his eyes.

Okay, not what I expected.

He dropped the phone on the end of the bed. "Think that's true?"

"What's true?" I asked, breathless at the look of determination in his eyes.

He crawled up from the end to hover over me. "That guys all over the world are jealous that I got you?"

His face was poised over mine and I was having a hard time forming words. "No, but the girls are probably hating me right now."

He kissed me, his tongue darting into my mouth. "Oh, I think the guys are definitely jealous. But that's their problem, because you're mine." His mouth came back down on mine.

The shrill ring of my phone made Cole pull his mouth away. "Sawyer's not going to stop, is he?"

"Probably not."

He groaned and dropped down next to me on the bed. "Cockblocked again."

"Let me talk to him and we'll pick up where we left off."

I hit answer and held the phone to my ear.

"Where have you been?" Sawyer snapped the moment the phone connected.

Cole lay next to me, all miles of bronzed skin and almost naked glory. "In bed. Where else would I be?"

"I don't want to know. Did you read the article?"

"I did." Cole's hand caressed up my thigh.

"And?"

Rebecca Brooke

His fingers continued upward, running along the crease where my thighs met my hip. A moan caught in my throat.

"Mari?"

"What? Umm . . . what did you say?" I batted Cole's hand away.

"Tell Cole to keep his hands to himself for five minutes so we can talk."

"Sawyer said—"

"I heard him," Cole grumbled. He stood up, a frown marring his features as he pulled a pair of basketball shorts out of his drawer and yanked them over his boxers. "I'll be in the kitchen."

The bedroom door slammed behind him.

"Finally," Sawyer said.

What was his problem? Cole didn't seem to be bothered by the article. I wasn't. The only damper on the morning was this call. "Don't start. Now what's so important?"

"Are you okay?" There was concern in his tone, but my irritation still bubbled to the surface.

"Cole's annoyed now, all because you want to make sure I'm okay. I'm pretty sure I sounded that way when I answered."

"He needs to get his panties out of his ass—"

"Sawyer," I warned.

"Fine. I'm behaving. And I know you. You bury that kind of shit down deep."

I sighed, some of my annoyance fading away. "I'm really good. Cole didn't care about the article, why should I?"

"Because you hate people digging into your personal life?"

I dug around on the floor, finding my underwear from last night and one of Cole's T-shirts. If I couldn't be in bed with him anymore, I'd take the scent of him wrapped around me. "It's bound to

273

happen—to all of us. I know you don't want to hear that, but the more we play to larger crowds, the more we'll be at the mercy of the gossip blogs and paparazzi."

The sound of a mug slamming against the counter came over the line. "Doesn't mean we have to like it."

I raked my fingers through my hair, catching sight of myself in the mirror. "No, but it also doesn't mean we can stop it either. Not unless they post something completely outrageous. If I throw a fit about pictures of me kissing my boyfriend they're only going to assume the worst."

Did I like having my picture plastered all over the internet? No. Did I want the gossip blogs to think I was embarrassed about being with Cole by asking them to take it down? That was a big hell no. It was just something that I needed to deal with, whether I liked it or not.

"Heath said the same thing," Sawyer murmured.

"And he knows more about the media end of this business than any of us."

I could hear his fingers drumming on the counter. "You're sure you're okay?"

"I'm positive. Now I'm gonna go and deal with Cole."

"Don't tell me he's pissed about the article." His voice took on a hard edge.

"I already told you he wasn't pissed about the article. He's the one who convinced me it didn't matter. He's annoyed at the interruption." No need to mention more how Cole was attempting to convince me.

"Fair enough. Go talk to him."

"I'll be home later."

I hung up and went to find Cole. He was sitting at the table, head bowed, a cup of coffee between his hands. I set my phone on the table and climbed over him to straddle his lap. "Why the glum face?"

He avoided my question. "What did Sawyer want?"

"He wanted to make sure I wasn't bothered by the article. What concerns me more is why *you're* upset."

"I thought he was trying to convince you to get it taken down."

I ducked my head, forcing him to make eye contact. "It doesn't bother you, right?"

He curled an arm around my waist and pulled me closer. "No. I like the world knowing you're mine."

"Then it doesn't bother me." I leaned in for a kiss when my phone went off again. My eyes shot to it sitting on the table, waiting for it to bite like a venomous spider.

"Who's that?"

"My mom," I muttered.

"Oh."

I climbed off his lap and pick up the phone. "I have to answer."

"I bet you do. Good luck with that." There was a gleam in his eyes when he stood and took another mug down from the cabinet.

I dropped into the seat he'd vacated and answered. "Hi, Mom."

"You have a boyfriend and you don't bother to tell me? I have to read about it on the internet?"

Cole set the steaming mug in front of me as I rolled my eyes. "Relax, Mom."

"Relax? Cole grew up around the corner and you didn't think to tell me you were seeing him?"

I dropped my head on the table. Warm hands curled over my shoulders, massaging out the tension the same way he'd done last night. I let my head fall forward to give him better access. "It's not like I had much of a chance to talk to you last time. You passed me around the entire office."

"And after that you couldn't call, text, give me some sort of heads-up?"

"Sorry, Mom."

"Well, are you going to give me any more details?"

And there it was. My mother had never been good at keeping her nose out. She was like a bloodhound when it came to sniffing out gossip. There was no way she was going to let this slide.

"You're too much. Cole and I met up again last fall when he came to one of the shows. We started dating a couple of months ago."

"He was such a cute boy in high school."

I knew Cole heard when his hands froze on my shoulders momentarily.

"The picture was hard to see. Is he still good looking?"

I peeked over my shoulder at the man who'd captured my heart with a guitar and a sweet smile. I thought about all the long, ropey muscles in his arms. The way they held me tight. The miles of rock-hard abs, and hard, strong thighs. "Even better."

"Are you happy?"

I sighed. "More than you could imagine."

"You know that's all that matters to me?"

"I do. Look, Mom, I just got up a little bit ago when Sawyer called me about the article, can—"

"Called you? You're not home?"

Heat raced up my cheeks. Cole chuckled behind me and I wanted to crawl under the table. Shit. I hadn't meant to give that away.

276

"Umm . . . not right now."

"Okay, I don't want to know anymore. Call me when you get a chance."

"I will. Bye, Mom."

A twenty-four-year-old woman shouldn't be absolutely mortified by their mother knowing she stayed at her boyfriend's place, but these weren't exactly normal circumstances. I mean, a picture of me kissing him was plastered everywhere.

Cole kissed the top of my head. "That was an interesting conversation."

I covered his hands with mine. "It's been an interesting morning. Think we can go to bed and start the day over again?"

"I think we can figure out something to do."

And with that, Cole bent over, flipping me over his shoulder and carried me down the hall.

ᗡᗡᗡ

A few weeks later things didn't seem so easy.

Cameras followed us everywhere we went. Even something as simple as getting groceries became a chore. For some reason, we'd become this fairytale couple to people who a few months ago hadn't even known my name. It was frustrating. Thankfully Cole took it all in stride. Not once did it bother him; at least, he never gave the impression that it did.

The band had been asked back to open another show and seeing as it was close by, I asked Cole to come with me again. I knew he wouldn't always be able to be there so I planned on taking advantage of it when he could. We hadn't spoken again about the possibility of being across the country from each other. If I was being honest, I'd actively avoided it. I wasn't sure I was ready to make those kinds of decisions—not with everything else going on.

Flashbulbs went off as we pulled into the venue. It made me really appreciate the covered entrance in the back; the one reporters didn't have any access to. It was disturbing to have my life and relationship dissected by the press, and I had started actively avoiding gossip sites and begged Sawyer to stop sending me links to different articles because I didn't need to know what the media thought about my relationship with Cole. We were happy, and that was the only thing that mattered to me.

Cole leaned in close as we walked down the hall to the dressing room. "You know how sexy you look?"

"Yeah, hiding from the press is real sexy."

"I love seeing your pictures on those pages. Reminds everyone that you're mine."

I opened the door to the dressing room. "And you're not mine?"

"Sweetheart, I'll be yours any way. . . any time you want me."

I guided him over to the couch and shoved him down on it, wanting to teach my dirty-mouthed, smart-ass boyfriend a lesson. Before he could utter a word, I had his pants open and his dick free. I stuck my tongue out and licked around the head, watching his eyes roll back.

"God, Mari."

I sat up on my knees and slid my mouth down over him. He dug his fingers into the leather of the couch and I gripped the base of his shaft, moving my head in time with each stroke.

Unintelligible noises left his throat. I knew he was close when he sunk his fingers into my hair, his hips beginning to piston into my mouth. I let him take control, my tongue sliding along the underside of his cock. His rhythm faltered. He held himself tight to my mouth as I swallowed down his release. He was panting, his eyes squeezed shut.

"Holy fuck, your mouth is good for more than singing."

I smacked his chest, and laughed as he hauled me into his lap and kissed me until my head spun.

A knock sounded on the door. "Twenty minutes."

"Every fucking time," Cole complained, releasing me so I could get ready for the night.

Cole tried not to pout while I finished getting ready, but I did notice his eyes slammed shut when I started to change. My skin heated with the thought that I turned him on so bad he had to close his eyes to keep his hands to himself.

Like the last time, Cole came with me on stage, watching the show from the wings. The energy in the place was electric, my performance driven by their excitement. I never imagined a time when Monty's words would ring true. The crowd strengthened my performance, but so did the man watching me from the sidelines.

I loved seeing Cole waiting for me backstage after each performance. Every time I walked off stage I went straight to his arms. What I didn't expect was to see Tom standing there waiting with him.

"Tom, this is my boyfriend, Cole. Cole, Tom is our rep from the label."

They shook hands, then Tom looked around at all of us. "I came by to talk to you guys. Why don't we go sit in the green room?"

"Lead the way," Jackson replied. Sawyer shot me a look and I shrugged my shoulders.

Tom led us to a door not far from the stage. He opened it up and gestured for us to go inside. We all found a seat throughout the room, but Tom stayed on his feet.

"I'll get right to it. We've been watching your performances, and as an opening act you're drawing decent crowds of your own. The band you opened for tonight has about eight weeks left on their tour and we'd like you to finish it with them as their opening act.

Monty leapt out of his seat. "Holy shit!"

"We're in," Heath said. He knew he didn't need to ask the rest of us. Just like the initial release, this was another big break for us. Another shot.

I turned to Cole who immediately kissed me, stealing my breath. "This is an amazing opportunity for you."

Tom continued talking. I wasn't paying as much attention as I should have been, but I did hear something about having two days to get packed and everything set up to be on the road. Sawyer could fill me in on the details later. I was more worried about how this would affect my relationship with Cole.

After Tom left, the guys went to pack up our equipment, giving me and Cole a few minutes alone.

He rubbed his thumb along the crease in my brow. "Why the frown?"

"I'm excited, but I'm gonna miss you."

He chuckled. "I knew this was probably coming. Things will be fine. This is what they make Skype for."

I wrapped my hands around his waist, tucking my face against his chest. For the longest moment I couldn't speak past the lump in my throat. "Will you come out and stay with me once the year is over?"

He lifted my face to his, his eyes tracking mine as he brushed his thumb over my lower lip. "Let's play it by ear. You may find life is crazy on the road."

"I still want you to visit me."

"Then we'll find a way to work it out."

CHAPTER TWENTY-SEVEN

Mari

Cole wasn't answering my calls.

We'd been on the road for a few weeks and still had three shows to do before we could go home. I missed him, and for all the times I tried to convince him to come out, he hadn't made the trip once. I wanted his arms around me. I wanted him backstage cheering me on. I wanted to feel him against me. I knew it was selfish, but that didn't stop me from trying to figure out a way for us to spend time together.

I needed coffee—needed the middle of the day pick-me-up. Of all the things I missed about Cole, his ability to make the perfect coffee was one of them. It was always the right strength and temperature. I reached the lobby, but one look out of the front doors and I knew there was no way in hell I was leaving the hotel. It seemed like every news outlet was waiting outside, cameras at the ready, flashes going off left, right, and center.

My phone buzzed in my pocket and I pulled it out. It wasn't Cole so I sent it right to voicemail. He was the only person I wanted to talk to right now. Everyone else could wait.

We still had a few hours until we had to head over to the venue so I grabbed a small coffee from the cafe downstairs. It wasn't great but it would have to do. I took a sip and shivered at the overwhelming strength as I pushed the button on the elevator and made my way back up to my room with every intention of trying to call Cole again.

I placed the card against the door and shoved it open, surprised to see the guys, minus Heath, waiting for me.

"Mari."

Alarm bells immediately went off. Sawyer's tone was cautious and Monty and Jackson stood on the other side of the room, their eyes everywhere but on me.

The hair on the back of my neck rose and I walked over and took Sawyer's hands in mine. "What happened?"

"Umm . . ." He glanced at the guys and then back at me. "We need to talk to you about something."

A lump formed in the back of my throat. What weren't they telling me?

My phone buzzed for what felt like the hundredth time and I pulled it from my pocket, only to have it yanked from my hands.

"What the fuck, Sawyer?"

He pressed his lips together and shook his head. "There's no fucking way I'm letting you look at your phone. Not until we talk."

"Then you better start talking. My phone's been blowing up for the last half hour, but I haven't had a chance to check it. And the press was camped out in front of the hotel. I was coming up here to call Cole, but he's not answering his cell." My hands were shaking. "What happened?"

Sawyer wrapped his arm around my shoulders, directing me to the small couch in the room.

"Let's sit."

I shrugged him off.

"I really think—"

"Jesus Christ, Sawyer. Just tell her or I will. You're only making things worse." Monty came to stand in the middle of the room, his hands at his sides clenched into fists. "The bastard doesn't deserve your protection."

Sawyer whipped around. "You think for one moment I'm trying to protect that fucker? I don't want to hurt Mari."

Jackson sighed. "She's going to be hurt no matter how long you take to tell her."

That's when I lost it. "Damn it! Someone spit it out. Now!"

The guys looked at each other, but it was Sawyer who cleared his throat. He swallowed hard and opened his mouth to speak. "A video was leaked to *TMZ* about an hour ago."

My muscles seized. "What kind of video?" My voice was so low I was surprised anyone heard it.

"Show her," Jackson urged. "Better she sees it with us here."

Sawyer pulled his phone from his back pocket and pressed to open one of the apps, handing me the phone.

Mari's Boyfriend Has Her Brainwashed

284

The article went on to name Cole, his parents, his job. But that wasn't all. The damn article described in vivid details the nightmare of my teenage years, complete with a compilation video someone had made of the most humiliating moments of my life.

The video showed four guys surrounding me. Sam in the lead of course, all yelling vulgarities.

"Come on, baby, you know you want to meet us in the back storage closet later."

"We can each use every hole you have."

"You know you want us."

You could clearly see the tears streaming down my face but I was trapped, my eyes are tightly shut. Then another guy came into view and muscled the other ones out of the way. Instantly I recognize the man as Cole.

"Don't be scared."

And that was where the video ended.

The breath in my lungs leaked out and I couldn't hold myself up any longer. My knees buckled and I slid to the floor, strong arms wrapping around my waist before I hit the floor. My throat burned but I didn't bother trying to hold back.

How had I not realized it was Cole who'd walked up and told me not to be scared? Not long after that, I'd cracked one eye open and to find them all gone. Worried that it was all part of the plan, I'd run away and locked myself in a stall for the rest of the period.

"That's not him," I sobbed. "Not anymore."

Sawyer sat on the floor and cradled me in his lap. "Why didn't you tell me how bad it was?"

I curled into his body, trying to hide from the world. "Do you think anyone wants to admit things like that?" I mumbled into his shirt.

I closed my eyes tight but the video just played in my memory, over and over. My stomach rolled and I bolted from his lap, straight into the bathroom. Feet pounded behind me. I threw up the toilet seat and purged everything from my stomach. A warm hand rubbed circles on my back.

"Breathe, Mari," Jackson whispered. "Monty's on the phone with Tom and the label's lawyer. They're trying to get it taken down."

A few minutes of dry heaving and I was sure there couldn't possibly be anything left in my stomach. A tissue appeared in front of me. I took it gratefully and forced myself to sit back against the cool tiles. My mind whirled with so many thoughts I couldn't keep up. Everything blurred around the edges.

The guy in that video wasn't the Cole I knew; at least, the one I thought I knew.

What if all of this was just another way to poke fun at Mariloon?

More of the article floated through my mind. Words I had tried to ignore when my eyes locked on them. They'd interviewed Brian. Of all the people we went to high school with, they'd chosen him. The interviewer wanted to know what he thought about my relationship with Cole and his answer made my throat close.

"This is better than the time he set it up to break her guitar. Cole is bada**. He really knows how to pull one."

Had Cole sent in the video to make a few extra bucks at my expense? He'd have no problem getting his hands on that kind of shit. Hell, he probably had it on his own computer.

Jackson squatted down in front of me. "Better?"

I nodded, afraid to speak and bring back the rush of tears. My skin felt too tight, my chest hurt, and all I wanted was a few minutes alone. Jackson must have picked up on it because he stood and tipped his head toward the door.

"I'm going to see if I can help Monty with the calls. Don't worry, we'll get this taken care of."

The door closed behind them and my head dropped back against the wall.

The silence was overwhelming at first. Whatever the guys were doing in the other room, their hushed tones left no way for me to hear the conversation. I closed my eyes and took deep steading breaths.

How had things gotten so fucked up?

I'd let my guard down and let someone in, that's how. I thought after meeting Sawyer that I'd become a better judge of character. Apparently not.

The pain in my chest at what I might have cost the guys was too much. I brought my knees to my chest and buried my head in my arms to muffle the sound. I didn't need to add any more problems to the list.

"Please don't cry." Sawyer's voice came from the other side of the door. I didn't answer, but hear the click of the lock and the squeak of the hinges as the door opened and he came closer and scooped me up from the floor. He carried me back out to the bedroom and took a seat, cradling me in his arms. I stayed there, tuning the world around me out. It was easier than facing the reality of what happened.

There was a knock at the door and Heath came bursting through the moment Jackson opened it. He took the seat next to us on the couch. "I'm so sorry, Mari. I was at the studio when the news broke. I've been on the phone trying to get it taken down since."

Monty sighed. "We've been doing the same. Any luck?"

Heath shook his head. "What about you?"

"Not really. Amanda from the PR department is working to come up with a strategy." Monty's eyes came to mine and he didn't have to say a word for me to see how sorry he was.

The last thing I wanted was for the most horrifying years of my life to be dissected by the world, but a close second was being a liability that needed a strategy for her career to survive.

A pounding started on the door and Heath jumped to his feet, racing across the room to glance through the peephole. Before anyone had the chance to ask who it was, Heath had flung it open and there was a brief moment when Cole's face came into view, but before he had a chance to speak, Heath threw his fist right into Cole's nose. The force of the punch sending him flying backward into the wall on the other side of the hall.

CHAPTER TWENTY-EIGHT

COLE

The school year ended a week ago and for the first time in my life, I was bored shitless. I sat on the couch, flipping through channel after channel, nothing catching my interest. Mari still had three shows to do before she'd be back home and while the phone sex was fun, I wanted more than my right hand for company.

It wasn't just about the sex, either. I missed her. Seeing her, spending time with her. I knew this was becoming her reality and I was really pleased she was getting to live her dream, but right now it really sucked for me.

Hayward and Cambria continued to call me. I hadn't told either no, which meant they were trying to outdo the other with their offers not knowing that my decision had nothing to do with what they gave me. I mean salary was important, but more than that, I wanted to make the decision with Mari. Couples didn't take jobs hours away without consulting the other. The one night we'd talked about it, she'd encouraged me to think about taking the job, but at the time I hadn't seriously considered doing it. Now, with her travel time increased, it didn't seem like a bad move.

Ryan yanked the remote from my fingers. "Dude, I can't take your moping anymore. You can't sit here all day, flipping through the channels."

"Why not? It's exactly what you're going to do."

"No, I'm gonna pick a show and watch it. You're going to flip, maybe stop at a channel, and have no idea what's on it 'cause you're too wrapped up in Mari and the job offers."

"You're right." I dropped my head on the back of the couch and scrubbed my hands over my face.

He flicked the TV off, turning to give me his full attention. "So what are you still doing here? She keeps trying to get you to join her now that school's out."

"I don't want to make the paparazzi worse. They follow her anyway, but when we're together they're relentless. It's lucky they don't think I'm interesting enough without her to camp outside of school or the house."

He lay a hand on my shoulder. "If she thought the paparazzi would be a problem she wouldn't ask you to go."

Ryan was right. She wouldn't keep insisting if she was worried about the reaction my being there would cause. I stood and walked to my bedroom.

"Where are you going?" he called after me.

"Wherever Mari is. I just have to look up her schedule."

I pulled the band's page up on my phone. I knew what cities she'd be in, but I couldn't remember the order. Her next stop was about a five-hour drive. I packed a bag for a few days, not knowing how long I'd be staying. I walked back into the living room to get my wallet and keys.

"If Mari texts you, don't tell her anything. I want it to be a surprise."

He rolled his eyes. "Dude, you better get flowers or something on your way. She's not going to be happy when she doesn't hear from you for that long."

I hefted the bag up onto my shoulder. "It's only five hours, I'll be there before dinner."

"Good luck and have fun."

Not twenty minutes into the drive, my screen on my dash lit up with a number I was starting to know by heart.

Hayward.

Knowing I couldn't ignore the call, I hit answer.

"Hello?"

"Hi, Cole, it's Michael from Hayward. How are you?"

"Good, I'm actually on the road right now." I switched lanes to pass a car moving way too slow.

"Well, I was just wondering if you gave our last offer any more thought? We'd really love to have you as our offensive coordinator starting this upcoming season."

It was still surreal that colleges were fighting over me for coaching positions. I was used to colleges fighting over me to play for them, but at my age to be responsible for every offensive play on the field was exciting and overwhelming all at the same time.

"Actually, I'm on the way to visit my girlfriend. I wanted to talk it over with her, before I make any decisions. Can I call you next week?"

"That sounds perfect. I look forward to hearing from you. Enjoy your weekend away."

Throughout the drive, the phone continued to ring, Mari's name lighting up the screen. It took all my willpower not to answer. A few numbers I didn't know popped up but, figuring they were telemarketers, I easily let those go to voicemail.

My car ate up miles, my focus on getting to Mari before Ryan spilled the beans. I'd texted Heath before I left to find out what room she was in. With the number on my phone, I navigated through the crowded streets toward their hotel.

As I got closer the traffic slowed to a crawl. Inch by inch I slithered along, my knee bouncing impatiently. It wasn't until I got closer to the parking lot that I realized what all the commotion was about. Every possible celebrity news organization was camped out in front of the hotel, their vans blocking all but one lane.

What the hell was going on? I picked up my phone to see what might have happened and found seven texts from Ryan and a ton of missed calls. I pulled up Ryan's text to see a link with a message.

Watch this before you get there.

Too late for that.

I opened the video and immediately wanted to vomit. It was one I recognized immediately from high school. I'd forgotten most of what happened that day except for what I did to Sam. I hadn't even remembered Mari being there. I also hadn't realized someone was recording it. It was from the last time I put up with Sam's bullshit. We never talked again after that. I watched the video play right up until it finished, just as I walked up to Mari.

"Fuck," I yelled. The important part was missing. Then again, I had no idea whether or not the rest had been recorded.

I scrolled down past the video, reading the article.

Sam Horton, a former classmate of Cosmann and Wallace, spoke with us about the incident. He felt sorry for Mari and wanted the world to know what kind of man she was dating. He considers her a friend and didn't want her to continue to date a man who was only interested in her fame and money. "I hope Mari will forgive me for bringing the video to light, but I think the world should know what kind of man she's with. Hopefully Cole will learn that he can't use people, and will find his way to forgiveness."

"Self-righteous motherfucker."

I punched the roof of the car, instantly regretting the action when a sharp pain shot through my knuckles and they began to swell. I had to get to Mari. If she'd seen that video I needed to tell her what happened afterward.

I climbed out of the car and made it less than five feet before the press started to swarm.

"Cole, can you explain the video?"

"Cole, are you only using Mari?"

"Are you here to claim your prize?"

The questions came at me like gunfire, rapid and straight to my chest. I had no intention of answering them, but that didn't mean I didn't feel each and every one of them like a shot to the heart. I dropped my head and pushed my way through the crowd, eventually making it through the doors and heading directly for the elevators. Nothing was going to stop me from getting to Mari. I punched in the number for her floor and the moment the doors opened, I ran down the hall and pounded on her door.

Before I got a word out, the door flung open and Heath's fist slammed into my face, sending me flying backward into the wall behind me. I felt the blood drip from my nose, but my need to talk to Mari overrode the pain. She'd obviously seen the video. I cupped my nose to contain the blood and stood to knock again.

"Mari, please, you need to listen. That's not me. More happened after that. Please talk to me."

I alternated between pleaded and beating on the door until the elevator dinged and I saw three security guards walking down the hall toward me.

"Sir, you need to leave," one of the men said.

It might have been stupid, but I knocked on the door again. "Mari, please. I swear I can explain."

One wrapped his arm around my chest, pulling me toward the bank of elevators. Two of the other guys took hold of my arms, keeping me from fighting back. By the time the elevator doors closed, all the fight had left me.

Mari wouldn't listen. Like I'd feared from the beginning, my mistakes were too much for her. One video and she believed the worst of me.

The men escorted me from the building, thankfully leading me out of a side door; not to preserve my dignity but to keep any scandal in their hotel down to a minimum. Head bowed, I walked to my car in a trance, trying to ignore the horde of reporters that surrounded it.

The questions they called out went in one ear then out the other. I yanked open the door and climbed into the car. Somehow, I made it out of the parking lot without hitting anyone. In a daze, I pulled back onto the highway. I hit Mari's number, not surprised when it went directly to voicemail. The ache in my chest grew with every mile I drove away from Mari.

I hit Ryan's number. "Dude, what the fuck?"

"I have no idea. I didn't see the video until I got there. I tried to see Mari, but she wouldn't answer the door."

"Can't say I blame her. What the hell was wrong with you in high school?" I winced at the judgment in his tone.

"I'm not that big an asshole. Sam's the asshole. The rest of the video is missing." I glanced in the rearview mirror to make sure no one was following me.

"What's missing? 'Cause, I gotta tell you, it looks pretty damn bad."

"After I told Mari not to be scared, I walked over and dragged Sam down another hall. I didn't pay attention to where she went. Sam swung at me and I beat the shit out of him. The last I knew, he'd been kicked out of school and arrested for hazing freshman members of the football team. I don't know what happened to him after that."

"Oh, shit. You need to tell her."

"I'd love to tell her . . . if she'd listen."

There was a rustling on the other end of the line. "Where are you?"

"On my way home."

"I wouldn't do that. There are reporters parked all along the street, waiting for you."

"Goddamn it." I slammed my fist against the steering wheel, my knuckles still smarting. "Okay, I'm gonna find a hotel somewhere and try to figure out what to do next."

"Call me when you get there. We'll figure out something."

"I don't want to drag you into this." I shook my head even though I knew he couldn't see it.

"Dude, I'm not gonna leave you hanging. We've been friends for years. We'll come up with something."

"Thanks, man."

I disconnected the call and when I was sure no cars were following me, I took the first exit in search of a motel. Some place that wouldn't worry about the gossip blogs and their bullshit.

I found a place a little bit from the highway. Thankfully, the guy at the counter was older than my grandfather and most likely wouldn't pay attention to anything that happened today. He gave me the key and I made sure to park my car in the back of the building to keep it from being seen from the road. I took my bag up to the room and flopped on the bed.

I needed a plan. Somehow, someway to prove to Mari that the guy in that video wasn't me.

But how?

CHAPTER TWENTY-NINE

Mari

The pounding had continued for another ten minutes before it stopped. The entire time I had my head buried against Sawyer's chest.

"Is he gone?" I asked, my voice muffled by the fabric of his shirt.

"He's gone. Monty called security to drag him out of here."

I sat up, swiping at the tears on my face. "I still can't believe I didn't know it was him that day. I had my eyes closed, not wanting to see the sneers on their faces, but I never even considered . . ."

Sawyer tried to bring me down to his chest again, but I fought against it. "I'm fine," I snapped.

"No, you're not. And you don't have to be. Any one of us would be a mess after everything that's happened."

I walked away from Sawyer, noticing for the first time that Heath had a pack of ice held against his knuckles. He looked up at me sheepishly. "I'm sorry, Mari, I convinced you to talk to him. I swear I had no idea."

"It's not your fault. Cole made his own choices."

My phone went off. I picked it up off the table to see Cole's name flashing at the top of the screen. I turned the whole thing off, not in the mood to talk to anyone, let alone him. Jackson threw his phone onto the bed. "As long as Heath's hand is okay, they still want us to play tonight. They think hiding will only make it worse."

"Of course we're playing tonight," I said. "Why wouldn't we?"

Sawyer walked up and, placing his hands on my shoulders, turned me to face him. "You realize that the media will be everywhere?"

"And that's exactly why we need to be out there tonight. The PR department is right. If I hide it makes me look weak. Going out there and singing my heart out proves that I'm stronger than they thought. That I will never let a man drag me down."

"Are you sure about this?" Monty asked.

I turned to Heath. "Is your hand okay?"

He watched me for a moment before tilting his head. "I'll be able to play tonight."

"Then it's settled. If you guys don't mind, I could use a little time alone to get ready." I couldn't believe I'd managed to summon up that much assertion. I didn't really need to get ready. No. Really, I just wanted to sit in the shower and cry, then lie on the bed with ice on my eyes to keep the swelling down.

Sawyer on the other hand ignored what I wanted. "I'm not leaving you."

I took his hand in mine. "You're my best friend and you know I love you, but right now I need for you to give me a few minutes. I promise I'll be okay."

I saw the war in his eyes; torn between giving me what I wanted and doing what he felt was best. Eventually he gave in, but not until he made me promise to call his room if I need anything.

I stripped out of my clothes and climbed into the shower, the water still cold, and as I slid down the wall of the shower, my ass hitting the cool porcelain of the floor, I didn't bother trying to hold back the tears. I needed to let them out if I was going to perform later. I sat and cried for so long, the water went from cold to hot and back to cold again. My fingers were so wrinkled I could have been mistaken for a grandmother.

Eventually, I pulled myself up off the floor, my heart in tatters. I dressed for our performance on autopilot; did my hair and makeup, warmed up my vocal cords. It was the same when I stepped out on stage. I could see the crowd cheering, see the delight on their faces, but I didn't get the same rush that I usually did, and even my own voice sounded like I was under water. In front of thousands of people, I went through the motions. We didn't have a bad show, but the enthusiasm that had been there from day one was gone and I didn't know if I could find it again.

If the guys noticed the difference, they didn't say anything. After the show I smiled for the cameras, signed autographs, gave a few short interviews, but it was all fake. I wore my mask and I wore it well. All I kept thinking to myself as I played the part of Mari from Jaded Ivory was, *two shows to go until I can go home and wallow in self-pity.*

The days passed in a blur of practices, singing, and traveling. The guys would try and get me to go out for a drink to take my mind off things, but I always declined. I wouldn't be very good company. I preferred to hang out in my hotel room. Netflix and ice cream became my best friends.

What hurt the most was the fact I'd actually thought Cole and I had something real. That maybe I could spend the rest of my life with that man. To think of all the times he'd praised me or helped me see a problem in a new light caused my chest to ache. With Cole, it was the first time I'd let someone besides Sawyer in.

That would be the last time I ever made a mistake like that.

CHAPTER THIRTY

COLE

The emails from both colleges, rescinding their offers, came the very next morning, one after the other. Both emails read along the same lines; while they loved my coaching style and knowledge of the game, they couldn't risk tarnishing their school's reputation.

And that wasn't the only thing weighing on my mind. As a result of Sam's blatant lies, I'd most likely lose my job at the high school. All night I tossed and turned, trying to come up with a plan of action, but without having the rest of the video to play to the masses I was pretty much screwed.

Ryan tried reaching out a few times, but I ignored his calls, more than happy to throw myself a pity party. In one day, because of some spiteful asshole, I'd lost the love of my life and my career.

My phone rang with my mom's number and I ignored that, too. My chest ached, my heart no longer a part of it. Really, I couldn't give two shits about the job, but the small glimpse I'd gotten of Mari's tear-streaked face . . .

It made my gut clench.

Forcing myself from the bed, I walked into the bathroom. Dried blood coated the area below my chin and heavy, dark circles rimmed both my eyes, and not the kind from lack of sleep. I touched my nose, pain reverberating through my head with the slightest bit of pressure. I was pretty sure it was broken. Bracing myself, I held both sides and pushed. My eyes burned as I bit back a curse. Not much a hospital could do for it, anyway.

The shower took forever to get lukewarm. During the entire time I was waiting, I heard my phone register message after message. After cleaning the blood from my face and pulling on new clothes, I felt more prepared to face the fallout. What I hadn't expected was a text from Jake, a guy who'd played on the football team with me in high school.

Cole. Long time. When you get a chance, call me. I want to help.

I weighed my options. Jake was more like me during high school. We'd both done stupid shit, but we never went too far. Then again, we hadn't stood up when we should have, either. I pictured the way Mari looked yesterday. Fuck it. Things couldn't get any worse. I dialed the number.

"Hello?"

"Jake? It's Cole."

"Cole. I'm really glad you called. Fuck, I owe you an apology for all the shit you have to deal with now. It's my fault, but I hope this can make up for it."

I lay back on the bed, careful not to drop down too hard and rattle my nose. "What are you talking about?"

"I'm the one who shot that video."

302

I sat bolt upright. "You fucking asshole. You gave that shit to the media."

"No. Fuck no. I was thrilled to hear about you and Mari. She deserves something good after all we put her through."

"Yeah, well that shit went out the window. How did the video get to the media then?"

"Best guess, Sam. I sent it to him after I recorded it. He threatened me, said he'd take me down with you for beating the fuck out of him. I think he realized after seeing it he was up shit's creek without a paddle and would have lost more than he would have gained had he turned you in."

Blood roared through my ears, my heart thundered in my chest. The video was the evidence I needed. "Do you have the whole video?"

"I do. It won't let me send it over the phone, though. The file's too big. I just need your email. It's the only way I know how to fix the mistake I made by recording it in the first place."

I gave him my email. "Thank you, Jake."

"Good luck getting Mari back. If you do speak to her, tell her I'm sorry for all of the problems I caused."

I hung up with Jake and started making calls. With the whole video in hand it was time to fight back.

Which turned out not to be as easy as I'd thought it would be.

The tabloids enjoyed the juicy story they had. They weren't interested in making a bad guy look good. Thankfully I was able to get Michael from Hayward to watch the video. He promptly offered me the job again, apologizing profusely for believing the gossip sites. He told me they'd work with me on getting the real video released.

Day morphed into night, the black sky reflecting my mood perfectly. Somehow, Ryan managed to send the reporters out front of our house on a wild goose chase. I pulled my car into the train station near our place and walked a few blocks down to where Ryan waited to pick me up. Even with the lack of lightning, I left my baseball cap and sunglasses in place. I climbed into the back seat, exhaustion settling over me like a blanket.

"Thanks for coming to get me." I tugged the baseball hat lower like it would somehow protect me from the shitstorm.

"Anything, man. I'm just glad it worked."

I sighed. "Honestly, I wasn't sure it would. But I'm glad it did. It'll be nice to be in my own bed, not looking over my shoulder waiting for them to find me."

"You do realize that they'll figure out where you are soon enough?"

I slunk further down into the seat. "I know. At least at home I have everything I need."

He glanced at me in the rearview mirror. "Have you heard back from Hayward or Cambria?"

"I didn't bother with Cambria since it was never my choice in the first place, but Hayward saw the video and offered me the job again."

"Are you gonna take it?"

That was the question. "I'm not sure yet."

On the one hand, if I took the job and somehow, someway I managed to get Mari back, we'd be living two hours apart. Then again, if she refused to even hear me out, being away from her might be for the best.

"What about the video?"

Even though I wasn't in the mood to hash all of this out at the moment, I couldn't be a dick about it after all Ryan had done for me over the last few days.

"The tabloids weren't interested in the truth. Not surprising, but Hayward's PR team is gonna try and use their influence to get the full video posted."

"At least it's a start." Ryan pulled into the driveway and looked around. "I think you're good. Let's get inside before they come back."

We raced to the door like thieves in the night. It was ridiculous having to sneak into my own home, but until the media lost interest, I was stuck with it.

The second the front door shut, I flopped down on the couch, dropping my duffle at my feet. I closed my eyes and let my muscles relax. There were things I needed to do like make some phone calls and check my email. I'd turned off all notifications on my phone after that first night. I didn't need to see the social media sites blowing up about me, speculating what an asshole I was. How I used Mari for revenge over my lost career, which happened to be the last theory I saw. The only notifications I left on were for calls and texts. I didn't want to miss if Mari tried to get a hold of me.

"Want something to eat? I can call for a pizza."

Like that the silence was broken. "Yeah, pizza sounds good."

Ryan turned toward the kitchen to grab a menu when I called his name. He looked back. "Yeah?"

"Thank you, for everything."

He smiled, but I could still see the underlying pity in his eyes. "Anytime."

He left the room and I knew it was time to face the rest of my reality. I grabbed my laptop from my bag and powered it up. Dread settled in the pit of my stomach at what I might find there. I sucked in a deep breath and opened the browser for my email. It loaded faster than I would have liked considering there were thousands of messages. Most of them from media sites looking for an interview, which I promptly deleted. Two emails stood out from the rest. One was from my school, scheduling a meeting to discuss my further role in the district. Who knew whether they planned to fire me or just remove my coaching privileges. Either way at least I had the evidence to take with me.

The other was from an unknown email address with the subject "You're just as bad as them," at the top. Nothing about the other email screamed spam, so I clicked on it hoping to figure out who it was from.

Mr. Wallace,

I trusted you. Thought you would actually stand up for the kids who were bullied. I never imagined you were one of the bullies. That you were still a bully. There is one thing I did learn through all of this and that's to stand up for myself and my friends. Mari is my friend. She deserves better than you. I won't let you bully her anymore.

Kristen Davis

I wanted to be mad, to punch things reading that email. The trust I built with my students and players washed away. And while I was thrilled she was taking a stand for something, I wish I could have seen it from a different perspective and not directed toward me.

I debated the appropriate response to her email. Responding to Kristen's email wouldn't be the most professional thing to do. With my job most likely on the line, would it really matter in the end. Right or wrong, I had to do what was best for Kristen which was to show her that her trust wasn't misplaced. She had a right to know that she didn't have to fear believing in the teachers. That we were there to protect her and we'd do anything to make it happen.

Damn the consequences.

I hit reply, making sure to attach the full video Jake had sent me the other day.

Kristen,

I'm happy to see you stand up for yourself and Mari. The world needs more people like you. I've attached the full video which WAS NOT released. I'll admit, I'm not proud of some of the things in that video, but not the way you think. I don't want you to lose faith in the people who are there to protect you and this is the only way I can think for that to happen.

Mr. Wallace.

Besides checking in with my mom again, there wasn't much more I could do for the night. I was out of ideas on ways to get her to listen. I'd sent the video to her email, hoping for a miracle. Then again, maybe this was the punishment I deserved for not standing up for her in the first place. I took my phone from my pocket, staring at it, willing it to ring, but nothing happened. I knew it wouldn't get me anywhere but I couldn't stop myself from calling Mari's number again. And like every time before it went straight to voicemail.

"Mari, please watch the video I sent. Don't do it for me. Do it for yourself. You need to see the truth of it all. More than that, I want you to know that I miss you more than I ever thought possible. Please, please just watch it. It's all there for you to see."

I was rambling. I ended the call and shoved my phone into my pocket. It wasn't the first time I'd called and rambled on and on trying to get her to listen. Deep down though, I knew she wasn't listening to any of the messages I left.

The next morning there was a knock on my bedroom door.

"What?" I pulled the covers over my head to block out the light.

"You need to get your ass out of bed." Ryan threw the door open.

"It's too early."

The covers were yanked off me. "It's two in the afternoon."

I glanced at the clock and groaned. "Shit. I didn't think it was that late."

He held out an envelope to me. I could clearly see the Hayward logo in the top left-hand corner. There wasn't a doubt in my mind what was in there.

"Thanks." I took it from his hands and tore it open. Exactly as I thought, it was a contract for the offensive coaching position.

Ryan watched me. "Are you taking the job?"

My heart picked up pace. I couldn't stop myself from looking over to where my phone lay silent on the nightstand and back to the papers in my hand. "I don't know."

He sighed and leaned back against the wall. "I know you're hoping Mari will see the video and call. Shit, I'm hoping that happens too. You guys were good together. But this is an opportunity of a lifetime. I'd hate to see you regret not taking the job to wait for her and never get her back."

I ran a hand through my sleep-tousled hair. "I know. I know. I'm not dismissing it completely. I just need some time to really think it over."

He nodded. "Don't wait forever. You don't want them to give the job to someone else."

"I won't."

I looked at the papers in my hands again. Ryan was right. I knew that, yet my heart still revolted at the thought of taking the job so far from the one woman who made my life complete. The room felt too small. I folded the papers and pushed them back into the envelope, setting them on the bedside table for safe keeping.

About a week and a half later I officially accepted the job. No matter how many times I'd tried to contact Mari, I couldn't get through. I had all the evidence of my innocence in my hands and I couldn't get her to listen. I figured putting some distance between us would make her rejection easier to deal with. Maybe someday she'd see the truth.

Maybe.

Mari

There was no way I was staying in another hotel, letting the media dissect my every move. The guys weren't thrilled with the idea of making a five-hour trip back that late, but they did it for me. I knew I was being a bitch, but I couldn't seem to stop myself. When we weren't performing I avoided any socializing at all costs, except when I wanted to get on the road earlier than we planned. I honestly didn't deserve them, how they took all my crap without complaint. The moment we arrived home, I went to my room and locked the door. I'd been holed up there ever since.

The first few days Sawyer tried to coax me out, and even though a part of me felt bad about it, I refused to leave the room. I needed time. This wasn't just a simple case of a broken heart. Ice cream and rom-coms with my best friend could fix that. This was a goddamn soap opera destruction of a relationship, complete with the unforgivable lies and massive embarrassment. It had been about a week since we'd gotten home and I was no closer to pulling myself out of the mess I'd landed in. The publicist and PR people for the label had done everything possible to tamp down the conjecture by the media. Not that I paid attention. I deleted all my social media accounts from my phone. I also refused to watch, read, or listen to the news. There was nothing about that day they could tell me that I didn't already know. The question I kept asking myself was how I could have been so wrong about Cole? Why didn't I see it?

Those questions are what kept me locked behind closed doors. I couldn't trust myself to be out in the world. Judging people's characters and deciding if they were worth my time. I'd tried it and failed miserably.

A knock sounded on my door and like every other time, I ignored it. Sawyer would end up leaving whatever food he made on the snack table he'd set up by the door when he realized I wasn't going to answer.

The knock came again. "Mari, we need to talk."

Not Sawyer, but Heath. I continued to stare at the ceiling.

"Look, I know you don't want to see anyone, but we need to make some decisions about the band as a group. Monty and Jackson are here too." He waited a beat for me to answer and when I didn't he continued. "We'll wait for you in the living room for as long as it takes."

The tone of his voice told me they'd wait all night or for days if they had to. My head and my heart warred on what to do. Sitting in my room had gotten me nowhere. I was part of Jaded Ivory. I put them in jeopardy with my decisions, the least I could do was listen to what they had to say, as long as they had no plans to talk about Cole. That was a topic I never wanted to bring up again.

Knowing that they really would wait, I forced myself from the bed and for the first time in days, I caught a glimpse of myself in the mirror. The sight that greeted me stopped me in my tracks. The woman before me looked like she'd been to hell and back. Blond hair stuck out in a million different directions and no, it wasn't in a hip, stylish way. There wasn't enough makeup in the world to cover the dark circles and red-rimmed eyes. I gave a brief moment of thought to the idea of showering before I met with the guys, but decided it didn't matter. The sooner we got this done the better. I planned on going back to my room when we were done. Eventually, I need to pull myself out of the funk, but today wasn't the day.

I padded my way out to the living room where the guys were talking in hushed tones. Sawyer's head snapped up when I stepped into the room. He jumped from his seat. The other guys glanced around the room, none of their eyes landing on me. I had a pretty good idea that they were talking about me. Not that I could blame them, I'd been an absolute wreck.

"Hey, Mari," Heath said, sliding back into his seat.

Sawyer stepped in front of me. "Are you sure you're up for this?"

"Maybe if I knew what we were talking about, but as long as the topic stays on the band and not my personal life, I'll be good." I couldn't even bring myself to say Cole's name. Sawyer nodded and led me to a seat in the living room.

Heath clapped his hands together to get everyone's attention. "I spoke with Tom right before we came over and the label wants us back in the studio. They want us to record an entire album."

Silence filled the room, but it wasn't hard to miss the wide eyes and open-mouthed stares. At least until Monty leapt from his seat with a loud whoop. The sound broke the tension in the room. Cheering, clapping, yelling. All of my worries of five minutes ago were pushed aside in that moment. Hugs were passed around as we jumped up and down throughout the living room.

"Guys," Heath yelled, gesturing for us to sit down. "I know everyone's excited but there's more we need to talk about before we celebrate."

Jackson rolled his eyes. "What else could possibly be so important it can't wait until after we celebrate?"

I noticed Heath glance at me, but just as quickly his eyes moved over the rest of the group. "Staying here. The last track took us almost two weeks to record. This would be a full thirteen to fourteen songs and we can't spend the next six months driving two hours each way. I think it's time we consider moving closer to the studio."

Monty nodded. "Makes sense. We could probably finish the songs sooner if we didn't have to worry about the drive."

"Think we'd find a place to rent with practice space?"

"Doubt we would need practice space with the studio right there."

The conversation swirled around me, but I'd stopped paying attention to who said what. It didn't matter. Not one of them brought up Cole, yet it seemed to come back to him anyway. I wanted nothing to do with him. So why did a part of me hate the idea of moving so far from where he was? It didn't matter how close or how far away he lived, he was still the same guy I knew in high school, he just got better at putting on the mask. Maybe moving from here would be good for me. Another fresh start. Another chance to put the past behind me. It worked the first time and as long as I didn't let my walls down it should work again.

When I looked up four sets of eyes were turned in my direction. "Why is everyone looking at me?"

Sawyer ran a hand through his hair. "Are you okay with moving away from here?"

I shrugged. "Why wouldn't I be?"

Heath chewed on his thumbnail. "Cole—"

I threw my hands up and stood. "I don't want to talk about him. Make whatever arrangements are necessary. Sawyer can find us a place and you guys just tell me when it's time to pack."

I didn't bother waiting for a reaction. I stormed down the hall to my bedroom, slamming and locking the door behind me. It was bad enough my own thoughts went straight to Cole when Heath mentioned moving. What I really didn't want to do was sit there and talk about all the reasons I might be upset moving far away from Cole. Tears raced down my cheeks as I dropped to the bed and pulled my pillow over my head. What a fool I'd been. I went and fell in love with the one man who I knew from the start would break me all over again.

A light tapping sounded on the door. "Keys, the guys left. Please let me in so we can talk."

I could have laid my soul at Sawyer's feet like I had so many times before, but for some reason, this time, I wanted to suffer on my own. Which left me ignoring Sawyer's plea again.

The pattern that started when we first arrived home continued. I left my room more often, but the moment someone tried to get me to talk I returned there for at least a day if not more. Sawyer tried a few times to get me to listen to him, but once it became obvious that I wouldn't talk about it, he would talk about anything but Cole. The ache in my chest grew with each passing second and I didn't have the first clue how to explain it to anyone. Why would they for one second understand how I could be heartbroken over a man like Cole? Except, I was. My heart was in a million pieces and I wasn't sure I knew how to put it together again.

Sawyer and I grew even closer than we were before. He made sure to find ways to keep me occupied. He avoided social media with me and we spent days binge-watching old 80s movies. He did everything possible to pull me out of the dark place I'd crawled into. When we were together he succeeded, but at night, alone in my bed I couldn't help but fall farther back in.

We were sitting in the living room watching TV and out of the corner of my eye I noticed Sawyer's leg bouncing up and down. Every once in a while he'd shift in his seat, watch me for a minute, then turn his attention back to the screen. By the fourth time he'd done it, I'd had enough.

I threw my hands up in the air. "What is the problem? Just spit it out already."

He rubbed the back of his neck. "I found us a place."

"And?"

"And I didn't want you to be upset. We move in in two weeks."

"Okay, so we need to start packing up the house." I did my best to keep my voice normal at the pain in my chest.

"Yeah. I can grab some boxes tomorrow." He sighed and his shoulders relaxed.

Rather than upset Sawyer more than I already had by completely withdrawing from him, I waited another half an hour before I stood and stretched. "I think I'm going to lie down and take a nap."

Sawyer nodded, but I noticed his eyes following me down the hall. I might have tried to play it off, but he knew me better than anyone. What I really wanted was some time to process moving on my own.

As I stared at the ceiling of my room, I knew I couldn't keep going on like this any longer. I hadn't sung a note in weeks. I'd managed to push everyone in the band away to the point they all walked on eggshells around me. I wouldn't let my dream fall by the wayside or push away my friends over Cole. It was my life and I was going to take it back.

I grabbed my laptop off the floor determined to find a killer recipe. It would at least be a start in the long list of groveling I needed to do. We could eat, laugh, and celebrate the start of something new together. After I apologized for the way I treated them of course. And even though it might hurt, hopefully we could hash out everything I went through with Cole and we could leave the subject where it belonged—in the past.

I searched the food sites I like until I found the perfect recipe. It wouldn't take that long to make and I was pretty sure we had all of the ingredients. If not I knew I could talk Sawyer into going out to pick up what we were missing. A notification at the bottom of my screen caught my attention. Over six hundred emails sat in my inbox. My spam filter was decent but apparently not good enough. If I was taking my life back, it was time to clean up the mess that built up when it fell apart.

I opened the app on my computer and cringed at some of the subjects. Anything that wasn't from an email I recognized I deleted immediately. My fingers were starting to go numb from all the clicking. About halfway through, I finally recognized one sender.

Kristen.

In all the chaos, I'd completely ignored her. She'd been coming out of her shell, learning that it wasn't her fault a few of the guys in her school were jerks. Up until the release of the video we'd talked at least once a week. Usually by text or email, but if I was free we talked by phone. I wasn't even sure if my phone worked anymore. Once the battery died, I hadn't bothered charging it again. There hadn't seemed to be a point. It was full of social media, phone calls, emails, and texts that I didn't want to deal with. And in my selfish shutdown I hadn't once thought of Kristen.

What kind of person did that make me?

I couldn't imagine what that video had done to her. She looked up to Cole, believed he'd do anything to stop the bullies only to find out he was one of them. The email was sent two weeks ago. She needed me and I failed. Well I wouldn't fail her anymore. I opened the email and was surprised to see an attachment.

Mari,

I can't imagine what the last few days have been like for you. I was crushed when I saw that video. I couldn't understand how Mr. Wallace could do that to someone. How the same teacher who stood up for me twice could hurt you like that? So I did what everyone is always telling me to do and I stood up to him. What I didn't expect when I sent him the email was for him to actually answer me. I figured he'd brush me off and delete it. So imagine my surprise when I saw he replied. But there was more to it.

I know you won't want to watch the video I've sent, but I really think you need to. You deserve the truth more than anyone. I'm not sure what you'll decide to do afterward, but please if you won't watch the video for you watch it for me. It would kill me to know I've kept the truth from you. You've done so much for me over the last few months, this is the only way I know how to repay you for it.

Kristen.

My hands shook as I moved the mouse onto the link for the video. What could she possibly be sending me? When I hit play, my stomach lurched at what appeared on the screen. It was the same clip I'd seen over and over again since the press released it. I hit stop. My chest felt tight, like I couldn't get a full breath in. Closing my eyes, I tried to focus on my breathing until the muscles loosened and I was able to pull in a full gulp of air. I switched back to Kristen's email with every intention of sending a "what the hell" reply, when her words caught my eyes. *But there was more to it.*

Of course I was the girl with the sadistic streak a mile wide, I pulled the video up again. Kristen begged me to watch it for her and that's what I would do before responding to her email. I sucked in a deep breath, bracing myself for the next few moments and hit play. Sam's voice made my blood run cold. To this day, the bastard's voice caused me to flinch. I tried to push it out of my head while I waited for Cole to appear on the screen. A few seconds later, broad shoulders that I'd recognize anywhere stepped on camera. He walked right up to me.

318

Don't be scared.

I heard his voice like he was standing right in front of me. I was shocked when the video didn't cut out. All the times it played, it went to black right after Cole spoke to me.

But there was more to it.

I sat forward on the bed, my hands gripping my thighs. On the screen, Cole stepped away from me and went right to Sam, grabbing his arm and dragging him down the hall. He shoved him into an empty classroom.

"What the fuck is wrong with you?" Cole advanced on Sam.

"Me?" Sam shouted. "What's wrong with you? We were just having a little fun with Mariloon."

"That's not fun. That's you being a prick with a superiority complex."

"Aren't you all of a sudden Mr. High and Mighty. Now that Cole's got his scholarship on the way to the NFL he's better than us." His lip curved into a sneer as he glanced around the room.

"Whatever you want to think, but I'm not gonna let you treat people like shit anymore."

Sam took a step toward Cole. "And what are you going to do to stop me?"

"Whatever it takes."

Cole turned his back to walk out the door when Sam grabbed him and attempted to throw a punch, but Cole was faster. He ducked and spun on his heel landing a punch to Sam's stomach. Sam dropped to the floor and Cole was on him in a second, landing shot after shot to his face. At one point the phone drops to the floor, but it still showed three guys pulling Cole off Sam. A hand comes across the screen and the video cuts out.

And I can't move a muscle.

I remembered the hall being empty when I opened my eyes. And I also remembered Sam being absent for two weeks after that. I didn't give a shit where he was, I just thanked my lucky stars I didn't have to deal with him.

My lungs burned and my vision blurred. Without thinking, I threw my legs over the side of the bed, my laptop crashing to the floor as I ran to find Sawyer. He was still in the same place I'd left him earlier.

"What's up?" he asked without taking his eyes from the TV. No words would come. When the silence continued, Sawyer glanced over in my direction. "Hey . . ."

One look at my face and he jumped from his seat and pulled me into his arms. "Keys, what's wrong?"

"Did you know?"

He leaned back and watched me. "Did I know what?"

"That wasn't the whole video."

He guided me over to the chair and pulled me down onto his lap. "What do you mean that isn't the full video?"

I brushed the tears from my face. "Kristen sent me the whole video. It doesn't end with Cole saying don't be scared."

He shook his head. "But I thought that was the last thing you remembered?"

"It was, but that was because Cole dragged Sam down to an empty room and beat the shit out of him."

Sawyer straightened in his seat. "He did what?"

"He defended me and I paid him back by believing all of the bullshit in those interviews. I let the past influence me and I was wrong."

320

Sawyer drew me close, rubbing light circles on my back. "You didn't know."

"Doesn't make a difference," I mumbled into his shirt. "I pushed away the man I love because I didn't have enough faith in him."

"You can't think like that. You didn't know about the rest of the video. It's not your fault."

I lifted my head to look him in the eye. "Actually, this time I think it is."

I buried my head against his chest and sobs racked my body. I'd have to find a way to make it up to him. To apologize for all the hurt I caused him. This one was on me.

There was a light knock on the door. "Come in," Sawyer called.

CHAPTER THIRTY-TWO

COLE

"Are you sure this is a good idea?" I looked across at Heath as we drove over to Mari's place. "How do you know Sawyer got her to watch it or read the article?"

"I don't. But if anyone can it's Sawyer. They've gotten even closer since all of this happened."

A boulder settled in my gut. I'd seen the shared gazes and light touches the two of them shared from time to time. It would appear that despite our time apart, the green-eyed monster was still rearing its ugly head. I reminded myself that they were just good friends.

It had been a few weeks since everything blew up in my face, and during that time, the band had been on the road. I hadn't given up, though. I spent most of my free time trying to come up with ways to get that video to Mari, or at least to one of the guys. It had taken time, but eventually I got

Heath to listen. I'd had to send the video to the band account from one called "ilovemari" hoping he'd open it thinking it was fan mail, but it had worked and he called me a couple of nights ago to tell me he wanted to help.

Apparently, Mari was as miserable as I was. With the publicity and hype surrounding the band, Heath had helped me get the real story about Sam to the PR department who gave it to the tabloids and that shit spread like wildfire. No longer had Mari been dating the former NFL prospect who only wanted her to boost his career. No, the media had done a complete one-eighty and now she'd been dating Cole Wallace, the man who'd tried to save her from the bullies. While it wasn't exactly the whole truth, only Mari and I knew that, and it was enough for people to quit looking at her like she was a pathetic victim.

I knew from the guys that she'd been actively avoiding the gossip news. Not that I could blame her one little bit. The strong, beautiful woman I loved had been once again broken by the mistakes I'd made.

But I loved her.

And if getting her back meant groveling or begging on my hands and knees, I'd do it. Mari was my world. I had to give it one more try.

We pulled up in front of the house and my whole body trembled as I stepped from the car.

"Relax," Heath said from the driver's seat. "Everything's gonna be fine. I'll wait here in case you need me."

I stopped and turned. "Thanks for everything."

"You're welcome and if things go your way, send Sawyer out to me."

I narrowed my eyes. "Why would I send Sawyer out here?"

He shook his head. "Damn, you really are in a sad state. It's been weeks since you've been together. I'm sure you'll need some time alone." He waggled his eyebrows like one of those damn cartoon characters.

Rolling my eyes, I started for the house again, each step more of a struggle than the last. I had no idea what I'd find on the other side of that door. There was the very real possibility she would slam it in my face.

I lifted my hand to knock, but then dropped it.

"Just do it," Heath called from the car.

I sucked in a breath and knocked.

"Come in."

Sawyer.

I swung the door open and stepped inside, and what I saw almost sent me to my knees. Mari was curled up in Sawyer's lap, her face buried in his chest as he placed a kiss to the top of her head. His hand stroked the soft skin of her back, up and down as he soothed her, exactly as I'd been longing to do.

"Mari, I think there's someone here to see you." Sawyer tilted her chin up and using his thumbs, he brushed the tears from her face. They shared a look before she turned, making no attempt to remove herself from his lap.

"Cole?" Her eyes went wide, her hand coming up to her chest.

Bile burned my throat, self-loathing pouring through me like acid. I shoved my hands in my pockets, hoping it would keep me from hitting a wall. I could do that later at the gym because I was really going to need to beat the shit out of something.

"There's something I want to say to you." I glanced down at Sawyer's hands wrapped firmly around her waist and closed my eyes. Acting like a jealous asshole wasn't going to get me anywhere, and I needed her to at least listen to me before she tossed me outside. "I just wanted you to know I love you, Mariella. But, I know I don't deserve you and hope that someone"—I glanced back and forth between Sawyer and Mari—"will make you happy one day."

She opened her mouth to say something but I just didn't have it in me to hear her say that I was right and Sawyer could make her happy. I spun and walked back out the door. Halfway across the yard I heard the front door slam.

"Cole, wait."

I spotted Heath leaning against the car, watching everything play out. His eyes bounced all over the yard, probably trying to figure out who to watch first.

I rolled my shoulders and turned to face her. The moonlight cast a glow over her features, making her seem untouchable. Nights of her in my arms flooded my mind, giving an edge to my tone. "What, Mari? What else is there to say?"

She walked up to me. My first instinct was to take a step back; to save myself the pain. It was very likely that this was karma coming to bite me in the ass. This was the world's way of making me suffer for my mistakes. For a brief period in my life, I'd thought losing my chance in the NFL was the end of the world.

How wrong was I?

I'd had no idea that losing the woman in front of me would hurt a hundred times more. There would never be another Mari.

She stood in front of me, waiting for something. For what, though?

"Look, I think everything is pretty clear." I gestured over my shoulder with my thumb. "I'm gonna have Heath give me a ride home."

Before I could take one step, her hand clamped around my wrist, dragging me back. Her eyes flashed and she stood on her toes and covered my lips with hers. At first, I held my ground, my lips unmoving as hers covered every inch of mine. But all too soon her taste, the feel of her body pressed against mine, became too much.

One last taste.

Like the night outside the tattoo shop, I sank my hand into her hair, holding her lips to mine. She gasped and I took advantage, slipping my tongue into her mouth. Her arms slid up my chest, wrapping around my neck. When I couldn't take it anymore, I stepped back, breaking the seal of our lips.

"I can't do this," I panted between breaths.

"You can." She moved closer and I moved back. "You have to."

I shook my head, trying to push her sweet, melodic voice out of my head. "I can't and, no, I don't have to."

"I love you." Her words were simple, honest, and they punched a hole in my chest.

"But not as much as you love Sawyer."

"No. My love for you is different and so much more." She came forward and took hold of my hand while I tried to catch my breath. "Please come inside, there's something you need to know, but it's not my story to tell."

In a daze, I followed her back into the house.

She loves me.

More than Sawyer.

Love.

She. Loves. Me.

326

No matter how many times the words passed through my mind, they still weren't settling in. Mari linked her fingers with mine and led me back into the house, guiding me to a chair in the living room. I took a seat and she sat down on my lap. The tables had turned in the last few minutes. Now it was me sitting with my arms wrapped around Mari. I glanced up at Sawyer, expecting him to be angry. But I didn't see any of the hatred or resentment I expected. His face was wreathed in a smile.

"Sawyer, please tell him. I can't lose him because he thinks you and I want to be together."

I looked down at Mari, then back over at Sawyer. What could he possibly say that would make me see their relationship differently?

He bent at the waist, resting his forearms on his thighs. "Besides my parents, only two other people in the world know this. One is sitting in your lap, and the other is outside waiting in his car. I know you have no reason to keep my secret, but I'll beg if I have to. I have no idea how it would affect Jaded Ivory and the contract. Not that I think it's anyone's business but my own, but I've worked too damn hard to have this taken away."

He stopped, dropping his eyes to the carpet and I waited for a moment before asking, "What's your business?"

Sawyer looked up at me again. When he glanced over at Mari, she nodded at him. "I'm gay, Cole, and I've known it for a long time. You're right when you say I love Mari. I do, but not in the way you're thinking. She's like a sister to me, and that's all she'll ever be."

Sawyer's gay?

How did I *not* see that one coming?

I shrugged. "Okay."

327

"Okay? That's it?" he asked, watching me warily.

"Yeah, okay. Look, as long as you're not fucking Mari, I personally don't give a shit where you stick your dick."

"Jesus, Cole," Mari said, swatting my shoulder.

"Why are you hitting me?"

"You could be a little less crude about it."

I gestured to Sawyer. "He's a guy. He knows what I mean."

Sawyer sat back in the seat, looking more relaxed than I'd ever seen him. "I do."

Mari shook her head. "You guys are ridiculous."

Feeling like I could conquer the world, I held her closer and kissed her forehead. "You love me?"

Eyes as clear as a Caribbean ocean gazed into mine. "Yes— I— Do." She emphasized each word with a kiss.

Unable to take any more, I cupped her face in my hands, slipping my tongue between her lips. What started out as sweet turned molten in a matter of seconds. Mari squirmed on my lap and my dick perked up. Just having her near, touching, even between clothes, and I was hard enough to hammer nails.

God, what this woman did to me.

My hand slid down her ribs to the hem of her shirt, needing to feel all that creamy, soft skin. A throat cleared.

Shit.

I held my hands up away from her. With her in my arms everything fell away. Including the fact that Sawyer was sitting across the room, watching as I groped my girl.

Mari glanced over her shoulder and flipped him off.

He stood, chuckling. "Hey, I gave you guys a minute to stop on your own, but since that apparently isn't going to happen, I'm gonna go see if Heath is still out there." His eyes ran all over the two of us, practically ready to fuck right there in the chair. "Yeah, I think I'm gonna stay there tonight. I do not need to hear what's gonna happen here."

With that, Sawyer grabbed his wallet and keys off the side table and walked out the door. Mari's attention turned back to me the moment it closed behind him. Fire burned deep in her eyes.

"Here, or my room?"

"While I would love to bend this sexy ass over the chair right now, I want to sleep with you curled up beside me." I stood with her in my arms and started for her room.

It amazed me how much I missed the feel of her against me. I stepped through the door of her room, not bothering to close it since I knew we had the house to ourselves.

I didn't bother stopping until I placed her on the bed, following her down. I took her lips in a heated kiss. Her lips were soft against mine. Every inch of me burned with need. My dick strained against my zipper.

"You have too many clothes on," Mari said, tugging the hem of my shirt up over my head.

Sitting up, I took it and threw it to the floor, before returning to divest her of the clothes covering all that creamy skin. I adjusted myself inside my pants at the sight of her pebbled nipples standing straight, reaching for me. Lowering my head, I ran my tongue over one then the other. The soft moans of pleasure coming from Mari were an aphrodisiac like no other.

"God, Mari. What you do to me?" I titled my face to the ceiling, trying to gain control of myself.

I ran my hands over every inch of her body. Caressing her breasts, moving down her ribs until my fingers found her clit. Toying with the sensitive bundle of nerves, I slipped a finger inside her body, gliding in and out in a rhythm that my cock wanted.

"Shit, Cole. Stop teasing me. It's been too long."

Damn, she had me. My dick was throbbing in my shorts. I was only torturing us both by prolonging things. I stood from the bed and dropped my shorts to the floor. After rolling a condom down my length, I crawled back over Mari and wasted no time slipping inside.

"Cole," she moaned, arching her hips closer to mine.

"I missed you," I said, capturing her mouth with mine. Our tongues danced an exotic cadence that matched my thrusts into her.

Pleasure raced down my spine and I wasn't sure how much longer I could hold on, as I felt her walls tighten on me. I slipped my hand between our bodies and thumbed her clit. The simple movement pushed her over the edge. Crying out, her body spasmed over mine, bringing about my own climax.

"I love you," I cried out, holding still inside her. Darkness pulled on the edges of my vision.

When my body was empty, I gazed down at the woman below me. Her eyes were glassy and a single tear tracked down her face.

I rolled to my side bringing her with me. "Why the tears?"

Her smile was radiant. "I'm just so glad you're here. I love you, Cole."

"I love you, too."

Later that night, my stomach was in knots over the one thing I'd yet to tell Mari. I'd been so excited about seeing her again, touching her, tasting her, that I'd forgotten to tell her something that was going to affect our relationship.

"I have something to tell you," she whispered into the quiet room.

My hand froze mid-stroke up her back. With a deep breath, I forced my fingers to move again. "What's that?"

She sucked in a breath. "The label wants us to move closer to the studio."

I held her tighter to me. "Really?"

She leaned up on her elbows watching me. "You're not upset?"

I brushed the hair from her face. "Not at all. Especially since I took the job at Hayward."

She jerked her head back. "You did? Why didn't you tell me?"

I glanced down at our obvious nakedness and back up at her. "It wasn't like I had much of a chance."

"Okay, okay. We were busy." She fell silent for a moment. "You really took the job at Hayward?"

I cupped her face in my hands. "I did. Now say you'll move in with me."

"What?"

"Move in with me. The university has already found me a house and I want you to live there with me."

Moisture pooled in her eyes. "Yes. I'd love to move in with you."

"Then why the tears?"

"Because until tonight, I thought all of this was lost to us. I love you. Thank you for not giving up fighting for me."

"I love you, too."

ROCK ME

I brought her lips down to mine and just like that, everything was right in the world. The woman who'd rocked me to my core was in my arms.

I couldn't have asked for anything more.

EPILOGUE

COLE

I blew the whistle. "Run it again."

It was the second week of practice. Mari and I moved our stuff in a month ago and I'd quickly settled into a routine. With both of our crazy schedules, it was nice to come home to one another. But with the start of football season coming up, and Mari having to go on tour, we knew there would be a lot of traveling for both of us.

The plus of the new job: once the season was over, I could join Mari on the road, if she happened to be touring at the time.

Everything was perfect.

The studio had sued Sam for libel, not that he had any money to pay. Apparently, after a three-year stint in jail for orchestrating a hazing incident that resulted in a freshman getting injured, Sam had had trouble finding work. He worked a landscaping job, but he lost that after the truth of the video came out.

Like he'd said in the article, maybe someday he'd learn from his mistakes.

The quarterback passed the ball. It was the perfect pass for the route we'd been running so I was shocked when it bounced off my wide receiver's helmet and landed on the ground. Heads started to swivel toward me. I dropped my clipboard and stormed onto the field.

"Caldwell, what the hell are you doing? You think the ball's magically gonna appear in your hands?"

"Holy fuck."

I turned to chastise the player behind me, and that was when I realized the entire offensive line was looking into the stands, along with the three other coaches out there with me today. I followed their line of sight and almost groaned at what I found.

Mari was standing at the bottom railing, watching the practice. Which wouldn't have been so bad, if it weren't for the shorts that barely covered her ass and the tank top that showed off her two new bird tattoos.

"Eyes on the ground, gentlemen, or you'll be doing suicides in full pads for the next thirty minutes."

Every helmet on the field dropped to the ground.

"Holy shit," I heard as I walked off the field. "Coach really is dating Mari from Jaded Ivory."

I hopped the railing and stood before her. "I think you have a fan club."

"The only member I care about is standing in front of me."

"Definitely words I like to hear. I thought you were in the studio today?"

334

She shrugged. "We finished early and I thought I'd come watch your practice."

I let my gaze roam over her outfit. "And you expect them to concentrate when you're wearing that?"

"What's wrong with it?"

I stepped closer and ran my hand along the curve of her ass. "Besides the fact that I can practically see the bottom of your ass? Absolutely nothing. I'm enjoying the view. However, I don't think my guys have enough self-control to keep themselves from eye-fucking you from across the field."

She smirked. "I guess I better leave you to it then." She turned, swaying that sexy ass as she walked. She stopped and peeked over her shoulder. "Don't be too late. I'll be home all by myself waiting for you." She waved and continued through the tunnel into the main part of the stadium.

I did the best to adjust my aching dick without being seen. Two hours left of practice before I could do anything about it. If there was one thing I'd learned about Mari in the last year, it was that life with her would never be boring. She'd hit her lowest and come out swinging, taking me with her in the process. Now she was on top of the world.

And I'd do my best to hold her up there for as long as she wanted.

ACKNOWLEGDEMENTS

Rock Me is a story near and dear to me. Being a band and choir geek myself, I remember what was like to not be part of the popular crowd. But I wouldn't change the friends I made for the world. If Mari can prove to just one person how strong they are, that they can do whatever they want, then my heart is happy. For years I've thought about Mari and where her story might take me. I'm so glad I can finally share her story with you.

Thank you to Marisa of Cover Me Darling. The second I saw this cover, I knew it was time to tell Mari's story and this cover couldn't be any more perfect for her.

Brandy and Kelley, you ladies always keep me sane, especially when I feel like I'm completely over my head. Thank you for always cheering me on, talking me down when I need it, and pushing me the rest of the time. I'm not sure what I would do without you. Thank you to Tracy, Miranda, and Alexis, your thoughts and notes are always a tremendous help.

A special thank you to Ryn of Delphi Rose. Rock Me holds a special place in my heart, so to hear such positive praise makes me happy dance. Thank you for always helping to make my words a little bit brighter. And to Judy of Judy's proofreading, thank you for finding those last little pieces to bring it all together.

To the bloggers and readers, thank you for giving Mari and Cole a chance. I hope you'll come back to see more of them in Sawyer's story.

Remember to always stand up for what you believe is right. Don't let the bullies win.

Keep up to date with new releases by signing up for my newsletter.

Love you all,

Rebecca   xoxo

Forgiven Series:

Forgiven
Redemption
Healed
Acceptance

Standalone Titles:

Letters Home
Coming Home
Just Once
Beautiful Lessons
Ryder
Second Chances
Traded
House Rules

The Folstad Prophecies:

Twin Runes
Elemental Runes

With Brandy L. Rivers – The Pine Barrens Pack Series:

Cursed Vengeance
Vengeance Unraveled

Coming Soon:
Taken (Traded Book 3) – Fall 2017

ABOUT THE AUTHOR

Rebecca Brooke grew up in the shore towns of South Jersey. She loves to hit the beach, but always with her Kindle on hand. She is married to the most wonderful man who puts up with all her craziness. Together they have two beautiful children who keep her on her toes. When she isn't writing or reading (which is very rarely) she loves to bake and binge watch Netflix.

Website
www.rebeccabrooke.com

Newsletter
Sign up

Facebook
https://www.facebook.com/RebeccaBrooke
Author/

Twitter
@RebeccaBrooke6

Made in the USA
Coppell, TX
07 May 2022